ABOUT THE AUTHOR

Jennifer Freeland qualified as a solicitor, specialising in criminal law. She began her career defending suspects before joining the Crown prosecution Service. For 20 years as a criminal lawyer and an advocate, she dealt with offences ranging from traffic matters to fraud, murder, and organised crime.

Jennifer Freeland lives near Chichester in West Sussex.

NOWHERE TO TURN

Jennifer Freeland

To my family, all ardent crime fiction fans.

CONTENTS

CHAPTER 1

TO WHOM IT MAY CONCERN. Of course, it should concern everyone really, not just those about to be named, because this isn't just a suicide note it is a documentary confession of an intent to murder. My intent to murder. I am going to murder an evil, evil man, a man who has encroached on every space in my life: my home, my work, my movements, killing all joy in living; a total invasion, of my being, my soul, leaving me stranded in an inescapable hell without hope of salvation. Those TO WHOM IT MAY CONCERN, those working in institutions I once valued; those I know as friends, neighbours, and work colleagues will, through my account in this document, learn how some of you too became a victim of this evil man's guile, unconsciously lining up with him with your pity and concern about my "mental" state.

Please believe me when I tell you that when you read my final words in this account, the last thing I want is for any of you to be racked with guilt. This is not about revenge at all. Those of you I knew before this brutal invasion I will love to my dying breath. I want happiness for you in your life and fulfilment, but I also want you to be aware, to know after I've murdered this evil being and am dead myself, how evil works so that you have some protection. I want those of you in authorities I looked to for help, but who ended up, instead, threatening to charge me with Wasting Police Time if I didn't stop bothering you, to know the truth. Bothering you, my God, I was fighting for my life and sanity, and you left me with nowhere to turn. You gave this evil man the green light to torment me to the end. You need to learn so that this never happens again.

I think I will succeed because, now that I know my life will soon end, I have nothing to lose. I don't have to struggle to keep my job, I can sell my home, use my savings, do everything needed to prove to you by evidence, that which you failed to find, see, imagine, or simply ignored. For the first time in a long time, I can feel some of my lost control of events returning and this feeling will grow.

I know that those who loved me but are no longer alive would not have thought me capable of murder or taking my own life. I know that many of you who still try to stay in touch with me, although less frequently than before, will be shattered that I could plan to kill someone. But, you see, I know this isn't the first time this man has done this. I'm told that he has no record, no convictions, but I know that he could not have achieved this level of expertise, this ability to drive the life force out of another human being without a process. I know that there was someone before me and I know that if I don't stop him there will be another after me, and then another. I must stop him. When those of you TO WHOM IT MAY CONCERN read this, you will understand that by simply taking my own life I would not have changed anything. My death would simply be filed under 'Tragic loss of life through depression,' and the evil invader will turn his attention towards another victim. So, I need to set out before you evidence that this tragic loss of life was not inevitable, you simply underrated the power of evil, as did I.

Before I name those of you TO WHOM IT MAY CONCERN, I just want, briefly, to tell you how this man first appeared in my life just over a year ago. Whatever representation of evil many of you imagine, it probably won't be the one I'm about to show you. That of course is why I didn't see it coming. So, a short background, and then your names, after which I will progress through my evidence, some already on record, the rest which I will collect and leave for you.   Here goes:

CHAPTER 2

DI Rory Hoskins walked into CID, looked at a group of detectives around the coffee machine and strode towards them. Before he reached the group one or two, noting Rory's purposeful advance, had already melted away to their desks, coffees in hand, 'back to work' expressions on their faces. Those who had been facing the coffee machine were taken by surprise and jumped at Rory's voice.

'Sorry to break up the coffee break,' he said crisply, 'but I'm still waiting for the evidence on the Clay conspiracy file.'

'Right, I've got the lads working on it right now,' DS Clarke Emery replied defensively. He tipped his head towards DC Johnny Hamilton. 'Now that Johnny has got rid of the woman crying harassment every five minutes, he's got a lot more time to deal with it.'

Rory's eyes swivelled in Johnny's direction, pinning him down.

'So, where are we?'

'I'll get what we've got to you shortly,' he replied, his manner cocky and vaguely challenging.

'Define shortly.'

Johnny's mouth lengthened. 'I had to finalise the harassment first in case we got any complaints down the road. Happily, letting her know that there was such a thing as a charge of Wasting Police Time seems to have worked.' With a grin, he added: 'Not that I actually told her that I was thinking of recommending the charge, no, no, just a little hint which, as I say, seems to have got her off my back, leaving me time to get up to speed on the conspiracy.'

'I want to see what you've got by the end of today,' Rory said.

The grin disappeared. 'Like I said -'

'And if you haven't got much, I want at the very least your action plan by close of play,' Rory interrupted. Out of the corner of his eye he saw the Sergeant drift off, leaving Johnny to fend for himself. 'Furthermore, I want the full harassment file now. I want to review it before we file it away.'

Very red in the face Johnny's voice rose as he defended himself from what he took to be an unwarranted rebuke: 'Everyone thinks she's a nut job. She's wasted too much valuable time accusing this miserable, inoffensive, little guy of acts one of which was false, a lie, he had a cast iron alibi.'

'I know, I've read our computer file, but I gather that there's a paper file printed off which was used for the applications at court, and I want it.' Rory said.

Striding over to one of three metal filing cabinets against the wall by the door, Johnny recovered the file, kicked the open filing cabinet drawer shut, returned, and presented it to Rory with a slight flourish. 'If you ask me, she was stalking him, not the other way around.'

It was on the tip of Rory's tongue to reply that he wasn't asking him, but holding his temper in check, just, he nodded, took the fat buff file, and walked out of CID. A second after he'd gone there was a collective sigh as detectives looked at each other, eyebrows raising, cheeks puffing out, but whatever Johnny had opened his mouth to say he thought better of when he saw two other detectives coming into the room. The Sergeant also noted the arrival of DC John Carter and DC Michael Flynn and throwing them a brief smile indicated to the others that they get back to work. It was well known that Carter and Flynn were two detectives DI Rory Hoskins valued highly. Nonetheless Johnny, aggrieved at his treatment from the DI, sauntered back over to the coffee machine and returning to his desk with a fresh mug of coffee, took his time before opening the conspiracy file on his computer.

Back in his office, Rory reshuffled the pile of paperwork on his desk and wondered what had happened to paperless operating. Most of the work they did, to be fair, was on computer but whenever files proved problematic a paper copy was usually generated and, with the cuts over the last few years, there were a lot of complaint cases.

Having insisted that he needed the paper harassment file, Rory now looked down at it, unopened on his desk, and wondered what the hell he was going to do with it. He should have told his partner, the CPS lawyer Thommi Carmichael, to keep her views to herself on his cases. But to be fair, he had introduced the topic himself. Now that Thommi was giving phone charging advice to police from home on a part-time basis, it wouldn't be appropriate to pass the file to her for a further review. Anyway, he didn't want to.

So, who to give the file to? Much as he'd like to pass it to John Carter, that would not be tactful and would put John in a difficult position vis-à-vis the Sergeant and Johnny Hamilton. One of his female DCs was on leave, another doing her Sergeant's exams, and Sarah Montgomery was on a course but had in any case made it clear that just because she was a woman it didn't mean she wanted to be landed with nothing but harassment, stalking, and sexual offences cases. "I like fraud, Guv," she'd told him. "And you owe me a break on the other stuff." In truth, the fact that Sarah understood computers and enjoyed complex cases with multi-handed suspects made her particularly valuable when it came to those sorts of cases.

Moreover, the victim had not actually made a complaint. The CPS had authorised charges against her alleged stalker twice and both times he'd been acquitted. It was only because Thommi had gone ballistic when he'd told her that the complainant had been threatened with a Wasting Police Time charge, something no one had asked his advice about and which he'd heard by chance, that he was taking an interest in it now. "You can't charge that without authorisation from the DPP, which you won't get in a million years, and all you're doing is ensuring that she cannot ask for help if she needs it," Thommi had said accusingly, eyes flashing, hands on hips.

Leaning back precariously in his chair, Rory mentally cursed Johnny Hamilton for threatening anyone with Wasting Police Time over a harassment case, particularly when the allegation was one of being stalked by a stranger. Johnny can try to split hairs by intimating that he hadn't actually threatened her with the charge but, if that was the case, why mention it at all? She may be a nut job, she had certainly used up resources which might have been better deployed to other more pressing cases, but stalking was a high-profile political issue and Johnny was the last person who should have been dealing with it. What the hell was Clarke Emery thinking when he allocated it to him? Johnny's swagger and his unerring belief in his own judgement produced results in straightforward criminal cases but he didn't have much time for what Rory knew he'd once referred to as "agenda driven bollocks." Although, in the past, he'd defended Johnny against Thommi's assertion that he was a relic of the canteen culture, Rory was now beginning to wonder whether there wasn't something in that view.

Still feeling slightly bruised by his scrap with Thommi, Rory looked up, suddenly inspired. Well then, if a member of the CPS was complaining, a member of the CPS could bloody well review the file. It would have to go to someone Thommi rated, or he'd never hear the end of it. Nigel Sheridan was her most trusted friend over at the South-West Central's CPS office, but Rory knew he was up to his eyes in a multi-handed people trafficking case. After a moment's hesitation, he thought "what the hell," the whole of the Criminal Justice System was up to its eyes in something and what are friends for? Rory picked up his phone.

CHAPTER 3

TO WHOM IT MAY CONCERN: I said I'd be brief, and I will. What is important in this document is the evidence I will put before you. To that end, although much of it is still to come, I will have to go over some of what has happened in the investigation so far because that is the start of the evidential process. Even though the magistrates declared that the prosecution had failed to come up to proof in two separate trials, and the evil genius walked away, throwing a glance of triumph in my direction, a rapid secretive movement of his eyes and lips, visible only to me, the evidence still needs context.

I first met this evil man, Billy Grant, at a London market in Barnes. It was a sunny and unseasonably warm afternoon in mid-September last year, and I was with friends who had insisted that I come with them because they were worried about me. Both my parents had died within a year of one another, and my fiancé and I split up six months after my mother, my surviving parent, succumbed to breast cancer. My friends supported me to the hilt then, even though I was bearing up pretty well. I told them at the time, they didn't have to worry; it was a relief when Timothy and I split up and I could grieve over my parents' loss freely. All the same, at the time, I was glad they twisted my arm that day, I was enjoying the market, eating home-made cupcakes, drinking cider, laughing, and then I saw a sundial for sale. It was almost certainly newer than it looked but small enough for my garden and quite expensive. Having just inherited enough to pay off a large chunk of my mortgage, I decided to splash out.

I have replayed that decision over and over in my mind. If I hadn't gone to the market and seen the sundial … if I hadn't made such a rash decision to buy it … if only. But I did go to the market, and I did decide to buy the sundial, and a round faced man with heavy jowls in his late thirties or early forties strode forward, elbowing aside a teenage girl minding his goods, and beamed at me. His face was very red from the heat and sun, and his hair was a mousy colour and thinning over a flaky pate. He was wearing a polyester shirt, revealing large sweat marks under his arms, and which was buttoned up to the last but one button at his throat, the gap enough to show the fleshy folds of his neck. He was wearing black trousers, shiny in patches which were more suited to an office than a market, and his highly polished shoes, contrasted strangely with what most people were wearing on that sunny afternoon. I remember thinking that perhaps he was older than I thought. There was nothing prepossessing about this man, but he seemed so pleased that I was going to buy the sundial that I smiled automatically back at him. That was the first mistake I made: Mistake 1. 'Always be kind to people who don't seem to have a lot going for them,' my mother had told me when I was growing up, 'you never know what people have been through.' The worst possible advice, darling, generous minded, wonderful, but deluded, Mum! But I too was a kind person then and I'd have responded in a friendly fashion anyway. If people smiled at me, I smiled back. Not anymore.

The next decision was how to transport the sundial home, it was small but very heavy and we'd all piled into one car to drive to the market. The rotund seller, twinkled at me and told me he'd deliver it, at the same time giving me a dog-eared card with the name Billy Grant at the top and Garden Furniture underneath it. I had handed over a considerable amount of money in cash and the card was the sort you could have designed online and printed off or had printed at a booth in a shopping centre. I wasn't a complete idiot, and you need to know that. I was a person grieving for the loss of her wonderful parents, but I wasn't depressed, and I was friendly and open and rational. I know that those TO WHOM IT MAY CONCERN will in the immediate aftermath of a suicide and murder initially decide that their view of the breakdown of my mental health was the correct one. But after reading this document, which will reveal the full truth, I hope you will be open-minded and honest with yourselves. Even though only one of you with me that day will be named in this document, I hope that all four of you who were at the market will remember me as I was that day. A rational, open, friendly, girl, eating cupcakes and drinking cider on a sunny day, not a basket case. As I said, this isn't about blame. I didn't see Billy Grant coming either.

I told him that I would have to arrange other transportation, but he then came up with an idea. He would follow us in his van with "Garden Furniture" painted on its sides, all the way to my place, and the two male members of my friends could help him erect the sundial in the garden. I agreed. Mistake 2. What a mistake! It gave the evil invader access to my address, my neighbourhood, and so much more. The one thing I didn't give him was my phone number or email. He asked me whether I would do a satisfaction survey on his service if he emailed me the form, but I declined. I may once have been a kind person, but I wasn't an idiot. Nothing about our business transaction merited a survey, as far as I could see he was a one-man band. I knew that my email had been shared by numerous organisations but due to recent attempts to scam me, I had become far more cautious about volunteering my personal contact details to individuals. Did I even then feel some sort of unease about Billy Grant?

Well, there you have it, that is how I met Billy Grant, the evil invader.

CHAPTER 4

Rory looked up when he heard a rap on the side of his open door and beckoned Nigel Sheridan into his office, indicating a chair for him to sit on. Nigel complied and looked at Rory, raising his eyebrows, and saying: 'Do you think we have no work of our own to do?'

Noting that, despite this pointed remark, Thommi's friend was looking resigned, friendly even, Rory relaxed and grinned apologetically.

'I know, I know. I'm hoping this won't take long, but before I put this stalker case to bed, I'd like a quick opinion from outside my office as to whether we should be looking at other lines of enquiry, whether -'

'Is this the harassment case where the alleged victim was threatened with Wasting Police Time?'

Rory frowned. 'I see that Thommi has got there before me. I should mention that she knows absolutely sod all about this case. I can give you an overview -'

'Just give me the file.'

Pulling a face, Rory handed over the large folder. 'I know that this looks like a lot of work, but you don't have to do it all at once, you can take your time -'

'Not a chance,' Nigel said as he pushed back his chair and rose. But, before Rory, startled by this abrupt interruption, could say anything further, he noted that Nigel had picked up the file. 'Find me a desk and leave me with this for a couple of hours, that's all I can spare. If possible, I'd like a desk away from CID, or I'll keep being asked about other cases.'

Rory nodded and stood himself. 'There's no-one in the old CPS advice office this afternoon, I'll open it up for you.'

In fact, it was nearer three hours later when Nigel's face appeared round Rory's door again. Sitting down, he put the file on Rory's desk and slid it firmly across to the other side of it. Rory's eyebrows rose, but despite this 'end of my involvement' action, the fact that Nigel had sat down meant that he had something to say.

'So, the good news first,' Nigel began. Rory was not comforted by this opening shot.

'In view of manpower considerations, there's not a lot wrong with the initial investigation,' Nigel continued. 'We charged Section 2 Harassment as violence wasn't involved and, at that time, there wasn't sufficient evidence for the either-way S4 stalking offence of causing "serious alarm or distress." Provided the evidence held up, we had a reasonable prospect of conviction. Either our victim didn't come across well, or the beaks found some other reason to acquit.'

On a sigh, Rory said: 'From what I heard, in the first case the magistrates probably felt sorry for the defendant.'

'Yes, I thought that was probably the case. The defendant has no convictions, the file paints him as a rather pathetic soul and the bench decided to give him a break so that he doesn't get a record. Give me a District Judge any day of the week on cases like these. Despite all the courses on harassment, when a defendant's course of conduct seems trivial, not many lay people really understand its effect on a victim unless someone they know has been targeted.'

Rory's attention was caught. Nigel was a clinically detached lawyer, but his insights into certain cases were revealing. As a boy, brought up on a rough Peckham estate, he had been the victim of racism and, as a teenager, of racial discrimination and harassment. Nigel had told Thommi that If it hadn't been for the tough love of a truly scary Jamaican grandmother his life would have turned out very differently.

The victim in the file on Rory's desk was a white, single woman, from a privileged background, a very different profile from that of the black senior CPS lawyer sitting opposite him. But Nigel knew what it felt like to be singled out for no rational reason and they both, it would appear, had that in common.

'I wouldn't criticise anything anyone did in that first case,' Nigel concluded. 'There are always other things we could have done evidentially, but it was a relatively minor case in a huge caseload, and it was good enough on paper.'

'Hang on, what other things?' Rory asked, shifting his weight.

'In hindsight, we could have countered Grant's assertion that most of the time his appearances in our victim's road and neighbourhood were accidental, by doing some investigation into the distances he travelled, providing evidence of alternative more straightforward routes to his claimed destination, that sort of thing.'

'Okay, sorry go on.' Rory braced himself for the bad news.

'On the second case, your guys should have done much more work, and I'd put my hands up to us sharing the larger part of the blame, because we shouldn't have authorised a charge without that work being done, if it wasn't for one thing.'

Midway through Nigel's sentence, to his shame, Rory had felt a bit relieved that any blame, if there was any, would be shared with the CPS, but that feeling collapsed with Nigel's final words.

'What one thing?' he demanded, the front legs of his chair slamming down on the floor as he leaned forward.

'The last statement from the victim which arrived after the decision to charge, and very close to the second court case, should have been flagged for a second review in view of its contents.

There was no way Rory could pretend he knew which statement Nigel was referring to, so twiddling his biro round his fingers, he said: 'Go on.'

Noting Nigel's quizzical expression, Rory responded with

a brief bark of laughter. He really should have read the case properly.

'In the last statement,' Nigel said, emphasising the word "last", 'the evidence the victim gives potentially complies with the causing "serious alarm or distress" stalking section. Had that been flagged by police, the review would have been made by someone in our Crown Court section where the difficulties in the evidence, the airtight alibi, and our failed application to get evidence of the first court case adduced on the grounds of a pattern of behaviour, would almost certainly have been picked up and the case discontinued until we had further evidence. From then on, all further evidence would have been reviewed by a Crown Court lawyer."

Rory took a deep breath and decided not to beat about the bush, he was rumbled anyway. He put up his hands and said: 'Okay, what was the serious alarm or distress suffered by our victim in her last statement?'

'The victim told the OIC that, due to Grant's persistence, she had to persuade her boss to change her working hours and, when that happened, there was a time when she didn't see him. But then Grant clocked her work pattern changes and continued to stalk her. As you know, changing routes to work and work patterns is one of the examples given under the Act.'

Rory looked out of the window, rocking back on his chair again and turning things over in his mind.

'One of my officers thinks she's harassing him, particularly since the victim was caught out when the defendant could prove he couldn't have done what she was accusing him of.'

Nigel's expression was sceptical, to say the least. 'Would that be the OIC by any chance?'

Rory realised that his officer's opinion would have been better left unsaid. Why he kept defending Johnny Hamilton when he didn't particularly like him, he didn't know, unless that was the reason, trying to overcome any bias on his part. Feeling a bit on the defensive, Rory added more robustly: 'To be fair, from what I gather, her evidence on that alibi is, at best, mistaken, at worst, manufactured.

But Nigel was having none of it. With a slight clip to his tone, he said: 'Look, stalking and harassment is all about control. He could have staged the whole thing to provide himself with an airtight alibi. I don't have time to expand on this now, but when my trafficking case is over, I'd like to do a lecture to police on Stalking and Harassment and I'll be using some pretty punchy examples.'

'Please do, but in the meantime-'

'In the meantime,' Nigel interrupted, rising to his feet, 'you send a sympathetic officer round to tell our victim that, having reviewed the file, there is no question of her being treated as though she was Wasting Police Time and ...' He broke off, then said, angrily, 'How any idiot could have done that when recent case law clearly demonstrates the devastating effect on a victim's life by being the target of an obsessive maniac, is beyond me.' He took a breath, shook his head and, in a milder tone, added: 'Ask her to report any further incidents, no, tell her to do so, and stress to her the importance of making detailed notes. From my quick take on the file, I'd be surprised if this was the end of the matter.'

Rory looked rueful but resigned. 'We could be inviting a complaint.'

'Mea culpa,' Nigel said over his shoulder as he headed for the door, but just before he reached it, he turned and said:

'It's a matter for you, but you might want to ask the OIC when the victim actually told him about her change of work pattern.'

Rory's expression was grim. 'You needn't worry about that.'

CHAPTER 5

CASSANDRA you are the first named person TO WHOM IT MAY CONCERN. My friend from university, my flatmate for that lovely year in London, the person I chose as my chief bridesmaid, before Timothy and I called it a day. Such a special person to me and will be to the end. But unwittingly, you were manipulated by the evil invader. I love you but I must show you and others how this manipulation came about. When I am no longer here, and neither is he, my final actions will at first tend to confirm the view the evil invader has persuaded you to believe. But I need to change that view, your view, by proving to you how I, you, and the authorities, were played by an intent so malign, so destructive, that it left me trapped and isolated, an existence in which every joyous moment, every precious memory, was slowly taken from me. You too were taken from me at the time I needed you most. You see, isolating the targeted person from family and friends is how controlling people maintain control.

I know that my saying this will anger and upset you. You will point to the times you telephoned me, the times you tried to get me out to the cinema, to dinner, to parties, the supportive texts you sent me, the U-Tube 'ha-ha' jokes you shared. You tried to distract me CASSANDRA, distract me. You didn't understand, you just didn't get that distraction wasn't an option. If I slept at all, the first thought I had on waking was to wonder where the evil invader was, where he was waiting; waiting to appear from around a corner, waiting to get on the same train or tube as me, waiting to queue behind me when I bought my newspaper, all the time wearing an innocent mask, until that swift silent secretive communication as he walked past me before reverting to the chubby cheerful chappie to all intents and purposes going about his daily business. Even though I learnt to avoid looking at him, my mind's eye registered the leer, the triumph in his glance, I didn't have to see it.

Finally, CASSANDRA, you will plead that you were the one who researched experts who could help me; you sent me the names of recommended top psychologists, grief counsellors, self-help groups and, finally, you offered to come with me to my doctor to demand psychiatric help for my depression. At that point, Cassandra, you were totally lost to me. You didn't listen, you didn't hear what I was trying to tell you. Like a fish attracted to the worm on the end of a hook, you took the bait and were reeled in. With every rotation of the reel, you bought into the easy solutions being peddled online and dangled before you, every one of them designed to cure me. Designed to cure ME, not the evil invader. But enough, this is about evidence:

Evidence: You are the first person I have named because you were there at the beginning. You were at the market when we first came across Billy Grant. After he and the boys had managed to get the sundial onto my patch of grass, you and I waved him off in his Garden Furniture van from my front doorstep. Let's quickly recap the evidence you gave at court in the first harassment case, because you were in my corner, and you didn't waiver then in cross-examination. Thank you for that, and when the full picture, the truth, is revealed, documented by evidence still to come, please remember how much I valued your support that day in court. Despite the verdict, the evidence you gave held up and was largely accepted by the defendant and his lawyer, even though you did not witness the first three times Billy Grant 'bumped' into me.

I gave evidence of those three occasions: the first when I was shopping in Waitrose. I wasn't initially concerned by the meeting, it was a supermarket after all, and I acknowledged his smile and greeting with a nod and brief 'hello' before walking on, but I was a bit surprised. I suppose it was because he was in a supermarket near my home, and he hadn't mentioned that he lived in my area when he had delivered my sundial. But when I saw him in the same aisle as me twice more, one time with him saying: "we can't keep on meeting like this," with a sly half sideways grin in my direction, I suppose 'uneasy' is the feeling I would describe. He didn't seem to be looking for anything on the shelves. I didn't reply to his comment, and I didn't let him deter me from finishing my shopping but when I was at the tills, I knew that he had joined the same queue. I'd seen him approach my till but not continue past it. I looked steadfastly ahead and, after paying, beetled out to my car, literally throwing my shopping on the back seat, so that I could drive away quickly.

The second time, when he appeared beside me out of the blue when I posted a letter in the post box at the end of my road, wearing the same grin and armed with a quick: 'it's a small world' comment, my unease notched up to alarm. My 'so it would seem,' reply was deliberately curt, and I walked quickly back home to avoid any further contact. I rang you, CASSANDRA, to tell you about these meetings and you decided to come over the next day and stay the night. That is why you were my first witness. You were in my sitting room when, on the third occasion, Billy Grant rang my doorbell, ostensibly to tell me something he'd discovered about the history of my sundial. He was scaring me now. I was glad you were in the house when I made it clear to him, I didn't want us to have any further contact and threatened to call police before slamming the door. But the funny thing is, you were the one getting even more steamed up about it then than me.

Because the case was relatively straight forward it was listed before Christmas, and we were so hopeful Billy Grant would be convicted and receive a Restraining Order before the holidays. God, that seems like a lifetime ago. You gave evidence. I don't believe he knew I had company when he turned up at my house because my blinds were shut, and curtains drawn. It was the last time he made the mistake of not knowing exactly where I was and who I was with. You told the Magistrates everything from hearing him ring the doorbell to what was said, because you remained in the sitting room when I answered the door. You heard our whole conversation, so there was no mistaking it was him I was talking to and, most importantly, you heard me tell him that the next time he spoke to me or came to my door I would call the police. I said that I didn't want him to come near my property again. Then, just before I slammed my door, you came out into the hall and looked straight at him, and he at you. He managed a quick 'hello' trying to sound friendly, but the door had slammed shut just before you let rip. It was vital evidence because the following day I opened my front door to a package wrapped in colourful paper with a ribbon around it and a note underneath it with the word: "Sorry" written on the note. That package, containing chocolates, was produced as evidence in the trial, and you were able to corroborate the fact that you'd heard me warn him I'd call the police, you remember?

My prosecutor didn't understand why he wasn't convicted. You, CASSANDRA, pointed out that he hadn't got anything in his past when it came to convictions or similar allegations. 'They must have just felt sorry for him and accepted that when he left you those chocolates with an apology, he was full of remorse.' When we left court, you added that you hoped the experience would be the end of the matter. Thinking about that I now wonder whether you, my creative friend with your awesome interior designs and a compassion for the underdog, were even at that stage taken in by his small blinking eyes and slight tremor of the mouth as he stumbled over his answers in cross-examination.

It might explain some of what happened in the second

prosecution ... but, before I go onto that, I'll say now, please remember me on that day at the market in Barnes, laughing, eating cupcakes, and drinking cider. It was and will be the last carefree occasion in my life.

I will not go into the quality of acceptable evidence I must produce for this document until I mention my second person TO WHOM IT MAY CONCERN. But I will state that the evidence you gave in the first prosecution, I regard as better than any other evidence because it was accepted by Billy Grant; it was simply the implication of his actions that was challenged.

So:

EVIDENCE 1:

The three occasions in under a week I saw BG: at Waitrose; at the post box; at my front door.

EVIDENCE 2:

The corroborated evidence of me telling BG that the next time he spoke to me or came to my door I would the call the police and that I did not want him coming near my property again.

EVIDENCE 3:

The package left outside my front door.

CHAPTER 6

DC Johnny Hamilton had the good sense to be out on enquiries, when Rory, picked up his phone to summon him to his office and when, later, Rory was facing DS Clarke Emery across his desk, he had calmed down considerably.

But, although the discussion taking place between the two of them was polite and professional, neither man thought it was going well, at least initially. For his part, Rory resented being made to feel that he was being unfair to a subordinate officer, even though he was choosing his words carefully.

'The advice I'm getting is that we should not have given an alleged victim of a stalker the idea that she was risking being charged with Wasting Police Time if she reported any further incidents. Apart from anything else, only the DPP can authorise such a charge and it's highly unlikely that he would do so.' Rory hoped that the word 'we,' including himself in the decision to take such a course, even though that decision was one endorsed by the DS and without his knowledge, would sugar coat the instruction he was about to give.

Clarke Emery felt patronised. He knew the law as well as anyone and he took a moment to calm down before saying: 'I didn't authorise anyone to threaten the alleged victim, but she had clearly been way off base regarding one of the allegations she made, and when I asked Johnny about the threat, he said he had simply mentioned the charge to get across to her the gravity of that error of judgement and I don't blame him for that. If she begins to lie to us and the Court to bolster her case, there are consequences Rory. One of those consequences is that it's highly unlikely that we'll risk another charge without independent evidence.'

Rory couldn't deny he'd made a good point. 'I know. But I was talking to an expert on stalker cases. His view is that stalkers are particularly cunning, and they often lay a trap for their victim to fall into. I don't know one way or another whether this was a genuine mistake on her part or not. However, much of what she said in the first prosecution was corroborated by others -'

'Mainly a friend of hers,' the Sergeant said, interrupting.

'And I'm told that the friend's evidence was not challenged by the defence.'

'That's correct,' was the response in a milder tone.

It was then that the discussion, unexpectedly, took a turn for the better. After a moment's thought, DS Clarke nodded and said: 'You know, I once had a case where the witness was fitted up by a defendant. It wasn't a harassment it was an assault.'

Rory leaned back in his chair and looked interested. The DS continued. 'After the defendant was charged, a car drove by the victim's shop at night while he was locking up. The victim turned as the car drove in front of the shop, before swiftly taking off again, and a voice said through the passenger seat window: 'You go to court against me, you'll be sorry.' The victim was convinced it was the defendant, particularly in view of the words said, but it turned out he had an alibi. He was at a friend's wedding reception and had numerous alibi witnesses. We thought it was someone he knew in the passenger seat with much the same build as the defendant. That count of Conspiring to pervert the Course of Justice was one of several on the Indictment and he was convicted of the others. We were lucky because the Jury might have taken the view that if there was doubt on one of the charges, there was doubt on the others.'

Relieved that Clarke had remembered that case, Rory said: 'Well, there you are, things can be staged although we don't know whether that's the case here. I'd like an officer go to the victim's house to tell her that she should report any further incidents.' Rory paused and straightened a pencil on his desk, hoping that what he was about the say wouldn't break the sudden rapport between the two of them and choosing his words carefully, he continued: 'It can't be an officer who's played any part in the last two prosecutions, someone else should take over the case. She sounds like a bit of a nightmare so that will be a relief to Johnny Hamilton.'

'It certainly will be. I hear what you say, Rory, but we are probably in for another deluge of phone calls from her.'

'Here's the file and let me know who you choose to take over from Johnny, just so that I have their back if there are any repercussions or complaints.'

Clark Emery hesitated a moment. 'Do you want me to tell Johnny to come and see you about that late statement?'

Rory took a moment to make up his mind. 'No, on reflection, I'll leave that to you, but it's a learning point we all need to take on board,' adding a second later, this time with a grin: 'After all Clarke, if it wasn't for that late statement, we could have shifted more of the blame for what's happened on the CPS!'

Clarke laughed and left, a relieved man.

Later that afternoon, Rory was pleased to find out that Clarke had reallocated the case to DC John Carter. Even though Rory felt that his Sergeant was too anxious to be popular with the DCs at times, that decision showed judgement and he applauded it.

It was late afternoon when Rory and John had time to catch up a bit. John was perfectly happy to go over to see the victim.

'Sort of apologise without really apologising,' Rory told him with a slightly guilty laugh. 'If I can avoid a complaint, I'd like to. I should warn you that you may regret this.'

'Yes, so Johnny tells me.'

Rory's ears pricked up. Something about his young DC inclined him to believe that he was interested in the case.

'It's highly unlikely that we'll charge again without a

lot of corroborative evidence,' Rory said, his piercing blue eyes holding John's. 'You've got a full caseload in your inbox and almost all of it takes priority.'

John's eyebrows shot up, rather comically. 'Tell me about it,' he replied with an acknowledging grin, before walking towards the door of Rory's office.

Rory stroked his chin where a five o'clock shadow was already showing and looked balefully at John's retreating back. Who the hell does he think he's kidding, he thought?

CHAPTER 7

It is so painful for me to remember the second court case, but I know that soon I will be beyond feeling pain and must hang on to that. Still, the recollection is so raw. It marked a watershed. Up until the conclusion of the case, I still believed in Justice and those who administered it and, more importantly, I still believed that love and friendship was unconditional or, perhaps, I mean unquestioning. I know that, taken to extremes that's not always healthy. I read once about a traitor whose devoted wife of many years did not know, did not for a nanosecond suspect, that he was a Russian spy. But I still can't believe how easily my closest friends could be swung by an evil intent. How cleverly Billy Grant managed to divide us, leaving me at his mercy. Naïve really, because politics and history illustrate only too clearly how people can be swayed by an evil demagogue. Easier still for one person, with a diabolical single-minded plan to destroy a chosen but random victim, to succeed in his evil intent.

TO WHOM IT MAY CONCERN, I am now expanding my list. In addition to you CASSANDRA, I am adding, DC JOHNNY HAMILTON, the officer in charge of my case, CHARLOTTE GREY, the prosecutor who decided to charge it, and COLIN FRASER, the Chairman of the Bench. I'd like to include Marcus Jenner, but I can't. He was brutal in his cross-examination of me, unnecessarily so, but he was allowed to be by the Chairman of the bench, and he was acting for the evil invader. He did his job. You see, despite being depicted as a deranged woman suffering from depression, possibly undiagnosed bi-polar, imagining things which aren't happening, or didn't happen, I can be rational, detached even.

So, the second trial: DC JOHNNY HAMILTON, I could tell when you took the first of my statements before Grant was re-charged, that your heart wasn't in this investigation. You hardly wrote anything about the finger shadow other than the date and time and it was clear to me that you didn't think I could have known who was on the motorbike. How I now wish I'd kept quiet about it. When I then told you that since the previous court case, I had seen Billy Grant in my neighbourhood eight times in the space of a week, you pointed out that there were no conditions placed upon him to stay out of the neighbourhood, since he'd been acquitted of harassment. I implored you to understand that, prior to my first meeting him, I had never seen him before. That's when you told me that he had moved since then, and my heart plummeted. Moved, moved into my neighbourhood? I feared as much. You couldn't give me his address it would be a breach of his privacy. HIS privacy, my God, what about my privacy?

You were reluctant to take another statement from me, following further incidents but I was desperate and kept ringing the number I was given until you came. I begged you to believe that his behaviour was not accidental, that you needed to listen to me, to hear what I was telling you. Billy Grant knew when I left for work, when I arrived home, when I went shopping on the weekend and where. He could only know this from having watched me. You wrote down what I was saying and even said it was suspicious but added that it was still just conjecture on my part. You took a bit more notice, and wrote more in your notebook, when I told you that, with the agreement of my boss, I had changed my working hours and when that happened there were a few days when I didn't see the evil invader. But then, it started again, he'd clocked the change in my work pattern and weekend shopping trips, and he'd adapted accordingly. Each time he saw me, Billy Grant gave me that look, that leering smirk, or sometimes he'd wave at me, except in the supermarket where there were cameras. Then he'd stalk me down aisles while pretending to shop by picking up products and either putting them back or in his basket. When I'd finished you sighed, DC HAMILTON, asked me to sign your notebook and said that one of the civilian staff would send me a typed statement for my signature in due course. No hurry then! The typed statement was produced so close to the court case that I had to go to the police station to sign it!

I had my notes of the numerous times and places where he'd appeared. My Exhibit! What a waste of time, DC HAMILTON. It turned out that even knowing the defendant's explanation for being in those places at that time; the dentist, the friend in another road, getting to know his new neighbourhood - the nearest pubs, shops, garden centres - you didn't investigate distances travelled, easier routes, or get a statement from 'the friend in another road.' This is my area, and I could have told you why some of his explanations made no sense and I don't even know where he lives.

In court, the only evidence which seemed to be in my favour was the CCTV from Waitrose. It clearly showed him in the same aisles as me on several occasions. Marcus Jenner tried to suggest it could have been the other way around, me happening to be in the same aisles as his client, but the CCTV told a different story, and he didn't chance his arm by pressing the point. Unlike when you were cross-examined, CASSANDRA. You had been with me on two of the eight occasions when I was accosted by Billy Grant, as detailed in my first statement, and two more occasions outlined in my second statement. But you conceded every suggestion Mr Jenner put to you. Yes, you agreed, Billy Grant didn't really do anything more than look over towards us both, yes, he could have been on his way somewhere, yes it could have been a coincidence. Couldn't you have said you thought it was unlikely because you had witnessed a previous occasion when he rang my doorbell, couldn't you at least have said that? You may have been stopped from talking about that case, but you would simply have been answering the question. Surely you could have tried. You didn't even point out that you thought it odd that you saw him four times out of the seven you had visited me. You looked a bit doubtful at times at the points Mr Jenner was putting to you, but that's about all.

Finally, I was humiliated in court, because you DC JOHNNY HAMILTON didn't get the CCTV evidence from the pub immediately or take a statement from the Landlord giving Billy Grant his alibi until after the pub had changed hands and the Landlord had moved to Spain. When I questioned you about the time lost, that's when you went on to threaten me with being charged with Wasting Police Time. Not in so many words, you covered your back. Just pointed out that there was such a charge and how important it was not to be tempted to stray from the truth by imagining things or getting coincidences out of proportion.

I know his pub alibi is what you and everyone else consider airtight, but I also know it is wrong. I cannot explain how or why, but I know I saw Billy Grant outside my window that night when I saw a finger shadow resembling the barrel of a gun on my wall. Billy Grant gave evidence that he had never ridden a motorbike, and it was confirmed in court that no such vehicle was registered to him. But I saw him on a motorbike the third of the eight times I saw him in one week. I put it in my first statement.

You had such fun in your cross-examination, Mr Jenner, such pleasure in removing everything I had to hold onto, every crutch, every hope. You asked me whether I thought this barrel of a gun facing upwards was symbolic of anything? Your expression was amused. I understood that you were hinting that I might have thought, or be suggesting, a phallic interpretation of the finger shadow. I didn't rise to your bait, at least I didn't do that. I did wonder, but I told the truth when I said that what bothered me was a threatening invasion of my home even from outside. But I caught the quick communication between Mr Jenner and you, COLIN FRASER, Chairman of the Bench. So difficult to describe the exchange between the two men. To me, it signified the mutual acknowledgement between them of my febrile imagination, even though the symbolic suggestion had come from Mr Jenner. Mr Jenner who stood, holding the lapel of his jacket, his carefully studious expression unable to disguise his delight that his own suggestion had been so easily accepted by you COLIN FRASER. You, the Chairman, with your slightly raised eyebrows and thickset girth exuding a kind of 'small fish in a large pond' pomposity which managed to dominate the other two magistrates sitting either side of you. I knew in that moment, that the case was over, that the evil invader would escape justice a second time.

But there was something else you said in cross-examination, Mr Jenner, which I didn't dwell on immediately because my thoughts were dominated by the acquittal and your silent communication with the Chairman. But it's something I've been worrying about since. You asked me if your client had ever had a friendly conversation with me about the West Country. I told him that we hadn't. You then asked me whether I knew the North Coast of Devon and, completely taken aback, I agreed that I did, I knew most areas in Devon. Looking briefly towards the dock, I saw Billy Grant's eyes light up, almost in surprise I thought, and I looked away immediately. You then asked me if I knew a place called Hartland and I replied that, years ago, I had driven through it with my parents and a friend, but we didn't stop there, so no, I didn't know it well. Your next question was about the areas I did know well in that area, and this was the one time, the only time, the young and less experienced prosecutor scored over you, Mr Jenner. He rose to his feet and told the Magistrates that this appeared to be a fishing expedition. If his client maintained that he had conversed with the complainant about specific places, then he should question the complainant about those specific places. Mr Jenner could hardly object, so he simply pointed out that it was his client's case that he and I had enjoyed a friendly conversation about the West Country and Devon, and that I had acknowledged it was an area I knew well and that I had travelled through Hartland.

But what a shot in the dark. How on earth could Billy Grant know about my trips to Devon? It was when I saw the photograph on my sitting room wall of my father and me sitting on a wall with boats behind us in a harbour that my heartbeat raced, and I had trouble breathing. For a moment, I wondered if the evil invader had gained access to my home and seen it and, perhaps, other photos in my albums. But I know that didn't happen; if he'd seen other photos, he'd have had other places to name. Then it hit me like a bolt that when you DC JOHNNY HAMILTON took my very first statement for the first trial, you did see the photo and we talked about our love of the West Country and the coast, and you told me you missed water sports. But my photograph was of a harbour in Cornwall not Devon, and you told me that you moved to South-West Central from being stationed in Cornwall. Neither of us specifically mentioned Devon or Hartland. You cannot have accessed my computer, evil invader, because otherwise you would have known about Welcombe in Devon, so that's a relief. But I keep wondering, I still wonder how you knew about my connection to that county.

CHARLOTTE GREY, Crown Prosecution lawyer, I have mentioned you because you didn't wait until you had Billy Grant's alibi evidence before charging. The young barrister, prosecuting on my behalf, said that he thought that alibi evidence should always be investigated before charge. But, more importantly, you allowed the statement of the pub landlord, which confirmed that Billy Grant had been at his party all evening, simply to be read out in court, under some Section or other. The Prosecutor in court was not, therefore, offered an opportunity to cross-examine the pub landlord on Billy Grant's movements. You insisted it was recognition evidence, corroborated by the documents exhibited by the new landlord, showing Billy Grant's booking, and his paid bill and, for that reason, you couldn't justify the cost of bringing the landlord back from Spain or setting up video-links.

After agreeing that the alibi evidence could simply be read, my only chance was if my evidence, and CASSANDRA's, in the first trial was able to be put before the magistrates. But the prosecutor told me that your application to allow this evidence, CHARLOTTE GREY, had been made at court shortly before the trial and failed. He couldn't understand why? I don't understand why? It's part of the story, part of what's been happening since the evil invader came into my life, part of what I'm told is known as 'a course of action.' How is Justice served by not letting the Magistrates hear the full story? Without the evidence in the first trial, and once you had the pub CCTV, why did you think you had enough evidence to proceed to trial CHARLOTTE GREY? By going ahead, I was then the one on trial and now I have nowhere to turn, and no trials left in me.

I escaped from court before the verdict because I knew what it would be. But what upset me most immediately after the trial, CASSANDRA, was when I told you about that brief communication I'd witnessed between Mr Jenner and the Chairman of the bench, you said: 'Men, they have a one-track mind!' You thought it was a joke! I know you realised immediately it was the wrong thing to say, but with the Billy Grant escaping justice a second time, it was like having the last crutch kicked from under me. Your words have no bearing on what I plan to do, CASSANDRA, I promise you, they simply underscored how impossible it was for anyone, even someone as imaginative and close to me as you, to understand what it's like to be singled out and targeted by a relentlessly evil person. But

I hope that when my ordeal is over, and you read this document after I have produced the evidence I need, you and others will understand.

So, to summarise: My key independent evidence in the second case is the CCTV evidence from Waitrose. I say 'independent' of course, because you made it clear to me, DC JOHNNY HAMILTON, that future charges, would have to depend on 'Independent' evidence. I was discredited, you see. The cast iron alibi would, in future, discredit anything I said without corroborating 'independent' evidence.

But there was something else. At the lowest point in my life, DC JOHNNY HAMILTON, you didn't limit yourself to your threat about Wasting Police Time. When I asked you why the pub CCTV video had appeared so late, so close to the court case, you were furious and warned me not to interfere in the prosecution, as though it was none of my business. Your face was set, your legs astride, firmly planted in front of me preventing my escape, as you told me to stay away from any of the witnesses as though I was the perpetrator, not Billy Grant. Then on witnessing my shock at your words, words which sounded like a threat, you suddenly gave a defensive laugh, recognising no doubt, that you'd gone too far, and you tried to shift the blame by reminding me that the defence Counsel had suggested that I might have been stalking Billy Grant down the aisles of Waitrose not the other way around. As I just stood there looking at you, you turned away, unable to meet my eyes and, with a wave of a hand, you tried to recover your ground by saying: 'That's rubbish, we know that, but I'm just saying you've lost two cases and Grant had an airtight alibi, so you need to take that on board,' and walked quickly away.

From that moment, I was under no illusion as to where you, a police officer, stood. But why the warning about staying away from the witnesses? Did you think I would go anywhere where I might meet the evil invader, such as a pub he frequented? But what if I did? I still wonder at your anger and defensiveness. But anyway, that was the end as far as we were both concerned, and your verbal attack had allowed you to avoid answering my question about the CCTV.

Now that I have laid out the facts of the second court, it is perfectly understandable why, with my own evidence discredited I have nowhere to turn.

From now on, I will add to the baseline evidence I have outlined in my document, with new independent evidence I will collect myself. TO THOSE TO WHOM IT MAY CONCERN, when this is over, it is important to me that you understand why I had no option but to take the actions I am about to take. Actions to release me from a living hell and to ensure that there will be no further victims of Billy Grant.

EVIDENCE 4:

CCTV from Waitrose.

CHAPTER 8

The signs of late Autumn were creeping in, but in view of a mild and sunny weekend being forecast, Rory had invited Nigel Sheridan, his wife Marla, their young kids, and John Carter to a barbecue. He'd made it clear that their invitation was on condition that no one talked shop and they had all agreed. He'd impressed upon Thommi that she too was under the same embargo and, although she'd raised her eyebrows rather haughtily at his injunction, for once, she didn't argue. That didn't mean anything, he knew. But he hoped that his words might at least mean she'd do no more than have a quiet word with John, rather than introduce any work issues for debate over food. Rory was still mulling over what to do about the stalker case, but that didn't mean he wanted a range of views on the subject. When John had turned up at the victim's property to reassure her that she would not be charged with Wasting Police Time, she wouldn't open the door to him. Rory supposed the next logical thing to try was a letter from him, via John, in case this time she did open the door. If she didn't, he could post it through her letterbox.

After marinating trays of Chicken, beef ribs, lamb, and lots of vegetables, Rory then thumbed through his Italian cookbook by Patricia Lousada. Marla was a pescatarian and, adding his own touches, he prepared a squid and prawn Italian pasta salad. He had already bought several rustic loaves, tomato bread and soda bread, at the food market. Surveying the kitchen table, Rory was in a more relaxed mood than he'd been in some weeks.

Having arrived back in Barnes on Friday night feeling stressed out, Rory had intended to try for a relaxed evening and weekend. He and Thommi could certainly do with one. Within minutes, his plan looked set to fail. The previous weekend, Rory had put his flat in Twickenham on the market with a view to combining the equity in his property with the equity in Thommi's cottage so that the two of them could buy somewhere together. However, on reaching the cottage he saw that there was no sale sign on it, which had been due to go up that day. Questioning Thommi about its absence, she had said that she just wanted to talk things over, to put an idea to him, before committing herself. She had looked towards him with what, in his exhausted state, he took to be a strange mixture of defiance and defensiveness. On the verge of losing his temper, Rory suddenly froze. Didn't want to commit herself to what? He knew that Thommi loved her cottage, but she had agreed to the plan. So, what was it she didn't want to commit to? Was it him, their relationship? Life had been testing recently but he loved her and wanted to spend his life with her. Had she had second thoughts? His world caving in, he nonetheless managed to say in a quiet voice: 'Do you want me to take my flat off the market?'

She shook her head immediately. 'I just had a thought, but if you don't like it ....'

'What?' he asked, raking a hand through his hair and feeling helpless.

Thommi faltered, looking at him in concern. 'Look, It's just an idea-'

'What?' He realised he'd raised his voice and added in a softer tone. 'Don't keep me in suspense.'

'Okay.' She lifted her left shoulder in a slight shrug, frowning at him. 'I just suddenly thought . . .' she began, and then spoke her next words in rush. 'I know that not everyone agrees with people having more than one property but if your flat would allow us to have a little property near your family in San Gimignano, we could let other people enjoy it too.' Looking anxiously at Rory, she shrugged again. 'It was just an idea I thought I'd run by you.' Looking around at their surroundings, she added: 'It's not as though this cottage is too small for us, as things are, but if you don't like my idea ...' she let her sentence trail.

Sheer relief was followed by Rory experiencing an explosion of emotions, all of them happy. The previous summer, he had taken Thommi to meet his maternal Italian relatives in Tuscany. His grandmother had died, but he still had the odd great aunt, several aunts, and uncles, and lots of cousins and second cousins living there. He knew that Thommi loved Europe and before they flew out to Italy, she had told him that, before her mother had died, her parents had taken the whole family camping all over Europe, exploring the countryside and ancient villages, cooking on gas cylinders and cooling drinks in rivers. All the same, Rory had initially been a bit tentative about how the trip would pan out. Despite Thommi's reassuring words, she had mainly experienced Europe from the vantage point of the daughter of a senior diplomat, living in grand houses. Rory's own family had smallholdings with olive trees and worked in a variety of occupations but were from a very different world. Moreover, having first met Thommi's father just after she had been stabbed under his watch, and felt the full force of his anger at police incompetence, Rory found it difficult to visualise Sir Casper Carmichael relaxing on a picnic rug in woods while cooling his beer in a babbling brook. But to his great joy, Thommi and his family had clicked immediately. She loved Italian food anyway and happily joined in with preparing meals, enjoying long lunches, looking to Rory to translate some parts of the conversation, but managing to follow quite a bit of it herself.

'Well, I suppose we should think about it?' he began cautiously but warming to the idea almost immediately. Seeing Thommi's face light up, he took a deep breath. 'Okay, well I've thought about it and let's do it!'

So, Friday night had turned into a celebration, and now watching Thommi putting cutlery on the outside table, as he finished his barbecue preparations, he felt mellow and happy and more relaxed than he had for a long time. Looking around the kitchen, and with the prospect of travelling to Italy with Thommi before long to scout out properties, hopefully with an olive tree in a garden, he felt for the first time that the Barnes' cottage felt like home.

As if they all recognised that there may not be many more occasions that year when barbecues would be possible, the lunch party had a festive feel to it the moment it kicked off. The adults chatted over Thommi and Rory's plans for a smallholding in Italy and put in their bids for future holidays while Nigel's kids ate hamburgers and chips with gusto and drank coke. It was only when John helped Thommi take the plates back to the kitchen before bringing out the puddings, that the two of them had a brief chance to talk about the harassment case.

'I gather she won't answer the door.' Thommi said. 'Are you sure she's actually there?'

John nodded. 'I'm pretty sure I saw an upstairs curtain move. Also, the postman turned up when I was still trying to hold up my ID, and he told me curtly that she was unlikely to open the door and he didn't blame her. Like an idiot, I didn't respond quickly enough, and he'd moved back onto the path to carry on delivering before I had a chance to speak.'

'Well, at least she may have a friend in the postman.'

'I hope so.' Looking out of the window to reassure himself that Rory was still occupied, talking to Marla, John added. 'We've written a letter, and Rory wants me to hand deliver it in the hope that, when I do, this time she will answer her door but to post it through her letterbox if not. That way at least she'll know that we're encouraging her to report any further incidences.'

Giving John a bowl of trifle to take outside, and picking up a plate of tiramisu herself, Thommi said: 'Keep me posted. If you have no luck, I might try myself to see whether she'll open the door to a woman. Oh, and can you lend me the pub video so that

I know what our stalker looks like? But don't tell Rory.'

Then, briefly checking that their guests were still deep in conversation, she added: 'You know this is down to us more than you. You might have served evidence late, but why didn't we Judicially Review that decision not to allow us to adduce the original harassment evidence? It was all part of a pattern of behaviour. And, if that didn't work, with such a weakened case we should have ditched it. We could have explained why to the victim and reassured her that we would nonetheless take any further incidences she reported very seriously.'

Nodding, John said: 'We've all let her down and she's now living life in a prison. I'll get you the tape and update you when I can.'

The two conspirators then walked into the garden with their puddings, just as Rory had turned his head in their direction.   As Thommi and John placed their bowls on the table, his arm sketched an arc over Thommi's offering and he said: 'This tiramisu is my aunt's recipe which Thommi and I prefer to most others. See what you think.' Inwardly smiling, rather loving Rory's words and expansive gesture, Thommi began spooning her offerings into bowls and the general chatter moved back to Italy.'

CHAPTER 9

There is another person TO WHOM IT MAY CONCERN I am naming with such gratitude in my heart and that is you, BOB, my wonderful postman. One of the little games the evil invader played was to get hold of my post. He hired, cajoled, rewarded, or in some other way persuaded a small boy to intercept a colleague of BOB's before he reached my door to say that he'd take my post in for me. Unsuspecting, the moment the postman had handed my post to "my nephew" and disappeared, the small boy must have gone off to meet Billy Grant to give it to him. I discovered what had happened by sheer chance and quite quickly.

Billy Grant had intercepted a letter from my solicitor regarding finalising probate on my mother's estate which confirmed that he had deducted his fee and put the remainder of the money into my account via internet banking. My account details were set out in his letter. Now, I want those TO WHOM IT MAY CONCERN, to take note of how brazen and crafty evil people can be. At the time you are at your most vulnerable, learning to deal with loss, they twist the knife. I reported this to the police, before CID became involved, but I doubted that I or they could ever prove that Billy Grant was behind this attempted scam. But I know and, by the end, I will have persuaded you that nothing that has happened to me since I bought the sundial at the market has been down to anyone other than the evil invader. It was just his bad luck that since I once worked as a paralegal for a large law firm specialising in white collar crime, I am savvier as a result.

On the day Billy Grant suddenly appeared when I posted

a letter in the post box at the end of my street, I had a kind of premonition. His eyes had briefly slipped to the envelope I was posting and, thinking about that moment, I remembered that I was expecting a letter from my solicitor. When I arrived home, I rang him up to learn that he had written to me first class the previous day, credited my account, and closed the probate one. After the call, I rang my bank and stated that I had reason to believe that my post may have been tampered with and that I wanted a security alert on my accounts. It was then that I discovered that the bank had received a typed letter that day, purportedly from me changing my address details. I told them, I had not changed my address and asked them for the address I was supposed to be changing it to. Rather than give it to me, I was advised that this matter would go to their investigation department, and I asked to be kept updated. In the end, it transpired that the address was a block of flats. Letters which did not match the names on the letter rack inside the front door were left on the floor. It would be very easy to gain access to the block by ringing one of the bells and intercepting post. I was sent a copy of the letter I purportedly sent changing my address. The signature was almost identical to my own. Now this is how forward thinking the evil invader is.

I know you will believe, at this point, that I am paranoid, but I know I can date the moment that Billy Grant picked me as his next victim. When he had his expectant face on at the market, he heard you CASSANDRA say to me something like: "Go on, spoil yourself. Your parents would have liked you to splash out and enjoy yourself." From memory, I think you may also have said that my mother would have wanted me to buy the sundial. Past tense. From that moment, the evil invader knew I'd suffered loss, I was vulnerable. He offered to deliver the sundial, so he'd know where I lived. Then, after he and the boys had carried the sundial into my garden, he took out another of those ridiculous "Billy Grant Garden Furniture" cards, with no information on them, scribbled something like: "Delivered" on it and asked me to sign it as confirmation of delivery. I did so, and he then had my signature. I was already the chosen one, his next victim.

When I saw you BOB and explained what had happened with my post, you acted like a friend and that is how I know that your colleague had handed over my post to a young boy. You investigated what had happened and apologised. When I told you, BOB, about what had been happening to me you didn't question my word and ensured that no delivery person from the post office would ever again hand over my post. But you went further. You ensured no postman would leave any parcels to me with neighbours or anyone else. If I wasn't at home, you, and your colleagues, would put notes through my door to collect my parcels and it was on one of these occasions, shortly after the second court case, that I saw Billy Grant again. Just like that.

I had parked in the only available carpark near the sorting Post Office and was walking towards it when I felt the hairs on the back of my neck rise. I know that's a cliché, but it's true. Don't ask me how, but I knew that Billy Grant was behind me. Perhaps it was because I realised that I hadn't ordered anything and didn't expect anything other than the return of papers to do with my mother's probate. But since most of the paperwork had been scanned or electronically sent, why would it amount to a parcel? I turned and there you were, the sly grin splitting your fat cheeks as your tongue lilted to the side of your wet mouth, and the loose neck folds below your jowls wobbling in amusement as you raised thick fingers in a finger wave. As always, I felt my stomach plummet.

It was an effort to walk calmly towards the entrance to the sorting office. I looked at the envelope being passed through the hatch, after showing my ID. It looked bulky. At that moment BOB, you appeared. As my eyes met yours you came forward. We inspected the envelope, no return address anywhere on it. I signed something to the effect that I was not willing to receive it and you walked with me out of the sorting office. I was a little ahead of you when a black motorbike swerved out from a side entrance into the road, but I saw the visor suddenly clamp down over your face, Billy Grant. You saw I wasn't alone, but although BOB saw the bike your action was too swift for him to see your face. After telling you BOB that I wouldn't be ordering any parcels or packages of any kind, you said that, if possible, you'd photograph anything that came in for my address, in case that was helpful in the future. But you're no fool, Billy Grant, you don't take chances, you just change tack and come up with something new to torment me.

But times are changing. I have just received money into my account from a loan I took out. If my home doesn't sell quickly, I may need more liquid funds than I have in my savings. I am now about to visit my doctor and get signed off for six months. Everyone will be repaid because the equity in my home will cover everything, and before long I won't need anything further anyway, and neither will you evil invader. I am already feeling stronger. I am going to wash my hair.

CHAPTER 10

Having parked, John Carter, letter in hand, walked up the now familiar path to the front door of the victim's Edwardian cottage. He noticed that the small grass patches either side of the path had encroached upon it. There were two tubs, one either side of the front door, with dead plants in them. He looked at the windows. It was 11.00 o'clock in the morning but blinds were shut across the large window to the right of the door and the smaller window to the left of it showed no light. The property had a barricaded look about it, as though under siege. Sighing, because he thought his chances of getting the harassment victim to open the door didn't look good, John rang the front doorbell. He waited, tapping the envelope against the hand which wasn't holding it. He stood back and looked upstairs. There was no twitching curtain but there was a small gap between otherwise closed curtains, enough for a person to see out. She was in there, he was sure of it, and he rang the bell again, standing back and wearing a smile as he held up his badge. No response. The only thing to do was post the letter. Instead, he walked away and back to his car.

Sitting in the driver's seat, John thought about other options. What if he involved Social Services? He knew that if there was sufficient concern, the police could break into the property on the grounds of fearing for someone's safety. Look, he had a letter, why not try posting it through the letter box first? He supposed it was because he wasn't really satisfied with it. It had taken several attempts to come up with a letter Rory was prepared to sign. The trouble was that, although privately conceding that Clarke Emery and Johnny Hamilton could have handled things better, Rory didn't want to give the victim any grounds for complaint by making unnecessary admissions. So, an apology, without actually apologising, was Rory's aim. But John thought that as a result, the letter was unlikely to inspire confidence in the victim. It read like a 'covering our back' sort of letter, saying the right things about contacting police in future, but without conviction. John wanted to speak to her and use words of reassurance. He wanted to give the victim his card and scribble his mobile on it. If only she'd – He suddenly became aware of a red van pulling up ahead of him and the same postman as before, stepped out of it.

John sprinted to catch up with him and when he did, the postman turned and gave him the same cold stare. John smiled and took out his warrant card. The postman didn't bother to look at it.

I've got a letter and I'd like to hand deliver it to the owner of this house, but she won't open the door.'

'After the way she's been treated, I doubt she will,' the postman said. 'I suggest you just put it through her letterbox.'

'Look, the reason I want to see her, speak to her, is to tell her that her case has been taken over by me and to reassure her that I am very anxious that she reports any other incidents.' John said.

After a moment of looking at John's face, and noting the sincerity in his voice, the postman relaxed his own austere expression. 'Look, I'll shout through the post box and see if she'll come down but I'm going to tell her you're here and she may not open the door.'

'Anything you can do would be appreciated. Just a minute.' Taking out a card, John scribbled on it. 'At least I can explain that I'm putting my card through the door and ask her to contact me if she needs to report or tell me anything, or just to talk.'

The two men walked up to the door and John saw that his companion had a couple of other letters for her as he knelt and opened the flap. John listened to him shout out her name. A moment later, through the open hatch her footsteps could be heard descending from above. Once she was at ground floor level, the postman said: 'It's Bob, love. Look there's a police officer here with a letter for you. He says that the reason he wants to give it to you in person is that he wants to apologise for what's happened and hand you his card in person. I've told him you may not want to open the door. He sounds genuine to me though.'

John registered Bob's interpretation of his words as an apology but didn't care. He could tell Rory, honestly, that those were not the words he'd used if a complaint arose out of it, but the fact was she was owed an apology.

There was a moment's silence and then the sound of a chain being unlatched and a bolt sliding back before the door opened far enough for her to look out. Bob handed his letters over and said that he'd wait until she'd shut the door again. This really wasn't what John wanted, but he didn't have a choice. Grovelling in front of a stand-up member of the community was not what Rory had in mind.

Moving forward as Bob stepped back, John found himself looking at a face that he might have described as beautiful if it weren't for dark bags under the eyes and an expression that was both cynical and haunted. The woman was clearly young, his own age, or very slightly older, with a mass of tangled blonde hair, defined arched eyebrows, and dark eyes. It was difficult to see their colour, hazel or maybe green. He caught a brief glimpse of a shapeless garment, such as a middle-aged woman might wear, hanging loosely over a slim figure, and her feet were bare. She wore no make-up and her whole demeanour was of someone who had given up on herself.

Forgetting everything Rory said, John spluttered: 'I'm so sorry about what you've been through. This is just a standard sort of letter because I couldn't get hold of you, but I wanted to give you my card and to let you know that you can ring me anytime if you want to report anything that's happened to you, any further sightings of this perpetrator, or just to go over anything. If I don't answer because I'm out, please leave a message and I'll get back to you.'

John held out the envelope to her but, although she looked at it, she didn't take it. He took it back and then held out his card. 'Please,' he said, feeling his face redden as he heard the pleading in his voice. Her eyes looked past him towards Bob, then briefly met his before she suddenly snatched the card out of his fingers and then closed the door. It was so quick that John didn't have time to ask her if anything else had happened but at least she'd taken his card. True to his word, the postman was waiting until he saw John leave. Looking back at the closed door, John debated whether to post the letter through the letter box anyway but decided against it. He turned back to the postman.

'Thank you very much,' he said. Then, on impulse, he pulled another card out of his wallet and scribbled on it, before asking: 'Do you mind if I give you this just in case you want to get in touch with me?' To his relief, Bob looked at him almost with approval, took the card, and went on with his rounds as John walked back to his car.

CHAPTER 11

To those TO WHOM IT MAY CONCERN, I am adding you DC JOHN CARTER. I am not a fool. I still have a radio and television and I am aware that a celebrity victim two days ago made the headlines by talking to reporters about her terrible ordeal at the mercy of a stalker. In her case, the evil perpetrator has been imprisoned for the second time for breaching his restraining order. The second time - My God, do you see? - once your system has been invaded there is no cure, just an occasional reprieve. But a bad press means that, suddenly, there has been a police and prosecution panic about whether I will make a complaint. Well, JOHN CARTER, you were chosen to come and sus out the situation with your schoolboy looks and educated manner. I did not take the letter, but you have nothing to worry about. This document will say everything I need to say. You played your part well but, apart from allowing yourself to be used as part of a public relations exercise, you have not been responsible for what has so far happened. I took your card because I felt that BOB, my friend, hoped I would. It is now in my bin, so don't worry about me wasting your time. It won't happen. All the same, and pathetically, I was glad I'd washed my hair when you saw me.

When I listened to what the celebrity had to say about her ordeal, it made me wonder, Billy Grant, how your previous victims managed to escape you. Or did they? I know from the planning that went into my own ordeal those previous victims exist. I know that there is only one way out for me and, for the sake of others like the celebrity, whose stalker came back like an evil virus, there is only one solution to stop you.

But I won't lie to those of you TO WHOM IT MAY CONCERN. There's a part of me that yearns for the solace of you believing that my final actions will be put down to the loss of two parents and a downward spiral into a depression so deep that I was not responsible for what I did. But I must suppress that yearning or nothing good will come out of my actions. I am not going to let you off the hook, you must understand what I and others have gone through. You must understand that there is now no part of my life untarnished by the evil invader. I am sitting on the beautiful rug my parents gave me for my 21st birthday and staring at my wooden flooring, the floor I stripped and polished myself. I felt such pride in my meagre achievement and although many tears were spilt when I lost Mum and Dad, there was so much to cherish. But now these are adornments in a prison. I don't have bars on the windows, but I cannot escape without knowing that somewhere Billy Grant is waiting. On the mantlepiece are photographs of my parents and me on holiday in Greece. Such a happy time, but now when I look at those photographs a knot starting in my stomach rises and almost chokes me. I am losing the ability to feel those times, to re-live those happy moments. I never realised that a part of memory is the ability to feel the moment.

I am sure that everything you, my friends TO WHOM IT MAY CONCERN, say about my mental state is partially true. You will reason that if I hadn't had a double bereavement in a short space of time, I would have coped better, I would have come across at court in a more rational way, I wouldn't have allowed things to 'get out of proportion.' But you must understand, it's crucial I prove to you, that you are putting the cart before the horse. If I hadn't had the double bereavement, I would not have become Billy Grant's next victim. Evil invaders identify vulnerability in a nanosecond and target it like a magnet and the only way I can prove this is by Evidence, Independent Evidence.

Today, now that I have funds, is the day, Billy Grant, that the tables begin to turn. I can turn them because I have nothing left to lose and that makes me as dangerous to you as you are to me.

CHAPTER 12

Thommi Carmichael and John Carter met in East Sheen at the home of Thommi's great friends who were away in Australia. John also knew the family from when, as a new addition to CID, he worked for Rory when Thommi was being targeted by major villains.

After tidying up the garden, the two of them returned to the kitchen where Thommi made coffee using an upmarket espresso machine.

Sitting opposite John at the kitchen table, she smiled down at her mug and said: 'I hope you realise you are drinking very superior coffee. I wouldn't be allowed a contraption like that because Rory's a devotee of his grandmother's method of brewing coffee, and he even uses a coffee sock. A dinosaur or what?! Having said that, he puts up with me using the traditional Italian coffee pot on a hob. But I have to say, this gadget of Nell's is very time saving.'

On the table was a CD, and Thommi pushed it across to John.

'I watched the CCTV from the pub, but I was unable to give it the time I wanted. But first, tell me about your visit to the victim.'

After listening to John's account, she frowned.

'So, she's living like a hermit. You know, she's probably suffering from depression. Going by what you say, if she's given up on her appearance, not taking a bath or a shower, that can be a sign of mental illness.'

'She looked perfectly clean,' John said. 'I mean, I obviously don't know what she does,' he added hurriedly, suddenly embarrassed by jumping in so quickly and protectively. In a more measured tone, he continued: 'Although she is living as though . . . well, as though she is trapped and, I'm guessing, afraid to leave the house, she didn't come across as someone who's completely let go of herself.'

After considering John for a moment, Thommi said with a sympathetic smile: 'Okay, well, that's good, but she has lost all faith in the prosecuting authorities.' She sighed. 'We've left her feeling she has nowhere to turn, but at least she took your card.'

'She hasn't contacted me though.'

'That's a shame. Thank God she has a friendly Postie.' Looking up from her mug, Thommi added after a moment's thought: 'If he was a bit cold with you to begin with, she must have told him something. I wonder if he has any information which would be helpful?'

'I wondered about that myself and I'd like to talk to him if he'll talk to me. The trouble is finding the time. I'm in trouble with the Governor for giving her my card as it is and he's piling this five-handed conspiracy to defraud case onto me.'

'If you can find time, I'll take care of Rory,' Thommi said with a laugh.

John looked dubious. 'Mm, his view is that we've done our best, if she refused to take the letter well, we offered it. She now has my card, so she has a contact, no brownie points from Rory for that, however, and we should leave things until she reports anything else. He also thinks that it would be difficult to take matters further without a hell of a lot of independent evidence after she remained defiant about seeing Billy Grant, on the night he had an alibi supported by witnesses at the pub and CCTV.'

Thommi reached across the table and tapped the CD. 'Talking of which, did you notice anything strange on the CCTV?'

'Well, you can only see Billy Grant at the beginning of the evening and the end, because his birthday party was in a private alcove. But you see him go into the alcove with his guests and leaving the pub just ahead of them at the end of the evening, which was well after the complainant's finger-shadow incident. I think I know what you may be getting at, though. When you do see him, he appears to be ensuring that he is prominently caught by the camera.'

'Exactly.'

'But that doesn't help us much. It's possible he got someone else to do the finger shadow, but the victim is adamant she saw his face.'

'Mm, I'd say that he could have got someone who looked like him, if it wasn't for the fact that not many people would resemble him. But I suppose it was a fleeting glance in the dark, even with a streetlamp nearby, he was wearing a helmet, and it was just his smile towards the window before roaring off which she based her identification on. From her point of view, who else would she think would do such a thing?' Then, after a moment, Thommi continued her observations on the CCTV: 'You know he has this jovial party look for the camera, but there's something about him.' Thommi looked out into the garden. 'He's not someone I'd want stalking me, that's for sure.'

'No.'

'Plus, did you notice, that when we see him at the beginning of the evening, before he goes into the alcove bit, he's showing off by buying drinks for all in a flamboyant manner, but although the other men and women are nodding their thanks at him and there are a few thumbs-up, they're all talking to each other rather than him? The same when he leaves ahead of the rest, even though it's his party.'

John picks up the CD. 'I'll have another look at it and I'll try to find someone who was at the party to speak to, just in case. But we have the Landlord's statement, both Landlords' the outgoing one and the new one, and I can't make it a priority, because I think the postman is my first port of call if I can find a time when he's on his rounds.'

'I agree. Look, you'd better get going, I've taken up far too much of your time. Leave those mugs, I'll wash them and lock up. But please let me know if she contacts you and whether you manage to see the postman. I'm still part-time so I might be able to help.'

John smiled. 'It will be good when the prosecution service has you back at the CPS office full time.'

'It's what I'm aiming for,' Thommi said. 'I'm feeling fine and back in control now and, although we're always in touch, I'm missing my daily interaction with Nigel and other colleagues.' With a defiant shrug, she continued in a slightly challenging tone of voice: 'Also, I want to get back into court.' Watching John, collecting up his statements and CD, there was nothing in his demeanour to suggest that he knew about her complete meltdown at the Crown Court a year after she was stabbed. Luckily the Judge, who was aware of what had happened to Thommi and what she must have gone through, had handled the situation well, despite shocked representations from the defence barrister who felt that she should be locked up for Contempt of Court at the very least. The CPS were constrained nonetheless to put her on light duties until she was appointed as an out-of-hours advice lawyer, working from home.

Raising his head after securing his gym bag, having put the statements and CD back into it, John nodded and replied in a neutral voice: 'I'll bet, and they'll be missing you. It's so hectic at the minute.'

Thommi smiled. She was in no doubt that John knew all about the incident, and in normal times referring to her opposite number in court as a "pompous, miserable, little prick,' would have resulted in disciplinary proceeding at the very least. But she was grateful for the collective amnesia of her friends, colleagues, the Judge and Court Staff. It would be a difficult moment when she stepped back into Court, but she would get over it. She would.

Just as John began walking away, Thommi stopped him by saying: 'Sorry, could I have the CCTV again? Perhaps I should just try to take a photo on my phone of Billy Grant with his friends in the background leaving the pub.'

With a shake of his head John said: 'No need. The defence served us with two stills of their client, which included the shot you're talking about. They're pretty good, I'll get copies over to you. Billy Grant's brief made a lot of those stills at the second trial I'm told.'

'I meant to ask, who defended him?'

'Someone called Marcus Jenner.'

'Oh my God,' Thommi said, with an eye roll. 'No wonder our victim feels so bruised. He's a smug self-satisfied bastard who loves throwing his weight around and enjoys shredding witnesses using sarcasm as his main weapon. I've come across him a couple of times in both the Crown Court and the Magistrates', but he prefers the Magistrates Court because he gets away with more. He has a way of buttering up the beaks by sentences like: "Your Worships will have come across this situation many times," or "As experienced Magistrates you will well know …," that sort of thing.' Of course, it doesn't work with everyone, the old hands see through it. But if it was a new bench and he was the one who got our application to adduce the evidence from the first trial thrown out, it explains a lot. We should still Judicially review that decision. I'm happy to draft it and I'll talk to Nigel. It won't change anything at this stage, but it would help in any future trial.'

'If there is one,' John said balefully.

'Well, I doubt Billy Grant will give up when he's had nothing but success so far.'

Throwing his gym bag over his shoulder, John brought an image of his first sight of the victim to the forefront of his mind. 'That's what I'm afraid of,' he said.

CHAPTER 13

To THOSE TO WHOM IT MAY CONCERN, I have my first new piece of evidence.

Today, I went to my doctor's surgery to get myself signed off work for 6 months. I dressed carefully and presented very differently to when you DC JOHN CARTER, arrived at my door. Today, I had on a fitted dress and jacket, and I was wearing shoes, shoes with a little heel. Professional woman! But I have a mirror and can see the Billy Grant effect in my appearance and so will my doctor. The last time I was at the surgery I told her that I hadn't been sleeping well, and there should be a record on my doctor's notes regarding my anxiety over the first Court case. I also told her about my parents dying. This morning, I expanded my account to include an update on what I'd been going through. I am giving those who investigate my suicide and Billy Grant's murder my permission to see my medical notes. You probably don't need it, but you have it. Not, as evidence of my mental condition, although that will be documented for those of you keen to cling onto that explanation for my actions, but because of the dates I went to the doctor. I came away with a sick note but it's not all I came away with today.

I decided to walk to the clinic this morning rather than get the bus. It wasn't until I was almost there that I knew you were lurking somewhere near, Billy Grant. My phone was in my hand, ready, but I didn't turn around until the last moment. I then spun 90 degrees and caught you before you had time to look away. The leer faltered for a second, and then you smiled, waved, and walked off. I know what your explanation will be.

You didn't know I was ahead of you and were shocked when I turned and, inexplicably, took your photo because you weren't doing anything. But my shot shows exactly where I was. I couldn't believe my luck. Beginner's luck. But we are at the beginning of the end, and I deserve some luck.

Firstly – POTENTIAL EVIDENCE arising from my photo.

DC JOHN CARTER, I think you will investigate matters more thoroughly than DC JOHNNY HAMILTON. Please now ensure the following is done. Please believe me when I say that just as Billy Grant's compass has faithfully directed him to my whereabouts, I too, have gained knowledge into his mindset. Going through hell is an education of sorts.

ACTION REQUIRED: I don't know when or where Billy Grant moved to, but you do. What I do know is that I first went to my doctor's surgery shortly after I was informed that Billy Grant had just been charged. Today, was only the second time I have attended since the evil invader entered my life. Billy Grant may, if he saw me the first time, already be signed up to the same surgery as me, but I'd taken him by surprise today, and he walked quickly away after I took his photo, so perhaps not. He will now be doing the groundwork for his defence, should he need one, so what's the betting he'll be on the surgery books now? He'll say that he signed up because he has only recently moved to the area. Look up the date he joined the surgery. Look at whether it is the closest one to where he now lives. Look up any dates he has attended there since he signed up. Had he made an appointment for today over the phone or did he go back there later in the day to register after I snapped him with my camera, having thought things over? Do what you were meant to do, investigate a crime.

I am now off work for six months. The head of Human Resources has made all the usual threats under cover of expressions of concern: 'You will need to see Occupational

Health for our own records, but I think you will find them very helpful . . . I do understand that it's very difficult for you to function with these things going on, but we can send someone from Occupational Health to your home . . . you will need to comply with the Company's policy . . . (through gritted teeth) well, I'll ring you in a week and we'll look to set something up then. Now you look after yourself.' I have my certificate, and this will all be over by the time the first verbal or written warnings arrive. In the meantime, I have work to do.

Billy Grant, evil invader, when I have finished my arrangements, the only way you can continue your campaign will be for you to come into my parlour. Knowing that the end is in sight has made me stronger. I am no longer cowering and racking my brains to think of some way to keep living and stay sane while all the time waiting for you to emerge from the shadows to torment me. How will you react when you find that to be able to continue your campaign you will have to come close, you will have to take chances, and doing so is going to make you vulnerable to being caught? I have my first piece of new evidence today. It is only the start.

EVIDENCE 5

Photo of Billy Grant behind me as I walked towards my doctor's surgery.

CHAPTER 14

John Carter ploughed on into the night working on his conspiracy to defraud case, his computer open and providing most of the light in his room. He switched between reading witness statements to documentary evidence exhibited by those statements, disclosure items, and downloaded CCTV and photographs. Beside him, was a piece of paper, only just lit by the computer, on which he jotted down points as he went along. There were five columns, and his jottings went into one or other of them. Finally, exhausted, and realising it was after 2am he shut the computer. He now knew enough about the conspiracy to defraud case to be able to summarise his views to Rory on the strength of the evidence against each of the five defendants the following afternoon. What he'd done was buy himself some time the following morning. The victim of the stalker harassment case had still not contacted him. Recalling her demeanour as she briefly looked at him from behind her front door, before she snatched the card from his hand and shut the door on him, spurred John into trying to intercept the postman the following day.

Sitting in his car, a little way down from the victim's house John waited. His phone rang on a couple of occasions but, as it wasn't Rory wondering where the hell he was, he cancelled the calls. After 45 minutes, however, he decided that he'd have to leave it to another day if the postman didn't turn up in the next five minutes. It was just as he was turning on his engine that he saw a postman coming from the opposite end of the street and sighed with relief when he recognised it was Bob. He caught up with him two doors away from the victim's house. Bob didn't look pleased to see him, but he wasn't particularly hostile either. John told him that the victim hadn't been in touch and received a shrug in response.

'Your lot weren't particularly helpful when she did contact you. I don't think she has much faith in the police anymore.'

'I know, but that's what I'm afraid of. Look, I know it's asking a lot, but can you tell me what you know? I don't want her shut up in her home and afraid to come out.'

The postman looked across two houses towards the victim's front door and his brow furrowed.

'I do the road behind hers,' he volunteered. 'Her garden had a small fence, now there's a new one which is much higher.'

'So, she's increasingly anxious. Have you seen this stalker?'

'Not so that I'd be able to identify him. I think you know about her post going missing when she came to the sorting office.'

John took out his notebook. 'Tell me anyway because I've only recently taken over the case.'

'She couldn't prove he was the one who did it, particularly since ...' He let his sentence trail before speaking again. John listened as the postman told him about the missing post, the measures he'd taken to protect the victim and what had happened on the day she visited the sorting office. 'Seconds after we walked out of the sorting office, I saw the motorbike speed past us. Sadly, I wasn't in time to see his face. She did, but when he saw she wasn't alone the visor went down,' the postman finished.

'Thank you,' John said, scanning his notes to see if there were more questions he needed to ask.

'Second thoughts, she might not have reported the bit about coming to the sorting office and the bike,' Bob said, his brow furrowing, 'but I think she did report the attempt to divert her bank account address to another one and the link between her post going missing and that.'

'Okay,' John said. Something was stirring at the back of his mind. He had read a short entry somewhere about uniformed police checking an address and wondered if it was related to what he was being told. Something actioned, but not proceeded with. 'Do you know the name of the bank?'

The postman gave him the name but added: 'I couldn't swear to it, and I don't know which branch or anything like that. But she thought the two things must be linked because the letter stolen was from her solicitor and it had her bank details. but she told me there was no way to prove anything. But like I said, I think she did report the attempt to divert her mail so you should know about that.' He shuffled his feet suddenly. 'Look, I probably shouldn't have said as much as I have.'

'Yes, you should,' John replied firmly. 'I'm going to try to speak to her through the letterbox, but if she doesn't reply I want you to promise that you'll report anything further.' Running a hand through his hair, he added: 'Look, do you know if there's been anything further?'

'I don't, but with the fence and everything ... but I don't think she leaves the house much anymore, and I know she's on sick leave so maybe he'll give up.' He paused for a moment. 'I'll let you know if I witness anything, but I have to get on now.'

It was as John was kneeling to shout through the letterbox, that he felt a hand on his shoulder and saw Bob there.

'I think I'd better try first,' he said. John gave way.

The postman called her name and said: 'It's Bob, love. Are you all right? Look the same young police officer is here. He wanted to know whether I had seen this stalker and I told him that I hadn't seen his face, but I had seen a motorbike speed away after we left the sorting office. I hope that's all right. He wants to speak to you.'

A voice came back. 'Thanks, Bob. I don't intend to deal with the police anymore. I'm fine and I don't want to speak to the detective. Please let him know.'

John heard her and sighed but, after the postman put

some post through her door and stood, John gave it one more shot: 'Please come down and talk to me,' he said. 'I know you've had a bad time and we could have done things better but give me a chance.' She didn't reply. John heard a sound behind him and turned as two people walked past after looking at him kneeling on the ground and speaking through a letterbox and he felt a fool. Waiting until they'd gone, he resumed: 'Look, please at least tell me whether anything else has happened.' The silence continued but, just before giving up, her voice sounded again.'

'There's nothing I want to report,' she said. 'One day you'll have everything there is, until then please leave me alone. I'm coping very well, and I don't want any further contact with the police.'

'You have my card, please let me know if anything else happens.'

'Thank you. Please go now.'

Standing up slowly, John debated whether he should demand she speak to him at the door or threaten to call social services. But on what grounds? She was off on sick leave, but she said she was fine, her voice was clear, her instructions were clear, she responded well to Bob. Wouldn't threats, particularly after what she'd been through just strengthen her resolve not to trust the police. He walked slowly towards his car. Before he arrived at it, his phone rang again. This time it was Rory.

CHAPTER 15

I'm almost ready for the evil invader, but not quite. The high fence at the back of my garden is up. To be able to see into my garden or get close to my house you will have to climb it, Billy Grant. The camera I'm having set up this afternoon, will trip the moment you touch the top of my fence. The camera is on my wall, and I can recover it through my upstairs window so, Billy Grant, there'll be a photo of you peering over my fence. Even if I can't get to the camera, the moment the photo is taken it is sent to my phone. It's a light sensitive camera which works at night as well as in daylight. Try explaining that away. But there are always things that can go wrong, no one need tell me that. Billy Grant might try to get to me via my neighbours' gardens. But my neighbour on the left has a hanging basket on his fence and shrubs and pots of plants up against it, and my neighbour on the right has a flower bed which, even at this time of year, still had some roses in bloom. But how likely is it that you, Billy Grant, will want to be caught in a neighbour's garden? I think that if I prevent you from stalking me, you will try to climb over the back fence.

I have also ordered two more phones. I am probably being over-cautious but, if anything goes wrong, I want a second phone which I will edit, and another I will smash so that it looks as though my original phone was destroyed in an accident. The evil invader must never have access to the phone I still use. I am thinking like a criminal, and these are my version of 'burner' phones. Sadly, you are not the only criminal now Billy Grant, but you are evil and, whatever others may believe, I am not.

I know those of you TO WHOM IT MAY CONCERN will ask afterwards why, when I had it, I didn't then give my evidence to the police? You will say that DC JOHN CARTER is a diligent detective as I believe he is, and that he would have pushed for Justice for me. You will say that I must be depressed to the point of being deranged because otherwise I would have given him the evidence. It is so difficult to explain why because, of course, much of what you say makes sense in the real world, your world. But when I have the evidence documented, I think it will be easier to explain. You need to understand the lengths to which I know the evil invader will go to destroy me before you understand why.

You think, at this stage I have choices. I don't. Choices are what people who lead your lives have. What if I handed over sufficient evidence for the police and CPS to charge Billy Grant again, and I accept that one photo is nothing like sufficient evidence. Sufficient independent evidence. What if, a different and more experienced person prosecuted on my behalf and the evidence from the first trial and the CCTV from Waitrose in the second trial, was admitted as evidence in the next trial? What if Billy Grant was finally convicted, and it's a big if? What next? A first conviction, no violence – My God, please redefine violence - what next? Don't worry, I will answer the questions before you TO WHOM IT MAY CONCERN have asked them, and by the end of this document, you will, you must understand, why I had no choice, or my actions will be in vain. It is difficult for me to hold things together as it is, but I am managing. I cannot let any of you, except Bob, into my existence anymore, and that includes you DC JOHN CARTER, or my resolve will collapse. But I'm looking to you all to restore to me in death what you couldn't in life. To those of my friends who have memories untouched by Billy Grant, please remember my wonderful generous minded family, and please remember me as I was that sunny day at the market, drinking cider and eating cupcakes.

My delivery of food is coming. I have ordered so much

that I can survive now to the finishing line. I am hoping that my next entry in this document will include Evidence, a photo shot of the evil invader.

CHAPTER 16

John entered Rory's office armed with the five-handed conspiracy to defraud case and met his DI's icy stare beneath those thick dark eyebrows, without flinching.

'Guv,' he said, before sitting down in the chair opposite him.

Rory looked at the file, at this stage a slim brown folder because most of the evidence was on the CPS and Police high security computer system, and then at John. 'So, what have you got for me?' he asked, his tone of voice brisk.

It took twenty minutes for John to give Rory a meticulous summary of the evidence, another ten to point out the weaknesses in the case against each defendant, ten more minutes to outline what action and further investigation was required, and five more minutes to answer one or two questions from Rory.

Forty-five minutes later, Rory leaned precariously back in his chair and, raising an eyebrow, said to his young DC: 'So, you covered your back?'

'Always,' John replied cheerfully.

'When do you find time to sleep?' Rory asked but continued before John could reply: 'I suppose there must have been a time when I could burn the candle at both ends but, if so, it was a hell of a long time ago. Not that you're off the hook. I want to know why, having given the harassment victim your card, you decided to slope off to see her again.'

'My main aim was to intercept the postman. Thinking over our conversation it occurred to me that she may have confided in him. I wanted to know why initially he cold shouldered me and to discover whether there had been any further incidents which he knew about, and we didn't.'

'And were there?'

'Yes, but something that happened before charge, and part of it was reported. I'm going to go over the CAD entries again.' At the end of his update, John added: 'She didn't tell us about the sorting office and motorbike because Bob didn't get a look at the person on it.'

'So, if it was Grant on the bike, it shows he has access to one even if he doesn't own it,' Rory said. After twiddling his pen, Rory shook his head. 'Doesn't help, unless we can crack the airtight alibi, which isn't likely although it would be good to get a statement from her on the missing post visit to the depot.'

'Yes, but she won't do one now.' John didn't add that he thought that Johnny Hamilton would have taken the view that it would be impossible to bring the post interception home to Billy Grant so would not have instigated further enquiries anyway.

'Well, if that's the tack she's taking, there's really nothing more we can do. If she's reported nothing further, then there's nothing further to investigate. Hopefully, there isn't anything.'

John hesitated and then said: 'I think from something she said there may be. I managed to talk to her briefly through her letterbox and she said: 'One day you'll have everything there is, until then please leave me alone.'

'So, you think that means that she's making notes about things but not reporting them until she thinks she has enough?'

'Yes, and that she's doing her own investigation into things.'

'What? By barricading herself into her house.'

John nodded. 'It's not likely she'll get far by doing that, but she's on sick leave now apparently so, theoretically, she has more time.'

Righting his chair with a thump, Rory looked his subordinate officer in the eye and said: 'Well, we don't, so from now on we get on with the work we have.'

'There are just a couple more enquiries I'd like to make so

that if there is a complaint we can say, hand on heart, we did what we could. But I'll do them in my own time. Also, the CPS may Judicially review the Magistrates' decision to disallow the evidence of the first trial to be adduced in the second, so if we get more -'

'Not good news there, I'm afraid,' Rory said, interrupting him. 'Nigel Sheridan takes the view we wouldn't succeed and Thommi, reluctantly, ended up agreeing with him. The problem is that it was argued that we wanted to adduce the evidence of the first case to bolster a weak second case; weak because of Billy Grant's alibi evidence on one of the allegations. That being the case, Nigel doesn't think that the Magistrate's decision is sufficiently "irrational" or "perverse" for us to win. Once the bad character decision went against us, the case should have been discontinued.'

'I think we're all agreed on that,' John said, in a slightly less measured way than usual.

'The trouble is that these cases are being fast-tracked because of their nature and there's not enough analysis of them. But should there be another case with allegations supported by independent evidence, and -' his eyes holding John's across the table, 'it's unlikely there'll be another case unless there is independent evidence, the same argument by the defence cannot be made. The CPS will also instruct more senior Counsel to prosecute or, if he can, Nigel will do it himself. Now -' Rory broke off and looked past John towards his doorway.

John turned to see DS Emery, standing there. 'I'm just leaving,' he told the DS, relinquishing his seat, and turning back briefly to Rory on his way towards the door adding, with a wave of his conspiracy to defraud folder: 'I'll get on with the further enquiries,' before walking down the corridor with a smile on his face. DS Emery's appearance had allowed him to forestall anything Rory was about to say after his "Now" which he didn't want to hear!

CHAPTER 17

Just another couple of days and I will be ready with my plan, but I believe that I may get some "independent" evidence because of an office safety measure I had put in place some time ago but haven't thought about for a while. Ever since my post was intercepted and I began to see Billy Grant almost every time I left my house, I told my colleagues that if any caller rang my office asking for me by name, and Billy Grant would certainly know where I worked, would they please immediately get a copy of the call off the office tape recording. In my managerial role, people don't usually ask for me by name as I don't man the phones or deal directly with the public.

Adding another name, to THOSE TO WHOM THIS MAY CONCERN, my lovely head of complaints, COLIN, suggested a further safety measure. Should anyone ask for me directly, any member of my team fielding the call would use a pseudonym, should the caller ask for their name. I have a list of the names, each of my team chose. The less the evil invader knows about people in my life, the better. But, more than that, if he tried to use an office contact of mine in any of his little games to torment me, I would know immediately it was him if one of the names my team had chosen was used. Well, today, COLIN, you rang me to say that a male had called and asked for me by name. You told him I was out of the office for some time and asked the caller what he was ringing about as you'd put him through to someone else who could help him. But he told you that he needed to speak to me personally and then asked for your name, and you replied: "Jack." He ended the call without identifying himself. I am waiting, Billy Grant, for some action on your part when you will use the name "Jack" to try to force a reaction out of me.

My net curtain is up at the back of my kitchen and my kitchen door to the garden now also has blinds. Later today my local garden centre is arriving to take away the dead plants in my pots outside my door, and to put large shrubs on my strip of land outside the front kitchen window. With my plantation blinds over both my front and rear sitting room windows, once my heavy pots of plants, which are hardy enough for this time of year, are in place it will be impossible for you to get near enough to see me, Billy Grant. I debated whether to get a solid wood door for the kitchen, but would you risk breaking in? You might imagine that the police have arranged for me to have a panic button somewhere and that I'd hear you. They did instal a panic alarm before the first case although I've never used it. I like to have some natural light, if only through the blinds, in my kitchen so, no, I don't think it's necessary for the reasons I've given.

After today, I am completely self-contained within my house. I don't call my property home anymore. I found it with my mother, but the thrill of the purchase, the memory of furnishing it, the love I and my family put into it, and the security I felt here, you have managed to ruin, Billy Grant. But what I now need is a fortress, not a home and, after today, that is what I will have. It's strange, I am feeling like I imagine soldiers must have felt sheltering on their hill on the eve of a battle. They and their comrades. To those friends TO WHOM THIS MAY CONCERN, I want you to know that I still think of you as comrades. I suppose what I'm saying is that now that some of my control over my life is returning, so are some of my memories, good memories. Billy Grant's invasion is not so complete.

CHAPTER 18

Thommi drove to Isleworth with one aim. There was a late autumn market there and she wanted to see if it was organised by the same people as the one in Barnes, where the victim of the stalker had bought the sundial.

Arriving at the field, next to a country Manor House, where the market was being held, she noticed quite a crowd. She bought a ticket and programme, which listed the contact details of the organisation which managed the market. Neither Billy Grant nor Garden Furniture were listed on the programme, but the names of some of the other stallholders rang a bell. Nigel had read out one or two of them to her over the phone which he'd found in the Barnes' market programme listed on last year's Grant file disclosure schedule.

There were quite a few food stalls displaying organic food products, jams, pickles, and including some home-made goodies including cupcakes, which Thommi remembered, the victim had eaten at the Barnes' event. After circling the field twice, Thommi approached a table selling local cider. She looked at the products while she waited for the stallholder to finish serving a customer and then instigated a conversation with him.

'I'm here to ask if, by any chance, you know a stallholder called Billy Grant. He was selling garden furniture at the Barnes market last year?'

He shook his head. 'I was there but I don't think I know him.'

Thommi took out the photo still of Billy Grant to show him, but he shook his head and after buying a couple of bottles of cider, she moved on. At least she now knew that there was a chance that other stallholders would have been at the Barnes market too. It wasn't until she took the photo out for the third time, that a middle-aged woman with a friendly freckled face, manning a cake stand, told her that she did remember him selling Garden furniture at the Barnes market.

'That's him,' the woman said in a musical voice. 'That's the one, he had a young lady helper, probably still at school and doing a weekend job. She looked after the stall when he wandered off.'

A young helper was news to Thommi. 'Oh, his daughter maybe?' she suggested.

'I don't know, but that would explain why she was there because from the way he talked to her no other teenager would work for him a second time.' The woman hesitated suddenly: 'Sorry, you said someone you knew had bought something from him and wanted to get in touch. Is he a friend?'

'No, definitely not,' Thommi reassured her with a laugh. 'Not someone I'd want as a friend.'

'Phew! I'm always putting my foot in it. He's not here today. I don't think I'd seen him before the Barnes market.' She looked around the field. 'I know most of the stallholders here and lots of them are now my friends. The reason I noticed him,' she said, nodding at the photo Thommi still held, 'is because he was not far away from my table and he ordered this young kid around until a customer arrived and then, literally, elbowed her out of the way. One minute he acted like a bully another, when there was a customer, he was all service with a smile.'

'Did he stay to the end?'

'Well, he sold a sundial to a customer and left the young girl looking after the stall while he took off in his van to deliver it. He returned sometime later, told his young helper to help him load the van and then dismissed her.' Frowning, the woman added: 'I heard her ask him for her money, so probably not his daughter thinking about it, and he told her he'd settle with her later, but that she hadn't been much use. She looked upset. He then got into his van and left. I doubt she'll see a penny of what she's owed. Good riddance, not a nice bloke. I hope he doesn't come to any more of our markets.'

Thommi shook her head and thought for a moment or two, while her new friend sold two Victoria sponges and a packet of brandy snaps to a couple of customers. Were there any other questions she should be asking?

'Did he have a lot at his stall to stow in the van?' Thommi asked when the stallholder was free.

'No, it wouldn't have fitted in. I saw the back of the van and it was full of junk, including an old bed, a motorbike -'

'Sorry, did you say a motorbike?'

'Yes, big black beast leaning against the van wall.'

At just that moment, one of the other stallholders wandered up with a cappuccino for Thommi's informant, so she waited, looking at the cakes, while the two stallholders chatted for a moment or two. Her friend then indicated Thommi.

'This lady, sorry I don't know your name?'

'Thommi, short for Thomasina, Carmichael.'

'Mine's Fran and this is Derek who has his own vineyard and his wines have received several awards.'

'Wow, I'll come over and look at them,' Thommi promised.

'Show him your picture of Billy Grant love.' Thommi did so. 'You were in Barnes last year Derek. Do you remember this chap?'

'He looks familiar. Something to do with garden furniture?'

'That's him. I can't remember why you said you wanted to know if I'd seen him recently,' Fran said. 'Is something wrong with the sundial?'

'No. I'm a prosecutor but I'm not here in any official capacity -,'

'Aha, stolen goods,' Derek said, with a knowing shake of his head.

'No, no, but I'd be grateful to know if either of you see

him again.' At this moment, Derek was hailed by a large woman standing behind a wine stall. There was a crowd waiting to be served. 'I've got to go. Give your details to Fran, and she'll give them to me.' He gave a wave and sprinted towards his table.

Thommi tore a piece of paper out of a notebook and wrote on it while Fran sold cakes to two other customers.

'Would you mind giving me your name and email or contact number?' Thommi asked when Fran was free again. 'I'm not an investigator, but a young detective may wish to take a statement from you if you wouldn't mind giving him one. His name is DC John Carter from South-West Central CID. I can't really talk about this now, but you've told me one or two things which might be important to an investigation.'

Fran looked puzzled, but readily gave Thommi her details after taking her card. 'I can't really add to anything I've told you but, of course, I'll give the officer a statement if I've said anything interesting. It'll be a first!'

Thommi smiled and took Fran's details before buying the last Victoria Sponge. She thanked her warmly, telling her she was now off to sample Derek's wine.

CHAPTER 19

I have a recording device on my landline but I'm not going to answer calls. If you ring me, Billy Grant, when you can no longer follow me, either you leave a message, in which case my recorded messages will pick it up, or you keep ringing until you are bored, or bored of leaving silent messages on my answerphone. The same goes for my mobile, but I keep this off for most of the time except when I pick up my messages. My landline isn't listed, but I have no doubt you will have found out its number. This is not the first time you have stalked someone, evil invader, and I am not underrating you. That was my mistake to begin with and, despite all the political soundbites and promises, the tightening of Stalking laws, the press coverage, that was your mistake too DC JOHNNY HAMILTON. Billy Grant hadn't touched me, there was no violence, no threatening emails or phone calls, he seemed to you to be a pathetic little loser and you didn't do your job, it wasn't worth your while, it was beneath you. Worse, you took Billy Grant's bait. I don't know how he pulled off his alibi, but he fitted me up and you were happy to have an excuse to throw in the towel. He played you DC JOHNNY HAMILTON because you don't understand how evil works, you don't appreciate the damage, the carnage, it leaves in its wake, you underrated him. That's me giving you the benefit of the doubt. I still think about your words on that last occasion we spoke. I'm not sure I even trust you.

I think you are different, DC JOHN CARTER, but I can't take the chance and it's already too late. I can fight my corner and leave you the Evidence to explain my actions, but my strength to do that stems from knowing that I will soon be free. Promise me, JOHN CARTER, even though you won't be able to make that promise to me in person, promise me that when this is over you will not say: "Lessons will be learnt," that empty get out clause for authorities to stage manage bad press, having failed to protect shattered lives. Promise me you will act on the lessons my actions will teach you. Actions not words.

Today is the first day of living in my fortress. I have one exception to my rule of avoiding all personal contact. BOB, I will speak to you through my letterbox and, if you say there is no one about, I will open my door to you briefly. I don't want any authorities intruding having been told that I may be harming myself and forcing entry to my fortress. BOB, I am relying on you to tell police that you have spoken to me and that I am managing fine. If they ask you, please tell the truth. I am fine. Now that I have a plan in place and I know the outcome, I am strong. That is why I must not let myself weaken. That is why, despite having another piece of evidence, I am adding it to my list rather than trusting the police with it.

So, my second piece of "independent" evidence! Yesterday, Friday evening, I received a typed note through my door. Very brief. It said: "I know you are on sick leave, but I wonder whether you would meet me tomorrow at eleven at the café around the corner from the office. Something has come up at work you should know about because it affects you. I don't want any phone calls or texts registering on my phone or yours. It will be a very brief meeting as I don't want anyone to see us together because I could lose my job. Hoping a Saturday is safe. Jack." I rang you COLIN, and you confirmed what I already knew. Colin had not put a note through my door.

This is evidence not even you will be able to brush aside. It won't have fingerprints on it, but I have put it carefully into a see-through envelope anyway.

EVIDENCE 6

The note put through my door by you Billy Grant. It cannot be from anyone else. You are the person who rang my office and you typed "Jack" on the note.

CHAPTER 20

John walked out of CID to the doorway giving him access to the police station car park. The moment he was sitting in the driving seat of his vehicle he returned Thommi Carmichael's call using his mobile.

'Sorry to cut you off earlier but Johnny Hamilton was hovering around. Tell me what you found out at the market.'

Thommi did so while John put his phone on speaker, then balanced it on his dashboard while he took notes. At the end of Thommi's account, there was a moment's silence.

'At this stage, I think I need a statement from you and, once I have it, I'll contact Fran and take one from her,' John said.

'I agree. It would be great to arrest Billy Grant for perjury or perverting the course of justice, but we don't have nearly enough to do so.'

'If we did that, and he came up with a plausible reason for a motorbike in his van all we'd have done is shown our hand too early. I think it's better to try to get some further evidence, if he's still stalking our victim, and question him about the motorbike as part of the interview.'

'I'll ask the clerk at court to forward me any notes of the second court case. I'd like to know whether our suspect simply said he didn't own a motorbike or whether he went further, i.e., said he had nothing to do with motorbikes, that sort of thing. I know that no motorbike is registered to him.'

'So, Fran called it a big black beast. Bob, the postman, said the bike that swept past them outside the sorting office at speed was black. The trouble is . . .' John sighed.

'I know,' Thommi said down the line. 'The pub CCTV, the Landlords of the pub, the fact that it was Billy Grant's own birthday party so it would be noticeable if he left in the middle of it.'

'I suppose he could have lent the bike to someone he'd paid to zoom over and do the finger shadow thing.'

'The victim said she saw his face, or part of his pace.'

'That could have been a genuine mistake. As you said, it was dark, and she'd have expected it to be him. The trouble is, it doesn't really take us much further unless we find the person who did ride over.'

'What if it was one of the friends at the party?'

'I need to find out more about Billy Grant's friends and try to talk to one of them.'

'It would also be good to find this poor helper who was with Billy Grant when he sold our victim the sundial.'

'That too.'

'I'll let you get on. I know you're snowed under. I'm going to contact the market organisers in case they can give me any more information. Keep me posted.'

'Just one more thing, which may be nothing. There's a sentence in the police log of one of the victim's calls to the station regarding her post going missing and being re-directed. Another sentence simply states that the address it was re-directed to has no known connection to Billy Grant, but it would be good to know what enquiries were made. However, our victim apparently accepted that there was no way of proving that this was him. I've asked for the call and, when I have a minute, I'll listen to it in case something's been missed.'

'The police log doesn't say anything else?'

'No. This was information entered early in the investigation when uniformed police were dealing with it.'

'Interesting.'

'Anyway, I'll keep you posted.'

As John came out of the door leading to the car park,

Johnny Hamilton walked up to him in the corridor.

'I've heard on the grapevine that our alleged stalkee – is that a word? – is not ringing up every five minutes.'

John looked at Johnny thoughtfully. 'She's not ringing up at all,' he replied.

'Aren't you the lucky one?'

'I'm not sure about that, Johnny. The impression I'm getting is that she's lost all trust in the police, has effectively barricaded herself inside her home, and that she may be sitting on some evidence which she's not now passing over to us.'

John watched his colleague's countenance change from one of casual enquiry into defensive mode.

'What makes you think that?' Johnny demanded.

'I spoke to her briefly, very briefly, and she told me that one day we'd have everything there is but until then she wants us to leave her alone.'

There was no mirth in Johnny's laugh. 'Don't fall for that load of old bollocks, she's manipulative, take it from someone who's been taken in already. It's probably just a new way of attention seeking.'

'Okay,' John replied calmly, 'but one thing I wanted to ask you is about a line or two in the early police log about her post going missing and being re-directed.'

Shrugging in an exaggerated manner, Johnny said: 'Even she accepted that there was no possibility of us proving that it was anything to do with Grant. That was early on when uniform was conducting the case and it was the reason it was passed to us. A flimsy reason, if you ask me but the fact that enquiries were becoming, what was described as, more complex, was the excuse to give it to us.'

'Oh right. Do you know what was done about that complaint?'

'Long story short, someone forged her signature, seemingly, on a letter to her bank redirecting her mail to another address. Uniformed officers went over to the address and none of the names of the flat owners matched Grant's.'

'Did anyone check whether he'd previously lived there?'

'For Christ's sake, John.' Johnny exploded. 'Grant is supposed to be a stalker not someone dealing in white collar stuff. This is a guy who, even on the allegations taken at their highest, has never rung her, texted her, laid a hand on her, we simply don't have the manpower to chase unpromising leads. We have much more serious cases.'

John simply said: 'Okay.' But his calm demeanour seemed to rattle Johnny.

'Sorry, I'm not getting at you,' he said in a milder tone. 'If I've made any mistakes or you want me to clarify anything, I'm around. Don't be afraid to ask me.'

John nodded. 'As you say there are more pressing matters,' and he began to walk on past Johnny towards CID.'

'Keep me briefed on how things go, and I'll help if I can.'

John turned briefly. 'Thanks Johnny.'

Like hell, John thought as he walked through the door of CID. Suddenly, he had a new line of enquiry.

It was just as Thommi was eating something, before her work shift, that Fran's call came through.

'I'm sorry to ring you, it's Fran from the Isleworth market.'

Please don't say that, on second thoughts, you don't want to be involved in any investigation or to give any statement, Thommi prayed. But that wasn't why Fran had rung.

'I just thought I'd tell you that when we were clearing up and I was telling my mates about our conversation, I hope that's all right, one of the stallholders, Matthew, had seen Billy Grant at the Barnes' market too. He recognised the description and saw the man beside his van with "Garden Furniture" written on it.'

'Oh good. Did he witness anything you didn't?'

'No, once he'd seen him, he kept well away. But he told me he'd had a bit of a run in with him at a market in Kingston over two years ago. It was over a prime pitch near the entrance to the market that both believed they had paid for. He said that he didn't remember the man's name as Billy but, in the end,

Matthew gave way when the organisers at the market begged him to settle for another pitch and gave him a deal on a pitch at an upcoming market.   Matthew said that the guy was turning nasty, and he hadn't seen him again until the Barnes market. But why I've rung you is that he said that at the Kingston market the guy had a van just the same, same make, as the "Garden Furniture" one but it had "Vehicle Accessories" painted on it, not "Garden Furniture."   That he did remember.   I didn't know if you'd want to know that.'

After profuse thanks and taking down Matthew's details, Thommi opened her mobile phone and, for the second time that day, dialled John's number.

CHAPTER 21

Friday night was the first time I slept through to dawn without waking. My last thought before drifting off was of Billy Grant tomorrow, skulking somewhere near the café around the corner from the office where we bought our sandwiches for lunch. He would wait in vain, hiding behind buildings, pretending to look in shops, wait until he could surprise me. But I wouldn't turn up. How would he react to his plan not working?

Then on Saturday morning, you COLIN wonderful friend and colleague, rang and told me to text over a photograph of the evil invader because you were going to be near the café at 11.00 a.m. and would snap a photo of him if he turned up. I could hardly breathe all morning then, and just a minute after I'd turned on my mobile, your photo pinged through by text. It was him. It was Billy Grant. You caught him, COLIN. I can't express what that moment meant to me. You, my colleagues, have been generous in your support of me but I couldn't help wondering if, after two failed court cases, some of you had also begun to doubt, begun to wonder if I was ill and imagining things. It would only be natural for you to do so. But COLIN, you have now put that to rest. Speaking to you on the phone, hearing you promise to do a full statement regarding the call you'd taken in the office, the name "Jack" you'd given when speaking to the evil invader, and exhibiting the photo you took this morning, I was so choked with gratitude tears were running down my face. You are also getting a copy of the recorded call made by the evil invader to my office and exhibiting it. I am so grateful, so, so, grateful. This is independent evidence COLIN, this is corroborative evidence DC JOHNNY HAMILTON, this is evidence that you Billy Grant will find difficult to explain away because in the photo you are walking away from the café having, as COLIN saw, just looked through its window. There are only so many coincidences DC HAMILTON that even you can swallow. Billy Grant doesn't live where I work, after all.

Sunday, I started sorting through my family photographs. There were so many, our smiling faces marking the thirty-two passing years of my life and bearing witness to such happy times. I now found I could relate better to those memories and live so many of them again. Then, suddenly, out of nowhere, I was once again crying, tears streaming down my face. It was better not to relate. I could feel my parents' hope for me to be happy and fulfilled with friends and laughter and, one day, children of my own. It took me an hour of pacing around my sitting room, lit mainly by artificial light because of my shutters, before I returned to my sorting. Taking a deep breath, acknowledging what my loved ones would feel if they knew how differently things had turned out but once more in control, I returned to my macabre task of "putting my affairs in order."

I woke up today, Monday, wondering how soon Billy Grant would react to one of his plans failing and had my answer almost immediately which slightly surprised me. I knew that it wouldn't be long before he'd come by my home when he failed to get close to me, to make eye contact, to leer, but I didn't expect it to be so soon. The failure of the coffee meeting had obviously unsettled him. I had hardly dressed when I looked through the small gap in my curtains and saw you, Billy Grant, emerge from behind your "Garden Furniture" van, parked opposite to me. You looked directly at my house and then turned around and began to put something through the letterboxes of my neighbours on the opposite side of the road. Cards with a contact number for anyone who wants to buy garden furniture, possibly? You are not on any bail conditions, Billy Grant, but you must still feel untouchable if you are willing to be seen in my street. All the same, I wonder whether some of your confidence drained the moment you took in the changes I've made to the house. No longer can you see through to any of my rooms, you won't know whether I am here, or whether I can see you. Already you know that I am no longer at work. I failed to turn up at the café yesterday. You will feel baulked. What will you do now? I watched you from my darkened room walk down the street opposite, as far as I could within my limited view. I then saw you return, still on the opposite side of the road to me. So, if in future any questions are asked, after all I took the photo of you near my surgery, I think I know what you will say Billy Grant. You will say that you didn't dare cross the road because you had been through two very upsetting court cases, and you didn't want to go near my home. You will say you were staying right away from me after the lies I'd told in court. But things have changed, and the evidence will continue to build because you won't be able to help yourself, Billy Grant. What does an evil invader do when he is prevented from invading? You will take chances and chances create opportunities for evidence gathering. I can think this through calmly now, I am feeling stronger. I can see my path and the end for both of us, although some way off, is in sight.

When you, BOB, turned up, I opened the door. Billy Grant now avoids being around when my postman delivers his post. I told you BOB what I'd seen and asked you whether you'd mind knocking on the door of someone across the road to ask whether they'd had a card put through their door. If they had, and they didn't need it, I asked you to see if they would give it to you. It was a big ask, but you didn't let me down. You had a parcel to deliver diagonally opposite and came back from there with a card which, the owner, a retired doctor, had picked up from his mat early that morning. Unfortunately, it didn't say: "Garden Furniture" it said: "Vehicle Accessories." But I am including it as evidence. Early in the morning, when the card dropped through the letterbox, is when I saw Billy Grant walking up the paths of the properties on the opposite side of the road. Evil Invader, you will deny knowing anything about a card stating: "Vehicle Accessories." It had a mobile phone number underneath, but nothing more. But BOB will tell the police that I asked him to go over to see if there was a card, my neighbour will say it was early in the morning, and there was a card on his mat. I will not ring the mobile number from my phone. I will not allow you Billy Grant to use a call from me in some twisted way.

But TO THOSE TO WHOM THIS MAY CONCERN who will be investigating the suicide and murder, and I am mainly thinking of you, DC JOHN CARTER, although I am sure you will ring the number on the card, please ensure you investigate it further. You can do this by seeing how many streets that card was posted through. Was it just this street? Had Billy Grant covered himself by putting cards through one or two others close by? Were any cards put through the doors of the streets where he lived? If the person leafletting only put cards through the addresses across the road from me and, perhaps the odd street nearby, that adds to my evidence of seeing Billy Grant early this morning. Please investigate properly because otherwise nothing will change. You and those others TO WHOM IT MAY CONCERN must understand the power of evil or it will continue to thrive with new victims surrendering their lives to the inevitable.

So, the evidence is building:

EVIDENCE 7

The photo on my phone, sent to me by my colleague Colin, of Billy Grant walking away from looking into the café, which is clearly shown in the shot of Grant. The café I and my colleagues in the office use for food and drink.

EVIDENCE 8

Awaited: Statement from Colin regarding his involvement and

exhibiting the photograph.

EVIDENCE 9

Awaited: Voice recording of Grant's call to the office and the statement exhibiting it. Independent evidence!

EVIDENCE 10

The card "Vehicle Accessories" put through my door at 0745 today.

CHAPTER 22

It was as John was driving back to the Police Station, having taken two statements, one from Fran Williamson, the other from Matthew Fisher, that a call came through from Rory.

'Are you coming back to the Nick this evening or going straight home?' Rory asked.

'I'm coming back,' John replied.

'Good. Can you drop by my office when you get here?'

John confirmed that he would, and the call ended. When initially he saw from the number coming up on his dashboard that it was Rory ringing, John had geared himself up for an argument if he was challenged by the DI on what he was doing continuing enquiries on the Stalker case. But the DI had sounded reasonable down the phone. Perhaps he didn't know where John had been.

Walking into Rory's office forty-five minutes later, however, Rory waived him to a chair and opened the conversation with: 'I gather you've been taking statements from two stallholders who have crossed paths with Billy Grant.' His voice sounded resigned.

John nodded as he sat down.

'Any good?'

'There's nothing that I'd want to invite our stalker in for a chat about now,' John said. 'But if the victim makes any other complaints, there is stuff in these statements which I think could prove useful.'

John passed the two statements across the desk and Rory read through them.

'He sounds a thoroughly nasty piece of work,' Rory commented.

'He is.'

Looking away towards his window and tapping his fingers on one of the statements while thinking things over, Rory added: 'Interesting that Matthew Fisher didn't recall his name, particularly when he says in his statement that he later made a complaint to the market organisers about Grant's behaviour after their argument in Kingston.'

'It is odd, because when Billy Grant was arrested over our harassment case, it was at an address which was registered in his name with the Council. He's moved since, but at the time of his arrest there were photos of him around the place, a council tax letter addressed to him, and some other bill.'

Rory sighed, and John, continued by saying: 'I suppose he could have used another name in Kingston. His van certainly had something different painted on it if it was the same van.'

'See what information you can get out of the organisers of these markets.'

'Next on the list,' John replied, pleased by Rory's encouragement to keep digging.

After another moment of staring into space, leaning back in his chair, Rory brought his attention back to John.

'Are there other enquiries you want to make?'

'Yes, I'd like to find out more about Billy Grant. I thought I'd go back to the pub which provided Grant with his alibi at court, to see if I can find out the names and whereabouts of any of the friends who were at his party that night.'

'What sort of questions do you want answered?'

John grinned. 'It would be good if the friends said that Billy Grant disappeared from his party halfway through it, got on his motorbike, and drove off, returning twenty minutes or so later.'

'Yeah right!'

'But seriously, I'd like to ask if anyone has ever seen him on a motorbike. If so, and the bike was black, it wouldn't be conclusive, but it would tend to tie in with Fran's evidence of a black beast in his van and Bob the postman's evidence of a black motorbike speeding past our victim and him when they left the sorting office.'

'A big 'if' but if it happened it would be a step in the right direction. Also, if the evidence stood up it would mean he lied at court.'

'It would be good to know more about Billy Grant's life, how well they know him.'

'You're going to have to be bloody careful with your questioning, the man's been acquitted. Twice!'

'Yes, but these two statements probably just about allow me to, well, have a conversation. I'll focus on the van and "Garden Furniture" and then hope that other stuff is volunteered. One question I'd like answered is whether anyone has seen him with a teenage girl and, if so, whether anyone knows who or where she is.'

'Mm. Difficult. But okay, see what you can find out but be careful. We don't want this creep accusing us of harassment or it might inhibit further enquiries.'

'No.'

After another moment or two of silence, Rory said: 'Be good if you could find enough that would allow us to go back to the victim's property to persuade her to tell us if anything else has happened. I don't like her saying to you: "One day you'll have everything there is." We must try to get back her trust because without her cooperation, none of this,' and Rory pushed the statements back across the table to John, 'is going to amount to anything.'

'That's what's been worrying me. It certainly sounds like she's keeping something or things back.'

With a head movement indicating the door, Rory said: 'Go off home now. Don't feel you have to stay up all night to make up for your enquiries on this stalker thing. Finish those enquiries on your shift and do the other work around them.'

John rose. 'Unless we get more from the victim, these

enquiries won't take long.' Arriving at the door, John hesitated and then turned round again. Rory looked at him enquiringly.

'One other thing I'd like to do and that's to go to the building where the victim's post was redirected to and take a photograph of Grant with me.'

'All right,' Rory said, nodding slowly. 'It's probably a long shot but go ahead, you never know. If by chance someone at the building does recognise Grant, then it's pretty good circumstantial evidence against him.'

'If there is any connection between Grant and that block of flats, I think it would be better than pretty good, Guv.'

CHAPTER 23

TO THOSE TO WHOM IT MAY CONCERN, I didn't sleep well last night. I tried to tell myself that it was nothing more than that I'd seen the evil invader early that morning, across the street. Seeing him has always been mind-blowingly unsettling. But I am a truthful person, and it didn't take me long to acknowledge that it wasn't seeing Billy Grant that was the cause of me tossing and turning. After all, I wanted him to give me opportunities to build evidence against him so that those of you I've named will learn lessons and other people will be saved the torment of perpetual invasion. No, the reason I didn't sleep well was that the, unexpected, strength of my new evidence made me wonder about whether I was doing the right thing, whether I should now tell police, re-evaluate my need to take the evil invader's life and my own.

I am not a psychopath or a person who carries hatred in her heart. But the moment I was honest about the root of my insomnia, I asked myself what difference the evidence would actually make? Would it, in fact, even guarantee that, third-time lucky, Billy Grant would finally be convicted? He is such a competent liar, such a successful puller of wool over other people's eyes.   After all, he has divided us. Would what had happened to me before, evidence in the two previous cases, be allowed this time into evidence or would you Mr Jenner work your magic on a new Chairman of the Bench arguing, in view of the fact I was proved to have lied about the finger shadow, that any bad character evidence of previous trials was prejudicial? It would only be the magistrates again because, although the evil invader has inflicted such injury to me and others, I know there are others, there is no physical evidence of violence. But even if he was convicted because this time Mr Jenner wouldn't hold all the cards, would his conviction change anything? If he was sentenced to six months in prison, given a restraining order, but walking free after serving three months of his sentence, what would that change? Nothing. The sentence is higher for breaching a restraining order I'm told, but a breach still needs to be proved. I know Billy Grant won't stop his harassment it would just become more nuanced. Nuanced – the new buzzword, you see I still have a sense of humour! - his targeting of me would go on and on. My mother always told me that dithering over decisions was the worst thing to do, once a decision is made, good or bad, things look up. Every time I think about the second court case I struggle to stop myself crying. I know that things have gone too far for me, I no longer have the strength to deal alone with life invaded by this evil presence. I want to stop others suffering this living hell too - decision made!

My walls may not have been breached, but the evil invader's actions turned the sanctuary of my home into a prison. Well, Billy Grant, it is now a fortress. To continue to do what you do, what you cannot help doing, turning my existence into a living hell, you need to be able to get to me. You need to take a chance, so you'll have to storm the citadel! There is no other option because I am here until I get what I need to end this hell, and I will last the distance because when I have what I need, incontrovertible evidence, the end for us both is in sight. The bitter irony is the knowledge that I can only free myself from you, Billy Grant, by bringing you ever closer to me. I hope that those of you I have named, those TO WHOM IT MAY CONCERN, will realise that even in my darkest moments I appreciated that having been invaded by the evil genius, we are locked together literally 'til death do us part.' Ironic or what?

I don't think you will appear today. You will realise that the card through the letterbox excuse may work once but is unlikely to do so if you appear in front of my house a second day running. But your choices are narrowing. What can you do? How can you torment someone who is cocooned and invisible to you? You will take chances. I won't pretend I'm not frightened, but the edge is taken off that fear by knowing there is nothing left for me to lose. The end is in sight.

Just in case something goes wrong, I have printed off these sheets daily and put them somewhere for you, DC JOHN CARTER, to find. I don't know how good the evil invader is with technology, but my guess is that he's good. I know I am stereotyping, but I think that closed-in controlling people, experts in manipulation, are good at technology. I want a paper document as well as the online one I hope to send to THOSE TO WHOM IT MAY CONCERN electronically. But computers can be hacked, material can disappear, and I'm taking no chances.

I was right, I haven't seen you, Billy Grant, today. Perhaps tonight you will try to climb my fence, but I think I'm being optimistic. It may take a little longer, but it will be soon. You won't be able to help yourself.

No evidence today.

CHAPTER 24

Driving back from a meeting on Police Budgets in Croydon, to avoid the snarl-ups on the London Road, Rory took a route back to Barnes which passed through an area near to where Grant's victim lived. On a whim, he diverted to see for himself the street where her property was. Although he didn't know the number of her house, John Carter had described it to him and when he slowly drove down the street, he spotted it quickly. The place is a bloody fortress, he thought, making a mental note of the number of the house. It was a dreary late afternoon of low clouds, but no light showed through the slats in the shutters or anywhere else in her house. Perhaps she was at the back of it. Rory drove on but, seeing a parking space ahead, pulled up so that he could jot down the number of the house, No. 14, and make a quick sketch in his notebook, for confirmation purposes. He recalled as he pulled out that John had told him that she had erected a tall fence at the end of her back garden. Turning left and left again, Rory drove down the street behind the victim's property and saw a new fence considerably higher than any of the others. Its location was the back of the house Rory had identified as hers. The fence obscured any view of the downstairs of the property, so it was impossible to tell if there was a light on there or not. Upstairs was in darkness with curtains drawn across the windows. He debated returning to the front and ringing her bell but decided against it. However slight, John had achieved some communication with her, and it was better to leave it to him, at least until they had more information.

The following day, Rory walked into CID and nodded to John to come with him. Once they were in his office Rory told him about his drive-by the previous evening, showed John his notebook with the number of the house he thought was the victim's and John confirmed that it was. The pots of large plants in front of the kitchen windows and flowerpots either side of the door were news to him, however.

'So, she's completely barricaded herself inside her property,' John said.

Rory nodded. 'Looks that way. The problem is that it might make things worse not better. While Billy Grant saw her in the street or in Waitrose, he didn't have to get close to her house to harass her. At least that remained a sanctuary for her.'

John shook his head. 'I wonder, you know. I wonder whether she's deliberately forcing him to come nearer her house so that she has a chance of getting something on him.'

'Well, it's a bloody stupid thing to do, if that is what she's up to. I know Grant hasn't got a record and hasn't physically assaulted her, but you never know what a stalker will do if control is taken away from him. She would be better off reporting what she has to us.'

With a wry smile, John said: 'I don't think that's the way she sees things.' His phone rang and he took it out of his pocket and looked at the caller ID. It was new to him. 'Sorry Guv, I'll just see who this is, and then cut the call.' But it was Bob, the postman.

'You remember I told you about the high fence at the back of her house,' he began, 'well I was delivering post in that road when I saw this bloke, medium height, balding a bit, fattish, standing looking at it. When he saw me watching him, he said, "good morning" and then walked off down the road, looking at other fences. There was something about him, and when he turned the corner, I walked quickly to the end of the street in time to see a van going by at some speed. From the glance I managed to get, I'm pretty sure it was him driving and the side of the van had "Garden Furniture" painted on it. There was no other person on the street. I haven't told her about this, she's been through enough as it is, but I thought I'd better report it to you.'

'You've done the right thing, Bob, and I need a statement from you. Would you recognise him again?' John saw Rory's attention fully focussed on him.

'I think I would,' Bob replied.

'Is there a time later today or tomorrow when I can take a statement?'

'Well, I can't today but tomorrow afternoon after my shift I could come over and give you a statement. It's the police station at South-West Central, isn't it?'

'It is. Are you willing to come here?'

'Yes, it's not far from where I am.'

They arranged a time and when the call was over John looked at Rory, who had heard the note of excitement in John's voice from the moment he'd identified the caller, and now said impatiently: 'Come on, what's Bob the postman got to say?'

Rory listened intently. 'So, now we know he's still at it.' He stroked his jaw in a characteristic gesture. 'You've got an appointment tomorrow afternoon to take his statement,' he resumed. 'Forget about your other work for the rest of today and tomorrow morning and make those outstanding queries on this stalker case. We'll talk after you've taken Bob's statement and look at what we've got before considering our next moves. We'll ask uniform to do the odd drive-by at her address but, with resources as they are, we can't do more than that at this stage.'

'Thanks Guv,' John said, as he headed out of the door.

CHAPTER 25

BOB, you only had a brochure for me today, and I've not seen a sign of the Billy Grant. It may take him a day or two to marshal his forces of evil and decide what next to do to try to torment me, so I must just get on with putting everything in order. I've drafted my will and I'm going to print it out. You told me that you weren't on duty tomorrow, BOB, so I'll leave it until the following day and then I'll ask you if you wouldn't mind getting a neighbour to come to my door with you so that the two of you can witness my signature. I'm a bit anxious about doing that because I don't want you wondering why I'm writing a will, BOB, and deciding to go to the police to report Billy Grant being seen by me across my street and you recovering the card. I know you are worried about me my wonderful friend but, trust me, nothing will change by you doing that. When I am free and the evil invader can no longer harm anyone, the police and those TO WHOM IT MAY CONCERN will see this document and the full evidence I will collect. Those named must see the full picture and the devastating consequences of evil. Billy Grant will take advantage of any half-measures now. So, when I ask you and the neighbour to sign my will, I'll tell you that my Solicitor has been badgering me about writing a will and make a joke about it. "What does he know that I don't, ha-ha!"

When you, CASSANDRA, rang me yesterday afternoon I gave you some information I am counting on you to remember. I told you it might be important in the future and to remember it in case I ever had more evidence against Billy Grant. I worry because although you can be imaginative, it didn't take long for

Billy Grant, that agent of evil, to manipulate you. You sounded sad and worried on the phone, and I know you were upset when I told you I needed the next six months off work to myself. I cried after the call. I promise you, to the last I will be so grateful for the times we had. I want you to know that now that the end is in sight, some of the evil invader's power over me has decreased and much of my feeling of helplessness has lifted. I can now remember good times and bring them to memory and feel them. So please remember that. I know you will be very shocked by events but know that I love you and remember me that afternoon at the market, laughing with you all, drinking cider, and eating cupcakes. But CASSANDRA, please learn from this document so that you can remain safe in the future, and I pray you remember the information I gave you yesterday, when the investigation has begun. My one huge fear is that those TO WHOM IT MAY CONCERN will never see this document. So, remember, CASSANDRA.

I don't know whether it was our phone call, but I had a very strange dream last night. I dreamt that I was falling, falling, and jerked awake, my heart racing. What upset me most was my anxiety because I plan to fall. Falling is what I plan to do, a few moments and then freedom. I must keep strong and focussed. I mustn't let myself weaken or this hell will continue, it will get worse.

The anxiety has stayed with me all day. I still think it may be a day or two more before you, Billy Grant, make your next move. You may be increasingly worried about the reason for my not turning up at the café. You may have rung the office switchboard, asked for Jack, and been told that no one of that name works there. I've thought about this too late to ring you, COLIN. The person answering the phone may have been a temp or may not, in any case, know about the arrangement I made with my team. Tomorrow, I'll ask you COLIN, to check with the receptionist to see if anyone rang to speak to Jack. If that's what you did, Billy Grant, it will be a new piece of evidence.

My anxiety is increasing when it should be receding. I must stay focussed.

CHAPTER 26

John caught Rory on his way out of his office to go home.

'I've had a conversation with one of the market organisers. Get this, she said they didn't have a stallholder called Billy Grant at the Kingston market two years ago.'

Rory stopped dead in his tracks. 'Christ.' With a nod he turned around and he and John went back to his office, although neither sat down when they reached it.

'I wanted them to release to me the names and addresses of all stallholders, but they've refused without a Court's Order.'

'Damn.'

'Look, I'm going to see whether Bob will let me come to his home to take a statement this evening.'

Rory looked at John, a calm and rational young man. The information they had was promising but not conclusive, or anywhere near that. But he picked up the tension in John's body language and Rory knew better than to question his young DC's instincts.

He nodded. 'Look, do what you have to do and let me know if you get anywhere. If he gives you enough to arrest Grant, we can ask for a warrant for the information the market organisers have. We'll have to go through everything we have first though. At the end of the day, Grant's fingerprints were taken after charge and, even if he did use an alias, nothing was known against him on the system, or we'd have found out.'

'I'll go and ring Bob now,' John said, heading out of the door, but turning again before leaving the office. 'If it's not enough I'll visit the pub tomorrow to find out if anyone knows the whereabouts of any of Billy Grant's friends from his birthday party. I'll take the shots we have of the crowd leaving at the end of the party. Even though the pub is under new management, it doesn't mean the regulars don't keep going to it.'

'No.'

'If I can find a friend of his, I can ask him or her whether he's ever called himself anything else. Either the stallholder at Isleworth has confused the Billy Grant at Barnes with the Kingston guy, or Grant used a different name to get his pitch at the market at Kingston, or he's using a different name now.'

'Yes. Oh, and warn Bob, the postman, we'll probably need him to do an ID parade at some point.'

'Will do.'

Bob invited John over to his flat early that evening. His wife, a cheerful looking woman with a neatly cut bob of silver-grey hair and wearing an apron with flour on it, opened the door to John and called out: 'It's the police love, I'm afraid they've caught up with you at last.' John laughed and was shown into a room where Bob rose to greet him, smiling at his wife. 'Sandra, would you mind getting us a cuppa or ...,' he turned to John, 'would you prefer coffee?' John told him tea would be great and Sandra left the room.

John took meticulous notes of Bob's sighting of the man looking at the victim's fence and then driving past in the van with "Garden Furniture" on its side. It was only when he asked Bob if he'd seen this man before, that his host hesitated: 'I can't swear to it,' he replied. 'But I think I have because I sort of remembered his face when I saw him. I couldn't tell you where or when, so I'm thinking it must have been on my rounds.' At this point, Sandra brought in a tea tray with two mugs and milk, sugar, and a plate of homemade biscuits, and then left them to it again.

Looking up after a mouthful of strong tea, John said: 'Bob, could it have been because you've had a description of him from anyone? From what you've told me, you know what's been going on. Did she describe the stalker to you?'

This time there was no hesitation. 'No, she didn't. I felt I should have asked actually.'

'Not when the two of you saw the motorcyclist speed off when you came out of the sorting office?'

'No, not then either. She's never given me a description. I don't know why. I could have kept an eye out for him.'

John made several more notes and asked one or two further questions. He then turned his notebook around and, as Bob went through the notes which he then signed, John finished his tea and ate a delicious shortbread biscuit. But as he was about to thank Bob he was forestalled.

'There's something else,' Bob said, and John picked up Bob's hesitation. 'I wasn't sure whether I should mention it because I don't want to break her trust. At least she opens the door and speaks to me, but Sandra thinks I should.'

'What is it?' John asked, once more alert and opening his notebook again.

'Monday mid-morning, I had a brochure to deliver to her and she opened the door. She said that she'd seen the stalker early on that morning across the road and that he'd posted something through the doors of the neighbours' opposite. She asked me whether I'd mind going to one of them and asking if they'd had something through the door and, if they didn't want it, whether they'd give it to me. I had a package for a retired doctor who lives diagonally across the road from her. It didn't need a signature, but I rang his bell. In answer to my question, he told me he'd walked past his hall early that morning on his way to his kitchen and turned when he heard something come through his letterbox. It was just an advertising card. He gave it to me, and I took it back over to her. She seemed disappointed when she saw it but cheered up a bit when I said that the retired doctor told me that he knew the time when it had landed on his mat that morning.'

'I don't suppose you know why she seemed disappointed?' John asked, looking up.

'Yes, she told me it didn't have the information she was hoping on it that's all. It's not surprising because it didn't say much.'

'What did it say, do you remember?'

'Yes, it said: "Vehicle Accessories" and it just had a telephone number underneath. Nothing else, not even a name.'

On a sharp intake of breath, John said: '"Vehicle Accessories" you're sure about that?'

'Yes, I'm as sure as I can be. Why, is that significant?' Bob asked, reacting to the intense interest he heard in John's voice.

'It is significant. Very.' John confirmed, as his pen raced across a page in his notebook. Looking up, John fixed his attention firmly back on Bob. 'Is there anything else she said about the stalker that morning? Did she mention anything about whether he had a vehicle? Any detail is vital.'

But Bob shook his head. 'No, just that she'd seen him look straight at her property and then turn and put something through some doors opposite. She said she could only see so much because she was viewing him from a crack in her curtains. That's all she said.'

John scribbled some more and then, once again, handed his notebook to Bob to read through again and sign, which he did.

'We don't really talk,' Bob volunteered, 'but ever since I helped her out by making sure her mail was never diverted again, she's trusted me. I hope she doesn't think I've broken her trust.'

'Bob, I'm going to level with you. It's very important now that she talks to us. I know, we all know, we've let her down, but we're going into overdrive now to make up for that. I believe every word she's said. I've more enquiries to make but I might need your help to gain her trust.'

'I'm off duty tomorrow.'

'Yes, you said, but I'll ring you after I've made my enquires. Please don't talk to anyone about our conversation.'

'I've talked to Sandra. She's the one who told me to tell

you about the man putting the card through the door.'

'She's a superstar,' John told him. 'She knows about that already, but don't tell anybody else.'

John had risen and Bob did likewise. 'No one else to tell, really,' he said, leading the way out of the door. Sandra came into the hall from the kitchen to say goodbye.

'He thinks you're a superstar,' Bob told her.

'A young man of judgement.' Sandra nodded complacently.

Rory had just handed Thommi a glass of wine when his mobile rang. He saw that it was John and picked up the call. As their conversation continued, Thommi sat on the arm of the sofa Rory was sitting on. Listening to his half of the conversation, she knew that something significant was being relayed.

'What's happened?' she asked when Rory returned his mobile to his pocket.

'I told you that John went over this evening to take a statement off Bob, the postman.'

'Yeah.'

'Well Bob had other information he didn't know was significant, but his wife had persuaded him to tell us anyway. It turns out that our stalker victim had seen Billy Grant early one morning. He looked directly at her house and then started posting something through the doors of the neighbours' opposite.'

Thommi made a Tch sound! 'Getting his explanation in ahead of time.'

'Yes, but Billy Grant doesn't know that we've talked to Matthew Fisher the stallholder you gave us. If you recall, I told you that Matthew remembered that Grant's van in Kingston two years ago had "Vehicle Accessories" painted on it, not "Garden Furniture." Well, our victim asked Bob the postman to see if he could get hold of whatever Grant had put through the doors of her neighbours' opposite. He did so and brought it back to her.

It didn't mean anything to her, but it does to us. The card he put through had "Vehicle Accessories" on it and then, simply, a phone number.'

'My God!'

'I know. We've got to find out what name he used in Kingston.'

'You do, you must, and soon.' Thommi put her wine glass down on the table and took a quick turn around the room. 'You know, given that Matthew remembered what was written on the van, that's probably why the name Billy Grant didn't mean anything to him. What's the betting he used a different name?'

'I know, we've already thought of that,' Rory said and then told her about the market organisers telling John that they hadn't rented a van to a Billy Grant for the Kingston market.

'He's got an alias. Look you need to get that list straight away.'

Rory shot a look at his partner from under his dark brows, as he'd done on previous occasions when Thommi had shown an inclination to lead one of his investigations. 'Me investigator, you prosecutor, remember?' he said. 'Getting the list is in hand but, firstly, John wants to make enquiries at the pub to see whether he can find a friend of Billy Grant's from his party with a view to finding out if anyone knows of any other name Grant uses.'

Thommi nodded and sat down. This time Rory did ask for her input when he said: 'But, what do you think? Do we have enough to arrest Grant on what we've got. Basically, it's Matthew's evidence that his van used to have "Vehicle Accessories" on it and Bob's evidence of seeing him outside the rear of the victim's property and picking up the card dropped through the neighbours' doors opposite with "Vehicle Accessories" on it.'

'You know what? You do. You also have the van with "Garden Furniture" on it, which Bob saw being driven away by Grant. Okay, what Bob told you the victim said about seeing Grant on Monday morning is hearsay, but Bob has effectively said that it was because of a conversation he had with the victim that he went over the road and retrieved the card put through that door. Get a statement from the retired doctor too. It needs to be specific on timing. Once you arrest him and it's obvious that we're continuing to investigate the harassment and stalking, you are much more likely to get our victim on board and she may have even more to tell you. Think about what she said to John: "One day you'll have everything there is." The moment Grant's been through an interview, you may need a quick ID set up unless he concedes that it was him Bob saw. At least, once he's arrested and it's an official investigation, you can then get a warrant. Depending how quickly things develop, you may get information about the alias from the market Organisers which will allow you to charge and remand him. If not, at least you can put conditions of bail not to go within a mile's radius of her property while outstanding enquiries are made.'

Rory took a long swig of his wine and looked approvingly at the bottle. 'Let's open another one,' he said. 'I'm thinking that we might be getting something on this bastard at last.'

CHAPTER 27

It's past midnight and I still can't sleep. Things keep turning over in my mind. Will everything disappear from my computer due to something the evil invader does? My printed copies are becoming copious, but they will still fit into my hiding place. But will you, CASSANDRA, remember our conversation, what I told you, when it matters. I'm surprised by how jumpy I am, considering that what's keeping me going is that it will all be over before long. It's a clear night with a three-quarter moon. Perhaps a prisoner, whilst longing for the release from torture by a firing squad, still dreads the raising of the firearms, is still anxious about the moment before oblivion. Oh my God, I see hands appear over the top of my garden fence, now a face, his face, and the camera flashes, it flashes, it flashes, and the face disappears. It worked. With shaking hands, I am reaching for my phone. Nothing. Yes, it's there on my phone, Just as I am about to lean outside my window and grab the camera, the image has come through. It is him, my phone confirms, the evil invader, peering over the garden fence. But what if my phone disappears?

If I forward the photo to any of those I have named in this document, they will come forward now, they will come around here, they may tell the police. I cannot have that happen now that I am so close to being free of this torment, free from you, Billy Grant. Deep breath, okay, I am adding you DEREK FRAMLEY to my list TO WHOM IT MAY CONCERN. My faithful Solicitor who dealt with both of my parents' wills and did so promptly and with great sensitivity towards me. You felt sad for me, losing my parents, and gave me the number to your personal mobile phone. I am now sending to your phone the photo. I am heading it: Photo to keep safe for me. I simply text: "Away now but will ring and explain when back." What will he make of a photo of the evil invader peering over my garden fence? He might think it has something to do with my post going missing. But when this is all over, the police will want to talk to my Solicitor, and you will show them this.

The sighting of you Billy Grant, has only increased my anxiety. You dropped yourself to the ground immediately you saw the flash of the camera. You must know that you have been photographed. You must wonder whether it is a police camera for my protection. You must now be expecting to be arrested. What will you do? It doesn't make sense for you to do anything more to incriminate yourself by further action, but you won't be able to help yourself. I am in a panic.

TO WHOM IT MAY CONCERN, I am about to print out the photograph to add to the rest of my evidence. I will put this latest piece of evidence with a statement from me exhibiting it, having seen Billy Grant peering over my fence and witnessed my camera flashing. Both will be in my hiding place, but I will only document the photo, because that is the conclusive evidence, the sort that speaks for itself. I don't think I will be surprised by the evil invader if I act quickly. He too will be in a panic. Initially, he will want to put as much space between himself and my garden as possible. He won't know how good the photo is. He won't want the camera flashing again. Well, Billy Grant, I think the photo is good enough. It pays to go top of the range. I must deal with this now and then sleep. I don't think he will be back tonight, and tomorrow I move to Phase 2 of my Action Plan.

I have so much now, I don't need anything more. Colin's evidence and the photo of you peering over my fence, is as good as evidence can get, and there is still the other stuff, the photo at my surgery, the card through the door. I am now at Phase 2 of my plan. If only I could sleep.

EVIDENCE 9

The photo of Billy Grant, peering over my fence. More conclusive "Independent Evidence" would you agree, DC JOHNNY HAMILTON? On second thoughts, perhaps I'll delete the last bit of the sentence. This document is not about revenge.

CHAPTER 28

When John said into his phone: 'On my way, Guv,' a few faces looked up and watched him walk out of the door. DC Johnny Hamilton voiced what all were thinking. 'What the hell is going on?' No one came up with an answer, but a sense of unease permeated CID as heads switched away from the door back to their computer screens. But Johnny continued to look thoughtfully through CID's door into the corridor, before standing up and sauntering over to DS Emery's desk. Sitting down opposite him, Johnny said:

'Have you heard anything new about that damn harassment case, Clarke?' he asked.

The Sergeant shook his head.

'Not really no,' he replied frowning. 'Just a lot of toing and froing. I know there have been no more phone calls and that she won't open the door to us.' He shrugged: 'Well, out of our hands now so let's just be thankful for it.'

'If she won't open her door or communicate with us, what on earth are they investigating? It's not as though there's another trial coming up.'

'Exactly,' The DS nodded in agreement. 'It's probably just a reaction to that actress or celebrity case in the press, Rory wanting to ensure that we've gone the extra mile before we close down the case altogether.'

Johnny looked at Clarke for a moment longer and then, seemingly satisfied that he wasn't holding anything back, rose to his feet, and stretched. 'We spend too much time worrying about complaints.'

Clarke Emery sighed. 'One of the things I hate about the job.' Then as if their conversation jogged his memory onto another potential bone of contention, he added: 'Before you go, Johnny. How are things on the Clay conspiracy trial?'

'I have a few enquiries of my own to make this afternoon and then with any luck we'll have enough to charge. I think we'll get home on this one.'

Johnny left Clarke looking a lot more cheerful than he'd been a minute ago.

Rory scanned through the whole of John's interview with Bob. When he had finished, he looked up at John: 'Thommi thinks we have enough to arrest Billy Grant.'

'I agree, but given that Grant seems to be out and about in the day should I just go to the pub now to see if I can get anything more from there? If I can interview one of Grant's friends, early afternoon, and it throws up anything additional, we can add it to the questions we're going to ask. We can then nick him tonight.'

Rory thought it over. 'Go ahead and I'll get a file opened. By the time you're asking questions, we'll have an ongoing investigation. I'll put down my authorisation to arrest Grant when he's likely to be home.'

CHAPTER 29

It was just as John had parked in the pub carpark that a call came in on his mobile. Seeing that it was Thommi, he answered the call.

'Sorry to bother you, I know you've got a lot on, but I thought I'd just mention something before I forget it. You remember I said I'd get the clerk's notes?'

'Yup.'

'Well, there was one line of questioning I find weird. Marcus Jenner asked our victim if she had ever had a conversation with the defendant about the West Country. She said that she hadn't. He then asked her if she knew the North coast of Devon. She agreed that she did, and that she knew most areas of Devon. She was then asked if she knew a place called Hartland and she replied that she had, with her parents, driven through it but never stopped there and she didn't know it well. His next question was to ask her what areas she did know well but, at this stage, our prosecutor rose and said words to the effect that this was a fishing expedition and that if his client had given specific places which he claimed they had talked about she must be asked direct questions. That effectively ended the questioning but gave Jenner an opportunity to suggest that she had conversed about Devon with his client.'

'That's the first I've heard about it.'

'I just thought I'd let you know.'

'Thanks.' There was a pause, then John added: 'Look I'm about to go into the pub where the party was held, but I'll think about what you've said. It's a pretty odd line of questioning.'

'It is. I'll let you go.'

Stepping through the door into the pub at midday, John noted that although it was half full, regulars were starting to drift in. He took out the stills from the CCTV evidence of Billy Grant looking straight at the camera at the beginning of the evening while buying drinks for the birthday crowd, then him entering the alcove and, finally, him leaving ahead of the others at the end of the evening. Going to the bar, John showed his warrant card to the new Landlord and asked him if he had working for him now, anyone who had worked there before the management of the pub changed. The Landlord nodded solemnly and pointed to a girl, also behind the bar who was serving a customer.

'Look, if you want to ask any more questions please go to that table and I'll ask her to join you when she's finished with the round of drinks she's serving now.'

John smiled his thanks and did as he was told. The Landlord hadn't returned his smile and John didn't blame him. A few minutes later, the young bar waitress, her dark hair scraped back in a scrunchy, heavily made-up, and wearing tightly fitted jeans with a rip at each knee, came over. She was also looking mildly pissed-off.

'Sorry to take you away from what you were doing. Hopefully, this won't take long. I'm DC John Carter from South-West Central police station. It's a longshot but I just wonder if you can help me out. I don't know your name?'

'Sally.'

'Sally, were you working on the night Billy Grant had his party?'

She sat down. 'Yeah, like I said to the other policeman.'

'Sorry again, I know it's irritating saying the same thing over-and-over again.'

She melted a little. 'Oh well, you're here now. What do you want to know?'

Looking around the pub, John couldn't immediately see any of the party guests from the photo shots, among the throng.

'Have you seen Billy Grant recently?'

'No, he's moved.'

'Okay, would you mind just looking at these photos. I'm hoping you might be able to give me a name of one or two of these people who were at his party.'

She looked down but didn't immediately identify anyone.

'This girl, for instance, do you know her?' John asked, pointing to someone raising her glass to Billy Grant, no doubt thanking him for the drink.

'I know her name's Bethany, and she still comes in here sometimes although mainly in the evening. I don't know anything else about her.'

'Thanks, Sally. What about this guy?' John pointed at the male who was half-turned towards Billy Grant but looking annoyed rather than grateful for the drink.'

'What do you mean?' she asked, screwing up her face.

John looked at her, confused. 'I just wonder if you know his name.'

'That bloke there?' she said, pointing at the same person John was still pointing at.

'Yes, him.'

'That is Billy Grant.'

'What?!'

John realised he must have shouted as he noted some heads turn. Sally looked at him as though he was an idiot.

'This guy here, with dark hair, is Billy Grant, is that what you're saying? The guy who had the party?'

'Yeah,' she said, nodding.

'Okay, who's this buying everyone drinks or, at least, it looks like that's what he's doing, this man here?' John said, pointing to the man he knew as Billy Grant, his voice tight with anticipation.

'I don't know his name, but he was buying everyone drinks. Billy was, like, annoyed about it, particularly when he followed Billy and his mates into the alcove for the dinner, carrying a bottle of champagne like he was gate-crashing or something.   Apparently, after giving everyone the champagne, he then climbed out of the window.   He wasn't in the alcove when I came in with the food, but he did later come back into the pub when they were leaving and tried to buy more drinks for them, but we were closing.'

'How much later?'

'Ooh, I don't really know, I was busy.' She thought for a moment. 'Well, not long before they left, so maybe two hours or something.'

'Sally, you are an absolute super star,' John told her. 'You don't know what valuable information you have just given me. But I need to find the real Billy Grant, do you know where he is?'

Sally was no longer irritated she was rather buoyed up and was happy to be helpful. Looking down at the photos she said: 'Well, this is his girlfriend Cathy,' pointing to a girl in the first shot. 'She's got a new job in Cambridge. After the dinner, on the night of Billy's party the two of them went on holiday and they were then going to look for somewhere near Cambridge to live.   I haven't heard anything from them since. Umm,' after a moment's thought she pointed to the man John and everyone else in the police had thought was Billy Grant and said: 'I think he knew Billy Grant and when Billy and his girlfriend were leaving to go on holiday and then to Cambridge, he gave them some money to stay in their flat because their lease hadn't run out.   I think he agreed to tidy the place up when he left so that Billy would get his deposit back. It didn't mean Billy wanted him at his party though. I heard him tell a mate that he was a "weirdo," and that Cathy couldn't stand him.   Anyway, Billy might know where he is, but I don't have an address for him, so you'd have to find him.'

After scribbling frantically in his notebook, John Carter turned it around and asked Sally to look through what he'd written thoroughly, and to sign it.

It was just as John was explaining to her that she'd later be asked to sign a witness statement that she interrupted him to say: 'That's a mate of Billy's, just come in.' John looked over. 'I'll read this through and sign it and then tell him to come over, if you like?' she said.

'That would be great,' John told her.

When a male in his late twenties, or thereabouts, came over and sat down introducing himself as Henry, John recognised him as someone in the CCTV photos, and he took him through the same process he'd gone through with Sally. Henry corroborated everything she said. Sadly, he couldn't give John as much information as he'd hoped for regarding the male the police thought was Billy Grant.

'I can't be sure, but I think his name was William but, other than that, I don't know anything because I'd never seen him before he was buying drinks for everyone.'

Nonetheless, he had a contact number for Billy Grant. 'I haven't been in touch for a while, we were more pub mates really, and I don't see him anymore. You know how it is, you're all going to keep in touch but then, in the end, you don't. He's got a management job in publishing so you might not be able to get him 'til this evening. I think he's also studying for an MBA at night classes some nights but hopefully you'll get hold of him before he goes out again. He lives near Cambridge with his girlfriend, Cathy. St Neots, I think that's what he told me.'

This time, John wrote (1) beside the picture of the real Billy Grant and (2) against the picture of the male the police thought was Billy Grant, and Henry signed a statement, identifying (1) as his friend Billy Grant who had the party at which he was a guest on the evening the photos were taken. He also corroborated the fact that the male at (2), he thought was called William, had bought drinks for everyone, followed them into the alcove with a bottle of champagne and, like a "fucking joker," had then climbed out of the window, and that he next saw him when they left the party, and he was trying to buy them drinks again. He signed John's notes.

When, finally, John left the pub his mood was a mixture of elation and trepidation. Sitting in his car, he rang the number Henry had given him for Billy Grant, but it was on voicemail.

John left his name and his police and telephone details and asked that he ring him back as a matter of urgency.   He then rang Rory.

There was a long pause at the end of the line after John finished talking, then: 'So much for the cast iron alibi,' Rory said on an exploding sigh. 'The moment you get back we'll drive over and arrest the bastard!'

CHAPTER 30

A new morning.   After I had hidden my evidence last night, I slept at last.   I don't believe I dreamt, and I am astonished that it is after ten and raining.   I feel much calmer. I cannot believe now, looking at my computer, how panicked I was last night, so on edge. In the cold light of day, I realise how valuable the photo really is.   What reason can you, those TO WHOM IT MAY CONCERN, find for the evil invader to jump up to peer over my high garden fence, other than that I have been telling the truth all along?   There is no credible explanation for his behaviour.   You note the "credible?"   It is lawyer speak.   You, Marcus Jenner, pinning me down with your sharp beady eyes, one eyebrow raised for effect as you moved in for the kill.   "I suggest, there is simply no credible explanation for you seeing Mr Grant at your address, when a pub full of people remember him in the pub at the same time you claim he was making finger shadows on your wall, other than that you made it up, is there?" Well, Marcus Jenner, find a credible reason for your client to be peering over my fence past midnight last night.

A new morning and I must now turn my mind to the next phase.   The difficulty with living in a fortress is that it will be near impossible to lure you here, Billy Grant, evil invader, without leaving my house.   It is my only problem.   I know how I will end your life.   I have the sleeping pills my mother was given to help her sleep when her cancer was advancing fast. Her doctor was a friend, there was no need for him to be careful about her becoming addicted, she didn't have long to go.   I have enough to drug you, Billy Grant.   I don't want you to feel pain.

This is not about revenge. But I must save the next victim; it is the only power I have left, the only thing I can do. You see, I know that you have done this before and would do so again if I simply took the easy way out. From the moment you chose me as your next victim, knowing that I had suffered bereavement, that I was vulnerable, to the stitch-up over the finger shadow, to moving into my area giving you the reason you needed for you to be at Waitrose, outside my doctor's, being in the vicinity, everything you have done has been planned. This was not a trial run, evil genius. You have done this before, and you will torment another vulnerable person again if I don't stop you. When you are helpless and asleep, I will smother you. I hope it will be quick and that you will not be aware of anything.

I will leave everything for you, DC JOHN CARTER, to find. I will by then be dead myself. You will find me at the bottom of cliffs on the North Devon coast, one of the most beautiful places I have seen, rugged and wild. As a child, I stayed in Welcombe, Devon, with my parents and I swam and rode seaside ponies and had picnics and I love that part of England. I want my last vision of this world to be of that time, that happy, happy, time and I will be free to feel that happiness because the power of the evil invader will have vanished, the invasion will be over.

It may be that I will have more evidence, Billy Grant, before my release from this world and your release from your evil urge to destroy lives, but I must now turn my mind to Phase 2. Your face over my fence after midnight has overridden any unfortunate moments of indecision I have had and struggled to suppress. Your action last night told me, in no uncertain terms, that while you live, I will never be free of you and I have no one to turn to, I have no family left to protect me.

But I am now going to end this document. As I say, the next phase may provide additional evidence and, if so, I will leave it to be found, but I have enough evidence as it is. My photograph of Billy Grant when I am visiting my surgery, the telephone call by an unidentified person to my office and picked up by Colin alias "Jack", the message from "Jack" which Colin did not put through my door, Colin's shot of you outside the café, the card you put in the neighbour's door which will be corroborated by you BOB and the retired doctor who can give evidence of when the card dropped through his letterbox. What I said to BOB and to COLIN and my team will also go into evidence at an inquest as 'hearsay' because I will be dead and cannot be summoned as a witness. I learnt that rule when there was some 'hearsay' evidence adduced by the defence because the pub landlord was in Spain and it was not practical to secure his attendance, or something like that. Finally, the timed shot of Billy Grant peering over my fence after midnight. If you add it now, to what went before, your evidence in the first trial, CASSANDRA, the package and note on my doorstep, the CCTV in Waitrose, it is more than enough.

I am now going to say goodbye to all of you TO WHOM IT MAY CONCERN. This is effectively a dying declaration as well as a confession of my intent to murder. In this document I have not used the, preferred, words 'taking my own life' because, far as I am concerned, my life was taken from me.

Everything I have said outside and inside the courtroom was true to the best of my knowledge and, if I made one mistake, it was an honest one, perhaps due to the paranoia that comes with the slow suffocation of life as you knew it by an evil intent. In order that you understand the power of this evil, I am now going to make some concessions.

I know that the loss of two beloved parents within a short space of time would not, could not, leave me unaffected. I know that when Billy Grant began to follow me, to turn up, to invade my space, it left me anxious and on edge and that the sorrow of loss contributed to my inability to cope. I know that in my desperation to explain the effect that being stalked was having on my well-being, my existence, I didn't always do myself justice in the courtroom. I am sure I came across as unbalanced and neurotic and there in the witness box was Billy Grant, blinking in sorrow, drawing on the sympathy of the magistrates, making my accusations sound out of proportion and overblown. But now look at the evidence. You may be right about my spiral into 'depression' but remember that often those who suffer with such a diagnosis, in their anguish, can no longer think of others. In taking their own lives, they can only feel the necessity for release, not the pain of those they leave behind.

I know that you CASSANDRA, will feel pain and I hate that and that is why I urge you to be happy and to know that I can remember the times we had with gratitude and love and that if there is one legacy you can give me it is to forgive me for not being able to see any option but the one I have chosen and to forgive yourself for not seeing or understanding my inability to do that. You are not alone in underrating Billy Grant, in not appreciating how malign his intentions were, how calculating, in believing him to be a sad creep with a crush but not a master manipulator. In your case, it was your compassion which allowed you to come to this conclusion. Remember that. But look at the evidence and learn. I am not Billy Grant's first victim and without stopping him, I will not be the last. It would have been so much easier simply to have ended my own life. Remember that too and, after this is over, know that I died still able to think of others, to act with others in mind and to remember love and friendship. Finally, and I know it will take time, let your overriding memory of me be that sunny day in Barnes, enjoying your company so much, laughing, eating cupcakes, and drinking cider.

When this is over, and all of you TO WHOM IT MAY CONCERN, have read this document and considered it dispassionately, as I urge you to do, I pray, I pray, you will understand what has happened. The shock of murder followed by suicide can only, initially, incline you towards horror and censure, but please grant me what the authorities could not do, and did not really try to do. You will note that I am not trying to get away with murder. I could, with the evidence I have collected, put forward, I suggest, a reasonable case for self-defence or acting while the balance of my mind was something or other. But I am not going to do that. I am an honest person as I have been throughout my ordeal at the hands of the evil invader. I am paying for my crime with my own life. Please look at the evidence, learn from it so that others can benefit from your knowledge, and in so doing, in heart as well as head, finally grant me Justice.

CHAPTER 31

As the police car drew up at the new address Billy Grant's Solicitor had given to the court, before his acquittal at the end of the second trial, Rory was astonished that it was only four streets away from the victim's.

'How the hell did he manage to get the bail variation this close to the victim?' Rory said.

John gave a shake of his head but said nothing.

'Did we oppose the change of condition?' Rory asked sharply, sensing that John knew the answer to his question.

'No, the police didn't oppose it,' he replied. 'I suppose Grant had been complying with conditions and the court case was coming up,' he continued, trying to find some mitigation for Johnny Hamilton's "the police have no objections to the change of address" memo that went onto the file that went into court.

As the two men strode towards a building which housed four flats, Rory spoke again. 'I'll deal with this when I get back,' he said uncompromisingly.

'Once the second trial was over, all conditions ceased anyway,' John reminded him.

'In view of what we now know, that's not really the point. Grant being legitimately a few streets away from her home gave him the excuse he needed for continually crossing her path.' Rory stopped walking as they reached their destination.

The address they had was Flat 2, but there was no name beneath the bell. John rang it. They waited, and when it wasn't answered he rang another bell. A female voice answered, and Rory said: 'Police, can you let us in?'

The intercom buzzed and they walked through and found Flat 2 opposite Flat 1 on the ground floor. Rory rang the bell. There was no answer. He rang again and banged on the door. A tired looking woman from the flat opposite, came out into the corridor.

'We're here to see Billy Grant,' Rory told her.

'You've missed him by a day, he moved out yesterday in a hurry.'

After a second, Rory took out his warrant card and said: 'Do you know where he went?'

'No, and I doubt the letting agents do either. I told them he'd left and earlier one of their staff came over. From what they said, he'd left it in a hell of a state before his lease had ended and, I daresay, owing them money, although I wasn't told that.'

'What estate agents?'

'Harlings, in the High Street.'

Rory thanked her and turned to leave when he heard John ask the woman whether she'd seen Grant with anyone, a young girl or anyone else.

'Not here in the building,' she replied. 'But a guy was arguing with him outside the building just before I heard Billy's door open and then saw him leave with his stuff. I was going to shut my window and saw them both.'

'Can you describe this man at all?' Rory said.

But apart from the fact he was white with dark hair and tall, the neighbour couldn't help further with the description. She was sure it was Billy he was arguing with, though.

After making a note in his book, John turned to her again.

'Did you hear what they were arguing about?'

'The only thing I heard was the man telling him he hadn't much time and had better move quickly, or something like that.' She thought for a second or two, before adding: 'He was angry this other man, but I can't say why. But Billy did move quickly, I can tell you that. It took about three trips for him to get his stuff and then he was out of here and I rang Harlings.'

'Are you absolutely sure that you didn't hear anything

Billy said to the man.'

'Well, he said something, but I might have misheard-'

'Don't worry about that,' John said.

'I thought he said something like: "But you knew, you said it was too late to change things." It was something like that. The other man then looked around and although I didn't have my light on, I think he saw me, or at least my open window, and he replied: "Did I fuck," and he then turned quickly and walked off. I think he's into all sorts, that Billy.'

'Did you ever see him with anyone else?'

'No, well I once saw him with a female who looked young in his van but when he'd parked, she walked off, so I thought maybe he'd given her a lift. I can't really describe her other than she was smallish, thin, young, and had, I think, dark hair. He's never had anyone I've seen in this building.'

Back in the car, Rory asked: 'What do you make of this tall guy?'

John shook his head. 'It's funny but, in my mind, I've never really connected Grant with doing business with anyone else. I had him down as a loner. But although his neighbour said he was arguing with Grant, the words the man said sound as if he was warning Billy to get out for his own good, although she didn't necessarily put that construction on his words herself.'

'No. I suppose if there was a business connection, I don't know drugs or something, and the guy thought that Grant had become a liability, that might explain his words.'

'It might,' John said: 'It seems to be a habit of his, leaving places he's rented in a hurry and in a bad state.' He had received a call back earlier from the real Billy Grant from which he'd learnt that the imposter "Billy Grant" who had given him a hundred pounds towards their holiday and told him that he knew a guy who would steam clean the whole place so that Grant could get back his deposit, was known by him as William Clarke.

'I knew him from when he had a vehicle accessories shop in Kingston so thought that I could get hold of him if he didn't keep to his side of the bargain. Also, he'd given us a hundred pounds towards our holiday some months back and stayed for a couple of weeks while we were away. That was fine. When we arrived back the flat was how we left it. So, this time, I didn't think anything of it, and he'd given me his card with "Vehicle Accessories" on it, so I thought he was legit. My fiancée, Cathy, and I got this great last-minute holiday deal and didn't really have time, what with getting our stuff into storage etc., to deal with the flat. We had an early flight and Cathy, who doesn't drink much, was driving us to the hotel at Heathrow after my farewell party at the pub. William turned up at the flat with his gear before we went to the party. We were already having some second thoughts about letting him take over the flat for the two weeks before the lease expired because we wouldn't be coming back to check it, and Cathy didn't take to him. But it was too late, so Cathy returned to him his hundred pounds and told him to put it towards the steam clean, to look after the place, and to make sure it was spotless. Anyway, when we were at the pub, he turned up. He wasn't invited to my dinner, but he insisted on buying all my friends drinks. He even bought champagne when we went to sit down and then climbed out of the bloody window.'

John had then interrupted to ask some supplementary questions, particularly about the exact time William Clarke had the use of Billy Grant's house when they left it some months ago. The timescale matched the police attendance at the flat to arrest the man they knew as Billy Grant for harassment.

'As we were in Cambridgeshire, he was supposed to put the keys through the estate agents' letterbox when he left,' Grant continued, 'but he didn't. When we tried to ring him after the Landlord told us that virtually the whole of my deposit had been used on cleaning, we didn't get anywhere, the phone was out of use. I remember he told me years ago, after I'd filled out some form at his shop for a guarantee on a purchase, that we had the same birthday, but that he was a year or two older. He reminded me of that when I saw him again. "I'm William from Vehicle Accessories. You used to come into my shop, and we share a birthday and first name." I remembered him because I'd felt sorry for him. He was a weird kind of a guy and a bit awkward. But after what he did to us, sorry is not the way I feel about him now. He'd better watch out if I see him again.'

'If you see him again, you don't do anything except ring us immediately and let us know where he is.'

'Yeah, well I didn't mean I'd attack him or anything,' Grant said, probably remembering that he was talking to a police officer. 'I'll ring you, don't worry.'

'Did he have anyone working for him at Vehicle Accessories?'

'Not that I know. I saw a schoolgirl in his shop once. I don't know whether she was a relation or not.'

John had finished the conversation by telling Grant that an officer from Cambridge would be taking a statement from him.

After Rory's terse call to CID issuing instructions to Clarke Emery and Johnny Hamilton, not to leave the office because their presence was required for a meeting when he returned, both Rory and John were silent for the first part of the journey back, both following their own train of thought.

'He must still be somewhere around here,' Rory said, breaking the silence. 'He was opposite the victim's property on one day this week, looking at her fence on another. I wish we had the number plate of his van. Why don't we have it? It must have been mentioned in the first trial.'

'He changed it apparently, before the second trial, although the new one still has "Garden Furniture" on it.' John paused, thinking about Rory's question, before adding: 'Matthew, the market trader, said that the van at the Barnes market was the same make and model as the one in Kingston except with "Garden Furniture" instead of "Vehicle Accessories" written on its side.'

'So possibly it was the same van but with different number plates,' Rory said, turning towards John with a despairing shake of his head.

'Yes,' John agreed, 'that's possible, thinking about it. I suppose it just didn't come up in the second trial because his stalking didn't involve his van.'

'Why would it. He lived just round the corner. We must get a warrant first thing tomorrow so that we can get everything there is from the market organisers on both the Kingston and the Barnes market stallholders and the registrations Grant used when he applied for the market pitches.' A moment later, Rory said: Let's stick to Billy Grant, for the time being, William Clarke, for all we know, is just another alias, and nothing came up on the PNC check under that name, but we might get some more info from the market stallholders.'

'Agreed,' John said.

"We also need to make enquiries of the District Councils in this area and in Kingston to see if there's been a change of address from a Billy Grant or William Clarke. Johnny Hamilton can do those. He can also get in touch with the letting agent to find out more about their lessee and whether he produced any references or bank details. I also want him to look into Grant's Vehicle Accessories business and find out where he lived then. Hamilton can bloody well now pull his weight,' Rory finished with some venom. Continuing after a moment, he added: 'Tomorrow, you go over to the victim's place with Bob, if need be, to fill her in on everything we have. Apart from anything else, she needs to be aware of what she's up against. If she's got anything to tell us, fucking well get it out of her and get her on board.'

'I will,' John said. He knew that he couldn't guarantee that, but Rory was not in a mood for John to point that out to him.

'The one thing in our favour is that he's still stalking the victim. If we can't run him to ground tomorrow, we'll run surveillance at the victim's property and arrest him in the act of continuing his harassment.' A grim smile spread across Rory's face. 'It will be something else to ask him about.'

CHAPTER 32

Rory hit CID with his presence like a tornado. 'Clarke, Johnny, my office,' he barked, turning on his heel. DS Emery shot out of his chair and even DC Hamilton didn't waste time following. It was now after seven and some of the detectives had already left to go home. One of the remaining detectives whistled when they'd gone, and several others looked towards DC Flynn for enlightenment, but Flynn doggedly continued with what he was working on.

After bringing the DS and DC up to speed on the developments, and noting the red colour spreading across Hamilton's face, Rory gave them both a list of enquiries he wanted completed by lunch the following day. John was also in the room and, although the DI had not behaved other than correctly, he felt profoundly sorry for Clarke and Johnny.

At the end of a gruelling ten minutes, Johnny spoke: 'I didn't think of doing an ID parade for the members of the pub to pick him out,' he admitted.

'We are where we are,' Rory said uncharitably, but John wasn't going to let him get away with that.

'Grant was originally arrested in a flat which was registered with the Council in his assumed name, he was on the pub CCTV appearing to be acting the host, he went into the alcove and, later we saw him leave ahead of the crowd. No one was challenging ID, I wouldn't have done one either,' John said, but then realised he'd made one mistake. He was too late to correct it before the DI jumped in.

'Our victim was bloody well challenging it.'

'What I mean -'

'I know what you mean.' After looking at his young DC before turning his attention to Johnny, Rory continued in a milder tone: 'I'm not actually blaming you for not holding an ID, but she's very far from being a nut job, Johnny, and, let's be honest, we haven't given this stalking case a very high priority. We could have done better with evidence gathering and the CPS could have made better judgements over their charging decisions. We now know we're up against a very devious, very calculating and, possibly, dangerous individual, and we have a victim who has no faith in any of us, with good reason. We cannot make any more mistakes. Now, are there any other enquires any of you think might help?'

By the time the meeting broke up, Action Points had been allocated to each individual officer for the following day, it was well after the shift ended and the group left Rory's office to go home.

In John's case, instead of heading towards his flat in Putney, he drove towards the victim's property, deciding to begin the surveillance straight away. He'd doze in his car and ring Bob the following morning.

It was as John was idly listening to the police channels on his way, that a call came through that gripped his attention. It was a call for Officers to go to an address and check on a single female occupant. John knew that address by heart. A Dr James Marshall who lived at No. 25, diagonally opposite the victim's rang 999 after hearing what he thought was scream followed by a bang or thud inside the property. He had gone across the road, pressed the doorbell, but no-one had answered it. The front door looked intact.

Putting his foot on the accelerator, John sped towards the victim's home. He heard the sirens approach when he was about four streets away. Divining that the cop cars would arrive at the front of the property, John decided to go down the road behind her house first.

As he reached the back of her house, he saw a white van

obscuring part of the fence and, on getting out of the car, noted two panels of the fence on the ground, hidden by the van, giving easy access to the back of her house. He locked his car door, now blocking the road, and ran to the fence. Looking through the gap, the first thing he saw were wires hanging down from a bracket by the side of her upstairs window. Had the bracket enclosed a camera? The next thing which made his heart jump was that her back door was ajar. John shouted her name but there was no reply. It didn't surprise him the open door told its own story. He stepped gingerly through the gap and on into the kitchen, making a mental note of where he trod for the SOCOs when they arrived to secure any forensic evidence. After entering every room, he confirmed that no one was in the house. On the one hand he felt relief that she wasn't lying injured, or worse, on the other he was pretty sure that she had been kidnapped and that didn't bode well at all. Retracing his steps, trying not to disturb anything, John noted that the kitchen door was splintered and had clearly been forced.

Getting back into his car, he drove up and down the street, looking at vehicles, before arriving at the front of the victim's property. Two officers were standing at her front door listening to another male who wore a dressing gown and slippers. John approached the group, took out his warrant card and explained his interest in the property in a few words. He also explained to PC Colin Henry that he'd entered the house from the rear of the property.

John ordered the uniformed officers to guard the front and rear of the property until they had further instructions and turned to the man in the dressing gown, who confirmed that he was Dr James Marshall, now retired. Taking out his notebook he asked the doctor to tell him what happened in as much detail as he could remember.

'I have a cat who normally reappears through his flap round about ten. He didn't tonight and so, at about 10.30 p.m. I opened my front door to see if I could see her. But just as I'd turned to look for her, I heard a scream and it seemed to be coming from this young lady's property. Almost immediately afterwards, I heard what sounded like a thud, something hitting the ground. I have noted recently that the very pleasant young occupant who lives here has changed. She doesn't really come out of the property to pass the time of day anymore. Lots of vans have turned up with heavy plants, obscuring her kitchen window, and she had a new door put in. One of the neighbours, Mary, told me that she now has a high fence at the back of the garden. We've been a bit worried about her. So, when I heard the bang and what I took to be a scream, I rang her doorbell, but I got no response, so I decided to call the police.'

'Have you seen any people loitering round here recently?'

'Well, not as such, but there was a man who I saw come up my path last week, early in the morning, who put a card with "Vehicle Accessories" on it through my letterbox. It didn't have a lot of information on it. Our postman, Bob, then came across and asked me whether anything had been put through my door and I gave the card to him. I saw through my kitchen window that he took it over to the young lady who lives here and, I think, he handed it to her.'

'Did you notice him drive away after he put the card through your door?'

'I didn't see him get into a vehicle, but I saw a van with "Garden Furniture" drive past my house and I thought that it was probably him that early in the morning. I remember thinking that I wouldn't buy any vehicle accessories from someone with such a battered old vehicle, in case they had fallen off the back of a lorry.'

'Did you get any of the registration of that van?'

The doctor shook his head. 'I know it was old, and noted an X reg. I think there was a W and the number 5, but I didn't get anymore, and I can't be absolutely sure.'

'Thank you, Dr Marshall. Did you get enough of a look at the man who put the card through your doorway to be able to identify him?'

The doctor took his time. 'The answer is, I don't know.

He was a pudgy fellow, medium height, balding a bit, and wearing black trousers and a white shirt, more what you'd expect someone working in an office to wear than a garden centre employee. As I say, I didn't see him get into the van and I can't be sure the same man who put the card through is the driver of the van passing my house. To be honest, it doesn't make much sense having "Garden Furniture" on a van and putting a card with "Vehicle Accessories" on it through my door.'

'You've been incredibly helpful, Dr Marshall, much more so than you think.' John turned his notebook around and asked the Doctor to look through his account carefully and, if he agreed with John's notes, to sign them at the bottom.

'Wait, there's more,' the doctor said, looking distressed. 'After ringing I came out of the house again and crossed the road towards her house. There was a car parked in front, it belongs to a couple down the road, and I walked around it to see if I could see anything, lights inside the house for instance, but I couldn't. I may be imagining things, but I did think a blind moved. I stayed for a while as I wasn't sure if I should wait until the police came but it was cold, and I could keep an eye out from my kitchen window. But I changed my mind soon afterwards and came out of my house again because I was worried. It was while I was dithering in the street, that I heard an engine start up to the right of me towards the end of the street and a large dark coloured van pulled out. I walked towards it, but it was dark, and it really shot around the corner, a little unsteadily at first. All I could see was an R and an X in the numberplate, but I couldn't see any writing on its side when it disappeared.'

Handing the notebook back to John after signing the bottom of his account, Dr Marshall said: 'This is serious then? Has she been kidnapped?'

John hesitated, but only for a second. 'It's too early to say definitely that this is what's happened, but I and these officers will now be proceeding on the basis that this is a kidnapping, yes.'

A black streak shot across the road and through the cat

flap of the doctor's front door. After advising the doctor that his help may be requested further, John told him he could return to his property after impressing upon him how essential it was that he say nothing about the incident to anyone other than the police. The doctor told John that he could rely upon his discretion.

Turning to the uniformed officers, John brought them up to date with the stalking investigation and asked them to carry out house to house enquiries where there were lights showing in any of the properties, both on the road they were on and the one behind which was the perpetrator's point of entry. He briefed them on the wording he wanted them to use. Any feedback should be reported to CID who would arrange any further enquiries early the following morning. He then rang the police station to put out an alert to all nightshift officers to look out for a van with "Garden Furniture" on its sides and to stop the van and arrest the driver. He also requested stop checks on any vans, with or without writing on its side, with the letters X, W, R, or 5 in its registration. Finally, he went back to his car to ring Rory.

Rory was about to follow Thommi up the stairs to bed when John's call came through. After listening for several minutes, he said: 'Christ.' Hearing this, Thommi came halfway down the stairs, sat on the landing, and listened to Rory's half of the conversation.

The moment the call finished she said: 'What's happened?'

Looking up Rory said: 'Our stalking victim has been kidnapped, almost certainly by Billy Grant.' He noted the colour drain in Thommi's face. 'I'm going over to the nick now to co-ordinate our response and give instructions to the night shift. John's staying at the house until the SOCOs arrive.'

Thommi said, her face white. 'I'll ring and brief Nigel, to see if there is anything, anything at all, in our files which might help.'

'Thanks. I'll keep you informed of what's happening

when I can.'

CHAPTER 33

Before going upstairs to prepare for bed, she had walked into her garden in her slippers and up to the sundial. All the evidence was hidden beneath it. It was cold but she didn't feel it. Tears were streaming down her face as indecision once more gripped her. Would she really be able to kill another human being?

That afternoon, she had taken out her mother's sleeping pills but simply looked down at them. Instead of grinding them up, almost unconsciously she put them back in their boxes. Afterwards, she had at least managed to feed numbers into her new phone with its new SIM card and downloaded some Apps. She sent some emails from it but invented mobile numbers for her friends or used some from plumbers or other service providers who'd given her their mobile numbers. The second phone she smashed, having destroyed its SIM card, hoping that if her plan failed and Grant outwitted her, he'd think she'd bought a new mobile because her old one had met with an accident and was now in pieces in a shoebox. That would explain the lack of data on her new phone. That way it would be easier to ensure that Billy Grant didn't get access to her real phone. Looking up at the sky through her tears, she noted that the stars were intermittently obscured by dark clouds shifting in the wind, their random turmoil suiting her mood. Sighing as she was about to return indoors, she suddenly stiffened when, for a second, she thought her back fence had moved inwards as though someone was leaning on it but wiping her tears away with the back of her hand, she decided it must be her imagination. The fence was as it had been since it had been erected, Billy Grant simply playing with her mind again. Retracing her steps, she went through her kitchen door and locked it. She turned on the light which lit her garden. Yes, everything was in its place. Tomorrow she'd be strong again and, if she wasn't, the cold light of day was the time to make decisions. She was so tired that every step was an effort. She'd practically come to a full stop.

It was as she came out of the bathroom in her dressing gown over a short nightdress and matching underwear, that she heard something, a sound, although one which she couldn't identify. She hurried into her bedroom and looked out at the garden. He was there, a round speeding shape rushing towards her back door. As she heard the glass smash followed by her door opening, she opened her window and threw her mobile phone across into the neighbour's garden and rushed back along the corridor towards the front of her property to the bathroom. Too late. She screamed as he began to run up the stairs. A moment later she saw his fist come towards her and the blow on her temple left her stunned as she crashed to the floor. She opened her mouth, but no further scream was possible. The evil, evil invader, had gripped her face and was pouring something into her mouth. She was choking and then, when the liquid stopped and just as she managed a breath, her mouth was taped. She closed her eyes to block out Billy Grant's face, a face contorted with rage, and a short time later a creeping sensation began to affect her limbs, a slow paralysis, affecting her ability to move and leaving her completely helpless.

She heard him swear under his breath and wondered if her scream had alerted someone. She could hear him moving along her corridor towards her room, then sounds of moving objects, before he returned. She kept her eyes shut, her eyelids already gluing up under the effect of the drug. Initially, her other senses didn't seem to be reacting to the liquid, if anything they were sharpening, compensating for her loss of movement, if compensating was the right word in such circumstances. She knew he had things of hers and guessed her computer, her new phone and, maybe, the watch and jewellery she had taken off before going into the bathroom. She felt some soft material wound round each ankle before he bound them together with rope or cord. The next moment, she felt her legs being lifted and a duvet cover pulled up her body to her waist. He then bound her wrists behind her back in the same way as her ankles, before enclosing the whole of her within the duvet cover, which he tied over her head. Finally, she was tossed up and over his shoulder in a fireman's lift, and she was being carried down the stairs. Terror was her overriding emotion, accompanied by a feeling of nausea. She concentrated on staying calm to limit the chances of choking on her own vomit but the image of this round, sweaty, and now violent man in control of her pushed back against her efforts. When he laid her down again, she heard him move towards her window. A second later, a ring on her doorbell, then another sound, a soft string of obscenities streaming out from under Billy Grant's breath. He was worried. Things hadn't gone according to plan. He then moved quickly in the opposite direction. She knew this from hearing his footsteps, the clank of something hitting the wall, followed by the sound of her back door being pushed further open, letting in the night air. She was now completely helpless to do anything to save herself, but something had upset him. The person who had rung her doorbell must have heard her scream.

It seemed an age before the kitchen door opened again but her sudden surge of hope died as she felt herself heaved over his shoulder, the smell of his sweat noticeable even through her covering, making her feel sick again. The temperature dived as they left the house, and he carried her across her garden. The next moment he pushed her through what could only be her fence. She fell onto the pavement, and he trod over her. She was hoisted up again as he weaved around something, presumably a parked car. Then the sound of the back doors of a vehicle, his van presumably, being opened, and she was picked up and shoved upwards into the rear of it, her body shielded from sight, no doubt, by an open van door. A moment later, the rear doors clicked shut, another car door opened then closed at the front of the vehicle, the engine fired, and then they were moving.

Moments later, she heard a siren, distantly at first and then louder. 'Fucking bastard,' she heard him say, still under his breath but more audibly than before, as the car turned and turned again, weaving away from the main roads she guessed. Suddenly it stopped, and she heard him get out. The back doors of the van opened again, and he rolled her to one side, his arms brushing her body as he reached for things which clanked as they were thrown to the ground. She felt the fresh air enter the compartment even from under her covering. The door remained open, and she could hear metallic sounds and thuds. Her heartbeat had quickened when she first heard the sirens, but as their sound faded into the distance, her brief surge of hope died. She guessed he was changing the numberplates.

As they moved on into the night, she felt her head swim. Things started to muddle, she thought she might pass out altogether, then she descended into a kind of drowsy disorientation in which nothing seemed to hold together.

CHAPTER 34

THE NEXT TWENTY-FOUR HOURS

It was a Saturday, but at 0600 hours Rory's office was full of DSs, DCs, and Nigel Sheridan, the CPS lawyer. Rory and John had already been liaising with senior police officers from Rory's office since the early hours of the morning. Senior regional detectives at DS level had been allocated specific roles in the investigation, starting with the Intelligence Unit analysts. An encrypted airwave frequency had been allocated to everyone involved in the investigation so that they could communicate via their car and personal mobiles without fear of the operation being picked up on other airwaves. A senior detective was in overall charge of the Automatic Number Plate Recognition System (ANPR) and Council CCTV. Every Force had telephone Intel Units and Cell Site recognition capability.

Word came through about a vehicle set on fire in a field south of Guildford before 0500 hours. A farmer had rung Guildford police station when he found the wreck on his field. The same SOCOs who had gone into the victim's house attended the site of the burnt-out van. Under hastily erected but powerful artificial lighting, they were careful in their initial inspection, it wasn't clear how long the vehicle had been in that state, there may still be bits of smouldering hot metal. Much of what they recovered had been bagged and taken away for inspection under laboratory conditions, but by the time they had finished they were able to report four things. (1) The number plate of the vehicle had been removed. (2) The van was probably set on fire between midnight and 0400 in the morning. (3) A coat of recently applied paint had twisted away enough so that a small portion of the side of the van revealed some lettering under the new coat of paint which would fit with a "G" for "Garden Furniture." (4) There was no evidence of a body in the van when it was set on fire. The members of CID sitting in Rory's office, breathed a little easier but relief was only temporary. Billy Grant still held the victim captive, they still didn't have a clue where she was, and he had kidnapped her just over seven hours ago.

'He no longer has a van,' Rory said. 'So, we're in the dark about any other vehicle he uses.'

'He has a motorbike,' John said. 'We need to look at all cameras for big, probably black, motorbikes with two people on them on the roads surrounding the farm.'

'There are a lot of side roads, cycling routes, without cameras in that area,' Johnny Hamilton said, turning his I-Phone to show the others his google map.

Rory nodded but said: 'Nonetheless, the chances are he's had to, or will have to, use a road with a camera, if only fleetingly, at some point on his journey unless he's still in the area.'

'I don't think he'll stay close to his burnt-out van,' John said. 'We have to hope, he doesn't use the bike to get to a vehicle parked off road somewhere.'

Rory shook his head. 'My guess is that's exactly what he will do if he uses a motorbike at all. I think there are too many difficulties controlling a bike, however powerful, with a reluctant passenger on board, even if she is heavily drugged and strapped to him.' Rory's chair was precariously holding his weight on two legs as he characteristically leaned back while he thought. 'He could have planned this -'

'I'm sorry to interrupt, Rory, but I think he will almost certainly have planned it,' Nigel interjected. 'I also agree wholeheartedly with your view that he won't be travelling around with our victim on a motorbike. It's more likely he'll use the bike to get back to where he was holding her after he'd torched the van.'

There were a series of nods around the table.

'So, first on the list,' Rory resumed, 'is looking at cameras for any vehicles crossing roads near the location of the burnt-out van in the early hours of the morning. If he's in a four-wheeled vehicle, it's likely to be a sizeable one. Righting his chair to the relief of those holding their breath, he added: 'We've got to move fast on this. We don't know how long we've got. The question remains are we going about this in the right way? Given that we know the perpetrator, should we be putting an all-out alert to other forces and the press?' He looked bleakly out of his window which simply revealed that it was still dark outside bar a thin beam from a streetlight. 'My instinct is still no at this stage, not while it's possible we may get a lead. Alerting him ...' Rory lifted a shoulder and let his sentence trail.

'I agree,' Nigel Sheridan said quietly. 'I'm not a psychologist, and you may want to talk to one, but from the experience I have on these cases, a stalker is a control freak and he'll enjoy the power he has over this victim. When she blocked his access to her, he went to considerable lengths to get to her, took tremendous risks, and so far, it's paid off. But the moment he knows that everyone in the country is looking for him, he'll feel threatened and a victim who's alive doubles that threat. As things stand now, there's a lot of information we have that he won't know we know. He may still feel relatively safe to plot for an end from which he will escape. After all, he's escaped justice twice so may have a false sense of security.'

'Yes,' John concurred. 'We need to investigate every possible lead before we put out the alert. He's probably holed up somewhere he knows, and he'll be waiting to see what's on the news. So far, we've talked about a missing person and that we are investigating whether this is due to criminal activity, and even that isn't in the public domain.'

Johnny Hamilton snorted. 'You're an optimist. The press will be joining the dots. Someone in the road will speak to them, someone will know that she's been stalked, Bob the postman, the neighbour who called us -'

'I've talked to both Bob and Dr Marshall, and neither will speak to the press until we say so,' John interrupted. 'Uniformed officers on the house-to-house enquires have done the same. We need the next 24 hours, so I think we get on with the enquiries now and we keep as low a profile as possible.'

Rory nodded. 'What are you planning to do?' he asked John.

'I thought I'd go to the place the victim's post was redirected to, then call in at the victim's property on my way back. It's important that I get to the block of flats as early as possible before people start leaving for work or what-have-you.'

Noting some puzzled glances being exchanged between other officers Rory elaborated: 'According to the victim's postman someone we believe is Grant, fuck that, someone we know is Grant, tried to redirect her bank accounts to another address where, purportedly, she had moved. One of the other flat owners may be able to give us some information, particularly if they recognise Grant's photo. Johnny, where have you got to on the Kingston enquiries?'

'I have two addresses in the area for a William Clarke. I'll go house to house to get as much info as I can.'

'While we're waiting for the results from the forensic team, potential evidence from the stallholders, and Flynn's enquiries, apart from ANPR, Council monitored CCTV, and door to door enquiries, anything else you can think of that we should be working on?' Rory said, addressing everyone in the room.

'Yes,' Nigel replied. 'It is highly unlikely that this is the first time he's done this. He's not got a record but that doesn't mean anything. We need to look at harassment cases which were reported but didn't end up in court and find the reason for that. His fingerprints may have been taken and then destroyed when no further action was taken, or the case was dropped. I would get in touch with police stations within a relatively wide radius and talk to both officers and civilian staff about any stalking or harassment cases they've had, whether they proceeded to charge or not, in the last two years and find out the names of those accused. He may keep to William and Billy, with a different last name or use a different name altogether, with an address and date of birth of a real person.' Taking a deep breath, he continued. 'If you think that any of the investigations you hear about sound remotely possible, if they have a similar MO, and the reason they were dropped was a suicide or death in the last couple of years, I'd look at those particularly closely.'

'What?' Johnny exclaimed. 'Why?'

Nigel smiled at the look on Johnny's face, but the smile didn't reach his eyes. 'You thought the victim was unstable, didn't you? A bit of an attention seeker, a time waster, with some issues. If he's done this before and, judging by his expertise in having everyone feeling sorry for him, from beaks to the real Billy Grant who lent his flat to him, he's probably been fooling the gullible for quite some time.' Nigel watched Johnny Hamilton's face flame, with some satisfaction. 'Being stalked takes over a victim's life, her peace of mind goes, depression sets in, isolation often leads to self-medication, booze, drugs, you name it. We don't have time to look at every vulnerable person who's come to the attention of the Criminal Justice System. We can ignore stalkers whose relationship has ended but won't accept it because that's not the case here. This type of perpetrator targets someone they deem vulnerable whether because of bereavement or being alone or for some other reason. If he went to the stage of diverting our victim's mail, he was going all out for total control and, given that he contacted her bank, he may have other ulterior motives. I may be completely wrong, but I have a feeling he will have crossed our paths in some guise before and we may get information from that, if we're in time.

Rory looked shattered. 'I'll get going with those enquiries and we may get something from her phone?'

'You've got her phone?' Nigel asked.

'We do but, on an initial examination, it appears it doesn't link with a computer. I'm guessing that was deliberate on our victim's part, and we don't have the computer.' Rory replied. 'We know she has a computer because we had to look at it as well as her phone, at the request of the defence team, to confirm that she had not received any emails from him, so we assume Billy Grant is now in possession of it. Our IT guys are going through her phone now. If there's are any links with her computer, other than texts and emails, we might be able to get something from the cloud, but it's a long shot and timewise ...' Rory shrugged.

Nigel nodded and rose. 'I'll get over to the Mags.,' he said but as Michael Flynn entered the room at that point, he waited to hear what he had to say.

'I've been in touch with some of the stallholders who were at the Kingston and Barnes' markets.' A few detectives looked at their watches. How the hell did he manage that? Michael smiled but reassured them that the people who answered their phone at the crack of dawn had been helpful. Some recognised his description of Grant as the man selling vehicle accessories at the Kingston market, and two of them said that a schoolgirl was helping him unload the van. Another couple of stallholders remember him with his "Garden Furniture" van from Barnes. One of them recalled the teenage girl at his stall.

'Fran Williamson, who saw the young teenager at the Barnes market, is already here doing a photofit,' Michael said. 'Once I have that photofit, I thought I'd go first to where Grant's shop used to be in Kingston and ask any shop owners nearby if they recognise the girl. If I don't get anywhere, I'll start with the local schools and colleges in Kingston and, if they don't come up with her name, widen my enquiries to other schools and colleges, emailing the photofit to them.'

'Can you let me know how you get on, Michael?' Nigel asked. He and Flynn were both members of the South-West Central cycling team and firm friends. 'If you manage to find the girl, that may prove to be a very good shortcut to knowing more about Grant and, more importantly, his known whereabouts.'

Rory agreed and told Flynn to go ahead on the lines he suggested.

It was as the meeting was about to break up, after Rory

told his team that he wanted updates on their enquiries over the secure line, that a piece of information came through. A van registered to a William Clarke was reported stolen yesterday morning. A young female voice reported it, stating that it was left in her care but had gone from a street she named in Kingston where she'd left it. She said her name was Fiona and she'd be in trouble with Mr Clarke if they didn't find it and then the phone went dead before the CAD team could get any further information from her.

'Like we said, Grant isn't leaving anything to chance,' Nigel said with a grimace.

Nodding, Rory turned to Flynn. 'Get back here if you can, Michael, otherwise get a room preferably in the nearest cop shop, but link in. Oh, and one thing I've forgotten to mention. When John and I were talking to the neighbour opposite Grant's flat, she said she had seen him arguing with a dark-haired male outside the building half an hour before Grant left with his stuff. She wasn't much help with either the reason for the argument or the description, but Sarah Montgomery is looking into that.'

'I could do that after the Kingston enquiries,' Johnny Hamilton volunteered. 'I know the area well.'

'So does Sarah, she lives just round the corner.'

For a moment Johnny looked set to argue but seeing Rory's set expression thought better of it.

The meeting broke up, chairs scraping back as the room emptied.

When he had his office to himself, Rory looked out of the window and picked up his phone. He wanted to ring Thommi just to hear her voice, but other things had to come first.

CHAPTER 35

She had been wrong. Her belief that there was nothing further Billy Grant could do to her that was more terrible than what he'd done already was wrong. The terror she felt now was greater than anything she had felt before. She was helpless and his power over her was complete. Despite her closed eyelids and covering, she was still conscious of moments of light from time to time before it faded again. She assumed that it was due to towns and built-up areas being replaced by more remote locations, the weaving and bumping of the van lending support to her belief; A roads being replaced by B roads, perhaps even C, all leading to one road for her. She had no doubt that he would murder her, but her greatest fear, as panic moved freely through her despite the imprisonment of her limbs, was not knowing what would happen to her first, what the evil invader had in store for her before oblivion mercifully put an end to her existence. If he touched her .... If he ...

She had no idea how long they had travelled before she found she could move her eyelids. The vehicle had begun to bump along, clearly now on a track rather than a road, and after a particular jolt her eyes opened. All she could see was her covering, but the process of defrosting had begun. There was no comfort in this. He would want her to be awake, to see his smirk as he gloried in his power over her. He would want her to suffer.

The engine noise changed, and the vehicle slowed and then stopped. She heard him get out of the van, then the sound of doors creaking and even, she believed, his breath as he, presumably, laboured to open them. Then he was back in the van and the vehicle crept forward for a short distance. The back of the van opened, and various things were thrown to the ground, the sound of metal hitting metal, before the moment she dreaded arrived. His hands were on her body, pulling her forward, lifting her out of the vehicle, as she tried to stem the waves of nausea causing reflux to rise to her throat. She knew that people had died choking on their own vomit but, even if this would be a more merciful end than the one the evil invader intended for her, instinctively she fought for control.

Outside the building, he put her on the ground in a sloping sitting position against a door and, releasing the top of the duvet cover he pulled it off her body past her waist before ripping the tape off her mouth. She instantly threw up over her nightdress and he recoiled. Her heart jumped at that small movement, that involuntary moment of disgust he couldn't disguise. As she watched him disappear, she felt that he'd allowed a miniscule chink of control to slip. He returned with a black bin liner and his rucksack from which he pulled out the clothes she'd left on her bedroom chair before she went into the bathroom. They consisted of her knickers, bra, and jeans. With a stream of expletives, mercifully still wearing gloves, he pulled the duvet further down, past the vomit line, and began to release her hands from their binding to get the nightdress off her.

'You try anything with your hands, and I'll tip more liquid down your throat to incapacitate you. Do you understand?'

She nodded, and moments later he had pulled the nightdress over her head and put it in the black bag, his mouth a moue of disgust at the presence and stench of vomit. Involuntarily her hands moved to cover her exposed breasts eliciting a short bark of laughter from him, but his next move gave her a temporary moment of relief. After looking at her bra, he shoved it down the bin liner to join her night dress, picked up her T-shirt and jumper and rammed both over her head and down to her waist before re-binding her hands. But when he then hauled her out of the duvet and lay her down on it, before working to unbind her ankles her terror levels shot up. With just her short matching pyjama bottom still covering her lower limbs, she braced herself for the worst. She closed her eyes, waiting for the moment when his gloved hands would grab at the elastic at her waist. But it didn't happen. Instead, she felt something pulled over her ankles and up her legs. She opened her eyes just as, with a grunt, he managed the final tug of her jeans. Startled, she saw him shove her knickers into the black bin liner to join her nightdress and bra. Then, rebinding her ankles with his gloved hands, he lifted her, once again, to put her body inside the duvet cover, but this time securing it at her neck. Catching something in her expression, his eyes narrowed, and he said savagely:

'Just not yet, save the best for last, ay?' and turned away.

But a slow realisation was dawning on her. His only physical contact with her so far was for practical purposes. Keeping her quiet after she screamed, drugging her, moving her from one place to another. His relentless targeting of her was always from a distance; sometimes a closer distance such as a supermarket aisle but, usually, not within touching distance. Partly it was to evade detection, but there was something else. He had hardly looked at her nakedness when he'd removed her nightdress. So far, he had never touched her unless he had to. No, whatever he planned to do when he murdered her, her dread of being helpless to prevent him inflicting the worst of physical intimate invasions on her was receding. Billy Grant was impotent she was sure of it. Whatever horrors he still had in store rape wouldn't be one of them.

Finally, picking up the can of water again he held it to her mouth with one gloved hand, holding the opening of the bin liner under her chin with the other. She choked but some of the liquid went down her throat. He looked at her for a moment, the familiar wet leer now back taunting her, his old self resurfacing, before drying her mouth and re-taping it. He then pulled a balaclava over her head.

Through the two openings for her eyes, she viewed her surroundings which included several outbuildings. Presumably the van was in the larger of them, the one resembling a hanger, one door of which she was leaning up against. There were similar corrugated iron doors on another building, a wooded door hung off an opening to a third, and a van, the sort which people use to sell refreshments at markets or fetes, nestled close to a squat brick office-like structure which is where he now dragged her. Once inside, he thrust her unceremoniously onto a chair. A light was switched on and a chain was thrown over her and tightened over the duvet around her waist before being wound around the chair, the other end then attached to a ring on a metal safe. The return of feeling to her limbs didn't matter, she couldn't move. She leant back against the chair as Grant walked outside again and, shortly afterwards, she smelt burning, her clothes, presumably, evidence that might implicate him in whatever was to happen to her. She stiffened when he finally returned and saw, through the holes in the balaclava that he had her computer bag. Taking out her computer, and sitting down at the table, he pulled it towards him and, with a triumphant glance over at her, opened it.

CHAPTER 36

Armed with the address, it was as John was driving towards the block that the first potential break in the case came through.

'Flynn has a name for the teenage girl who used to be at Grant's Vehicle Accessories shop in Kingston,' Rory said. 'Someone in a neighbouring shop looked at our photofit and said that the schoolgirl he sometimes saw in Grant's shop looked a bit like that and he identified the school uniform as belonging to the secondary school on the east side of Kingston. Flynn called the school's headmistress, emailed her a copy of the photofit, and she identified the girl as Fiona Marsh. The headmistress told Flynn she had a report of a conversation between Fiona and her teacher at school which might be helpful, after he'd managed to convince her that third parties could justify sharing information without a warrant where the wellbeing of a young person was concerned. He's on his way over now.'

'Brilliant.'

John arrived at the address, which was a standard 3-storey brick affair containing six flats. Stepping up to the front door, he rang every bell until the intercom on of them answered. After identifying himself, a male appeared at the main door and let him in. His name was Paul Cameron, he was a first year University student studying psychology at Roehampton University, wearing jeans and a T-shirt, and giving every appearance of having only recently got out of bed. But when John showed him a shot of Grant, he was alert enough.

'Oh, him, yeah,' he said, then looking at a wire basket on

the floor he continued: 'He's still got some post coming in. He picks it up. We had a flat owners' and tenants' meeting the other day, and we're going to tell him we're not keeping it for him anymore. He hasn't lived here for a year, apparently.'

John picked up five envelopes, and his heart missed a beat when he saw that although four of them were addressed to a William Clarke, one in the same pile had the name of the victim.

'I'm taking these, Paul. I would now like to talk to you to find out anything you know about this man. Can we go to your flat?'

'I guess,' Paul's expression was one of anxiety.

They walked up one flight of stairs and Paul unlocked his door. Turning around, rather red in the face, he said: 'I had a bit of a party last night.'

'I was a student once too,' John replied smiling and taking the only chair with nothing on it. When Paul sat on the bed, John told him that there was a serious allegation brought against William Clarke, police were unable to trace him at present, but it was essential that they do so.

'I don't really know him,' Paul said apologetically. 'I came after he left. In fact, this was his flat. I've just let him in a few times and pointed to his mail.'

'There's an envelope here addressed to a woman.'

'Yeah, well he asked us to keep hers too and kept saying that he would soon do a re-direction of post but would pick it up in the meantime. That was, like five, six, months ago, but he hasn't, mail keeps coming.'

'Who was the female, do you know?'

'He told me she was his girlfriend, that she was going to move in with him and so redirected her post here but then he decided to move himself.' Paul shifted on the bed. 'I never saw her but, like, the couple upstairs don't believe she is his girlfriend.'

'Why is that?'

Thumbing at the ceiling, Paul said: 'Miranda upstairs says he won't have had a girlfriend. He didn't like women. She's another reason we're telling him we're not keeping his post and the next time he rings a bell no one's letting him in. Apparently, he was creepy with Miranda, following her sometimes, asking her questions all the time, until Bob, her boyfriend moved in. He's a big bloke and straightened him out apparently. He thought Miranda was on her own. Next thing, he's moved.'

'Do you have a telephone number for Miranda.'

Paul shook his head but said: 'I've got an email for her. We're all sent minutes of our management meetings and hers is on that.' He stood up, moved to his desk, and opened his computer. John briefly stood, scribbled down her email, then gave Paul two of his cards.

'Is she likely to be back later?' John asked.

'Yeah, she works for the Council.'

'This is important, would you knock on her door when she's back, give her my card, and ask her to ring me as a matter of urgency. Keep the other one yourself.'

'Okay, will do.'

When they were both seated again John resumed: 'When was the last time you saw William Clarke?'

'Like, ten days ago, thereabouts.'

'Now just think for a moment or two. Is there anything, anything at all that he said in conversation that might give us an insight into his character or, better still, an idea of where he lives now?'

Paul sighed, but more at the attempt to dredge his memory than because he objected to being asked questions.

'Okay, he told me the reason he hadn't changed his mailing address up to now was because he was being harassed by someone and that he believed this person had intercepted his mail once. He said he'd had to contact police and that the person harassing him had tried to say he'd done something, but the police believed him.' Paul paused again. 'He was a weirdo, but I felt a bit sorry for him. I mean he looked odd, wearing black office trousers which were a bit shiny cos they were old, and socks over the summer, and old-fashioned shoes like your Dad would wear, and these polyester shirts. He was always sweating, and he had what Miranda called his 'wet mouth' look. I thought she was a bit mean, he couldn't help his looks, but she told me women would see a different side of him and that I was, like, naïve. But all he did was smile and ask for his post.' Looking thoughtfully at John, he added: 'But now you've turned up and you're obviously investigating something serious, so Miranda was probably right.' He grinned. 'Great psychologist I'm going to make.'

John smiled back. 'Did he say where he'd moved to?'

'No, but he said he'd bought something down the A3 somewhere. He told me he used to have a shop in Kingston, but it didn't make much money and that someone had left him some money in a will and that he'd bought some land. That's why he moved out of the building, he told me. He didn't say anything about Miranda or Bob. I didn't really know whether the harassment thing was true, but post for his girlfriend, if that's who she was, did arrive here.' Paul lifted a shoulder. 'I don't really know what to believe.'

'Could you be more specific about where he bought the land?'

'He said it was a leafy area, and I think he might have mentioned it being south of Guildford but I couldn't swear to it. I got the impression it was kind of off the beaten track and he was working on it, so maybe he couldn't live there yet. In fact, yeah, he said he'd redirect his post elsewhere cos his address wasn't ready to move into yet. Honestly, that's about it.'

'What about the will? Did he say who'd left him the money?'

'No, but he said the person had a daughter he looked after sometimes. I got the impression maybe that's why she'd left him the money. He said the daughter sometimes worked for him, but then he told me he'd given up his shop once he had the money.' Paul lifted a shoulder and frowned as though he was thinking through the discrepancies in Grant's account for the first time. 'Like I said, I don't know what to believe.'

'Did he say anything else about the person who left him money or the girl. Any names?'

'No, he never said any names. That's about all I've got. Oh, except he said the daughter self-harmed so he, like, helped her when he could. That's all, sorry.'

John rose. 'Don't apologise, you've been more helpful than you know. If you think of anything else, however trivial, please contact me. It's important, and it's also vital you and Miranda don't mention any of this to anyone. Don't forget to tell Miranda to contact me straight away but let me explain to her why.'

Paul was also now standing ready to see John out and he looked at the card John had given him. 'Okay, will do.'

'Would you mind giving me your phone number in case I need to contact you?'

'No, not at all,' Paul said, reeling off his number.

John jotted it down in his notebook and took his leave.

CHAPTER 37

He had taped the ends of his fat fingers so that he'd leave no fingerprints, after which she watched them play her computer keyboard like a piano. She had always suspected that he would be a computer nerd. For some time, his brow was furrowed in concentration, then the folds around his neck wobbled and she could see his loose mouth split into a grin. He turned briefly in her direction, his eyes disappearing into his cheeks, and she could only think that it was because he'd managed to break into her document. He turned back to the screen.

She could only watch him through the holes for her eyes but despite the balaclava and tape tight on her mouth making her face hot, she welcomed the fact that it masked some of her dread. There was something manic about Grant's concentrated glee. Whenever he turned her way, she tried to look away, but she was mesmerised by his concentration, and she inevitably looked back. After some time, he picked up his phone. Judging by his movements she guessed he had turned it off earlier. Opening it up, she saw him raise the phone to his ear and heard him speak.

"Okay, half an hour. Don't be late but don't get caught speeding. When you arrive, we need to move quickly."

Her stomach turned over, there was someone else involved in this.

Billy Grant's attention switched back to the computer and he began to type. Watching him, part of his tongue now poking out of his mouth as he concentrated on his task, she could only assume that he was either deleting or editing her text. After a while, her best guess was that he was editing it. For the first time since her brain had almost calcified, dimming her capacity to think, she felt something, a feeling akin to relief at the realisation that, if he was editing her text, her mobile phone ploy must have worked. The evil invader thought that he was in possession of the only source of her document. Her anticipation had outwitted him. By changing her account, he would be providing evidence against himself. Every word he was deleting, every word or sentence he was adding, was one more chink in the chair of evidence mounting against him. She watched his movements with a weird fascination. It was a big 'If' and she tried to damp down the first stirring of something resembling hope. It wasn't as if the outcome would be any different, the cavalry wouldn't arrive in time to save her. But it would mean that her actions might save other victims and that THOSE TO WHOM IT MAY CONCERN would be confronted by the true scale of Billy Grant's depravity, and that things might change.

Suddenly, he leant back, stretched, and closed her computer, before looking at his watch. He stood up and she clenched her stomach muscles as he walked towards her, his eyes gleaming. He reached her and leant down to meet her eyes with his. He didn't touch her, just held her attention like a rabbit caught in headlights.

'So, you thought you could get the better of me, did you? Funny thing, your plan is not a million miles away from mine, but you've helped by supplying the finishing touches.'

The venom in his tone was unmistakeable despite the softness of his voice. He was pumped up, glorying in his power over her. With an effort she closed her eyes.

'I'd keep them open if I were you,' he continued, almost in a whisper, and she felt his breath on her face. 'They'll be shut for a very long time. You see I'm going to give you your wish, a parting gift. Oh, not the part where you kill me, although that's still there in your document. That's what people will see, what they'll remember.' He laughed. 'But I am making a change. When you see your beautiful view for the last time, you won't be jumping into thin air, you'll be hanging. Murderers hang, don't they, or they did? It's more fitting. You'll be feeling a rope tighten around your throat, cutting off your airwaves. The rest will be just as you now say will happen in your document. As always, your own stupid belief that you could get the better of me, has helped me out.'

A second later, the sound of an engine broke the silence and amplified as some sort of vehicle approached their location. Grant stood and, behind her, she could hear him open the office door. His words meant that her whole world had suddenly spun onto a different axis. If the evil invader intended to stage her suicide, the person arriving might be an accessory but not her executioner, at least not yet. So, who was it?

CHAPTER 38

When John arrived outside the victim's property, he walked over to a vehicle opposite her front door and the window of the driver's side wound down. The vehicle was a Skoda Octavia. Looking up at him as he leant down was DC Shirley Cox.

'No-one's been near her front door,' Shirley told him. 'There's the odd curious glance from neighbours but that's about all.'

John nodded. 'Thanks Shirley, I hope, we all hope, that this surveillance won't have to last long.'

Shirley smiled at him sympathetically and then said: 'Hang on, someone's approaching her door now, a female.'

John turned and the two of them saw a slim brunette with long curly hair approach the door and ring the bell. She seemed agitated, shifting from one foot to another and then standing back and looking up at the top windows.

'A friend of hers?' Shirley suggested.

John looked at his watch. 'Damn, I'm expecting an update in fifteen minutes. It may be the friend who gave evidence in court on her behalf. If so, I do need to speak to her but not until after the call.'

'I'll sit with her in this vehicle until you've finished. You can then interview her.'

Nodding, John said, after turning back and watching her banging on the door again: 'Thanks Shirley, but I don't know what you should say to her in the meantime.'

'Look, I'll play it by ear. Sometimes the only way to

keep people quiet is to tell them what's going on,' and taking the decision out of his hands, Shirley opened the car door and walked across the road.

John watched as Shirley identified herself to the visitor and then began to cross the road himself as Shirley guided her towards the car. He didn't turn back but entered the house with his keys.

A quarter of an hour to go. John stood in the middle of the victim's sitting room and looked around. He had opened the slats of the plantation blinds but not put on any artificial light. He liked what he saw, a wooden floor instead of a carpet with a beautiful rug covering the centre of it and an original Victorian or Edwardian fireplace. Against the walls either side of the fireplace were bookshelves full of books which, judging by the titles, were a mixture of those inherited and those bought by the victim. The "Complete Works of William Shakespeare" was on the same shelf as Jilly Cooper's "Riders"; "Little Women" was wedged beside "The Gruffalo"; "Pride and Prejudice", sat next to Georgette Heyer's "These Old Shades"; and on the other side of that were three of J K Rowling's detective stories, written under the name of Robert Galbraith. It was a testament to a world of solid, perhaps privileged, middle- class existence, a safe world. A once safe world full of happy prospects and certainties now turned upside down.

Turning to the far end of the room, John saw that taking up most of a Victorian table near the window, in contrast to the cheerful muddle of new and old in the rest of the room, there were neatly stacked photo albums with printed lists documenting the photographs. Further lists topped paperwork including bank statements, legal documents, and there was also a single sheet of paper listing personal items, with the names and addresses of people to be contacted as persons "To Whom It May Concern," with some instructions. A chill travelled up his spine as he remembered Nigel's words: "If the reason was a suicide or death in the last couple of years, I would look at that particularly closely." Is that what these lists were about? Is this what that monster had done to her, driven her towards?

Opening the photo albums one by one, knowing he had no time to browse, but flicking quickly through John was left in no doubt that the victim had been a cherished member of a loving family, that her childhood had been happy, her teens full of parties, her university life full of promise followed by a successful career, and anger shot through him like a knife. Anger and guilt. The life of this happy young woman had been systematically taken over and destroyed and when she needed help, when she needed the police to do what they were meant to do, apprehend criminals, they had let her down.

John took out his phone a couple of minutes before the meeting. Not all the team could link in, some were still in the middle of on-going enquires but had reported back so that Rory could pass on any information they had. After John had given a succinct account of his interview with Paul Cameron, Rory agreed with him that it was difficult to know whether what Grant had told Paul was true, but he'd get someone to check a property register using the names they had for him. 'Why, given his stalking habit, would he volunteer information which might harm him?' Rory asked.

'He may think that nothing will harm him,' John said. 'He's got away with so much that he might think he's invincible, otherwise why would he risk kidnapping his victim?' He realised too late that this was not exactly a tactful opinion to voice with Johnny Hamilton on the line. Too late.

'We don't yet know everything the victim herself might have had on him,' Rory replied. 'We now have the three photos from her phone, one of Grant in the street opposite a doctors' surgery, one – and this is damning – of him looking over her fence, and one of him looking through the window of a coffee place, and the phone is still being interrogated. But she may have more and the tech. thinks that she's deleted things which can probably be recovered. However, given the photos, particularly one of him looking over her fence, he may have thought that this time she had him on the ropes if she reported him to police again. On the other hand, her barricading herself into her property, blocking his ability to stalk, may just have been too much for his sick mind.'

There was a murmur of agreement. 'There's also what looks like a bracket for a missing camera on the outside of her property overlooking her garden,' John said.

The discussion then moved on; they had no time for speculation which was unlikely to lead anywhere. The DS in charge had received CCTV so that he and his team could look at every bit of evidence on ANPR within a 20-mile radius of the burnt-out van and to check the number plates of every vehicle from midnight until 0500 hours to establish ownership of the vehicles. Another officer had shown, using charts, that it was difficult for a motorbike or overland vehicle to travel over more than 15 miles of rough land from the site of the fire without hitting a road with a camera on it, hence the chosen radius.

'A police helicopter is looking at remote locations near the burnt-out van,' Rory said. 'Once you've interviewed the victim's friend, John, get over here and we'll go to the sites and liaise with officers in the Guildford area.'

Every police officer at South-West Central and neighbouring police stations were aware of the clock ticking.

It was just as the phone conference was about to end that Michael Flynn came on-line fresh from his meeting with Fiona Marsh's class teacher. 'I went to the school. Fiona Marsh's form mistress told me that Fiona is a bright girl but that her work had declined dramatically halfway through her A level year.'

The gist of Flynn's visit was that, after speaking to Fiona, the teacher had found out that her mother had come under the influence of a male called William Clarke. Fiona had actually referred to him as a 'stalker.' Her mother had initially been frightened of him and had called police, but she was drinking at the time and no action was taken. She dropped her allegation, in any event, when he persuaded her that he could help her, and that her daughter could work at weekends in his shop. Fiona said to her teacher that he was "looking after her mother's money" but she thought he was stealing it, although he did give her work which he paid her for. Her mother took her own life eighteen months ago and Fiona dropped out of school.

There was a sharp intake of breath. 'Neither the Headmistress nor the teacher thought about reporting matters either to social services or us because Fiona told them she was leaving because she had a job.' Flynn said. 'She was coming up to 18 years old, and she hadn't reported witnessing Grant stealing from her mother. She was angry about her mother's suicide, but her anger seemed to be directed at her mother rather than Clarke even though she referred to him as "the weirdo." The Headmistress was both defensive and upset when I questioned her, but she did tell me that the mother of a schoolfriend of Fiona's had told her that her daughter had seen Fiona working at a market near London. Apparently, Fiona had told her friend that William Clarke had charge of her money until she was 21 years old. In the meantime, she had to work for him. The friend's mother was worried about the situation and the Headmistress told me that in view of my questions she wished she'd investigated it more, but she was just up to her eyes in work.'

'Jesus,' Rory said, and there were murmurs all round.

'We need the mother's Will,' Nigel said, 'and, in addition, we should get all the information on the report the mother made to police now as it may reveal more about him and where he has been living etc. in the past.'

There was silence for a moment before Rory spoke. 'We now know that Fiona Marsh is the young lady at the Barnes market and that she at least has a licence to drive a motorcycle and possibly a full driving licence; she must be nineteen now. Michael, can you get onto the DVLC and keep digging from the Fiona Marsh angle.'

'Will do when I'm back. I'm about to visit the mother of Fiona's friend.'

'Second thoughts, I'll get cracking on the police report. Clarke can you find out about the Will and do the DVLA enquiries. You go ahead interviewing the friend's mother Michael and then get back here unless your enquiries point to other leads.'

Rory then reeled off a series of further instructions and the meeting ended.

Opening the front door of the victim's property, John nodded across to DC Shirley Cox who then spoke to her companion. As the victim's friend walked towards him, John could see that she was crying.

CHAPTER 39

She caught her breath when she saw the girl walk into the office building, feeling the tape tighten over her mouth. It was the same girl who had been at the Barnes market, she was sure of it. But there was no means of communicating with her, she was helpless. She saw the girl look across at her, saw her mouth open, and her brow furrow and then the evil invader spoke.

'Don't look at her. She's been trying to steal your inheritance.'

'But what . . .?' The girl looked frightened.

'Don't worry, she's free when she tells me what I need to know to get the money back for you. Come over here, I'll show you what's on her computer.'

There was nothing she could do. Whatever Billy Grant had typed into her computer it had the effect of keeping the girl from making immediate eye contact.

'I've got some work to do in the shed with the van and cars. Come over to the door where I can see you and keep a look out. Don't go near her, she's a manipulative cow who's tried to steal your mother's inheritance.'

He came over and twisted the balaclava so that the holes for her eyes were covered, and any opportunity for eye contact had disappeared.

She heard the office building door open and felt cold air sweep in which helped with her rising claustrophobia.

'Stay here until I'm finished,' she heard him say to the girl.

Minutes later, she heard the same creaking as when they'd first arrived. Presumably from the doors of the large building where he'd parked the van being opened.

She was completely blind, but she did the only thing she could think of. She shook her head and then moved it. With her head movements she began to sketch a number, the phone number on DC John Carter's card which, despite her initial plan to throw it away, she'd rescued and, from it, memorised his mobile number. She paused when she'd finished and then started again. She had no means of knowing whether the girl had looked her way or not until, at the third attempt, she heard her begin to repeat: "07 …". She nodded but then shook her head when one of the numbers was wrong and did the movement again. She waited for the girl to speak again, and her heart felt like it would explode when she didn't say anything, but she managed to continue to do the same movements as before. Three times, with a gap in between, her head sketched the numbers. She had no means of knowing whether the girl had seen them or correctly interpreted them. Then an intake of breath by the girl and Grant's footsteps.

'Right, we're locking up. I've moved your moped out of your car because I want you to follow my van now and give me a lift back before you return to London. Come on, we've got to be quick.'

'Won't she be smothered?' the girl piped up.

'No, it's a knitted balaclava not a plastic bag,' he replied, but a moment later he'd swivelled it round so that she could see again, before pushing the girl ahead of him and out of the office door. She heard the key in the lock. Looking down at her chains, she was completely helpless to do anything about her situation, she couldn't move, couldn't speak although being able to see was better than feeling completely cocooned. Did the girl correct the "4?" Did she carry on looking, did she get the number on her phone so that she could ring it? If she could at least save this girl, that would be something she pleaded, as though offering up a silent prayer. That would be something good she would leave behind when her own fate was sealed.

The next thing she heard was an engine, the van, followed

by another vehicle igniting, then the creak of the doors and vehicles leaving.

CHAPTER 40

John now recognised her face from some of the photo albums. She was a university friend of the victim and they had also shared a flat together for a while.

'Please sit down,' he said, indicating the sofa opposite the fireplace. 'I think your name is Cassandra, isn't it? If I'm right, you also gave evidence on your friend's behalf at court on two occasions.'

She nodded, blew her nose, and tried to control herself but the moment she said: 'I can't believe she's been taken,' the tears spilled over again.

Waiting a moment as she once again tried to regain control, John then spoke in a more business-like tone.

'Cassandra, it's important you concentrate now. Firstly, will you tell me why you came over this morning?'

This brisk approach and having a question to focus on seemed to do the trick. Cassandra took a shuddering intake of breath and nodded. She did, however, leave the sofa to pace in a somewhat theatrical way and, as she began to speak, what she said was punctuated by nervous hand and arm movements.

'Okay. I rang her yesterday,' she began, 'she and I, well we hadn't fallen out in an argumentative sort of way, but she wouldn't see me anymore. She thought I'd let her down in that second court case. I know she did.' She turned to John and spoke in a voice full of appeal. 'I was told by the barrister who was prosecuting that I couldn't mention the first case, I wasn't allowed to. In the second case, I did say that I had seen Billy Grant in the street, and that he looked over at us, but his barrister kept saying that, as he lived in the area, I couldn't say that he was there for any reason connected to my friend, and more and more questions like that and, not being able to mention the first case, I couldn't give a reason why I thought it was deliberate. Without being able to give one, I couldn't say that he wasn't going somewhere, going shopping, whatever. What else could I have said?' She threw an arm out towards John.

'Understandable. Go on.'

'She thought I should have said that the reason why I didn't think he was there by accident was because I'd seen him before and, when he came to her house, because of what he said then, even if his barrister did try to stop me.'

John thought so too, but all he said was: 'Court procedure is very difficult to follow sometimes, go on.'

'Well, I just knew I'd let her down and then I sort of made a stupid joke,' she batted a hand in the air as if swotting an imaginary fly. 'It was after he got away with it again in that second case. She was very upset at the way things had gone. She'd caught a Magistrate pass a look at Billy Grant's barrister and it was like a male bonding kind of thing over her allegation she saw Billy Grant drive off after the so-called phallic finger shadow on her wall, and I made some silly comment about men having a one-track mind and I meant to make her laugh, but it had the opposite effect. I knew the moment I'd said it, it was a mistake. But she really is a completely different person to the one I knew. My friend who used to laugh so easily and who everybody loved to bits, but you can't get near her now, she's depressed but refuses to acknowledge it.'

Again, the appeal for understanding, but although he nodded encouragingly, John didn't say anything. Picking up on his slight hesitation, Cassandra stopped waving her arms about, looked him straight in the eye, and said, as though challenging an unspoken accusation:

'The fact is it wasn't me who lost the case for her, she made a mistake. It couldn't have been Billy Grant who did the shadow because lots of witnesses saw him elsewhere. Look,

I know this horrible little man has been the cause of her depression but it's not the only cause.' The appeal to John's sympathy was back. 'She lost both parents within the last year. They were a really, really, close family so she must have been grieving, and I know she was. She also broke up with Tim, her fiancé, and Billy Grant just added to it. Don't you think?'

'I imagine he did add to it,' John said, realising what the victim was up against, not simply because of the prosecuting authorities' mismanagement of the victim's allegations but also because her friend, like them, had totally underrated Billy Grant.

'I did everything I could to help, but everything I did was wrong.'

John didn't want to stop the flow but neither did he want her to divert the conversation away from the victim towards her own feelings of being hard-done-by.'

'I'm sure you were a good friend,' he said. 'So, you rang her?'

'I did. I wanted to see her again. I wanted to say sorry, but she wouldn't let me, she said that she was off sick for six weeks and she needed that time alone. I begged her to see me, but she wouldn't budge. All she said was that the one thing I could do to help her was to remember what she was about to tell me because it would be very important one day soon and to tell the police what I'd said. Well,' she amended, 'she said to tell you.'

John caught his breath: 'What was it she said?'

Cassandra collapsed on the sofa like a rag doll, shaking her head, both arms rising upwards in a helpless gesture. 'It doesn't really make sense.' She said and stopped. John waited. A minute later, Cassandra continued: 'She went back to the day at the Barnes' market, the day we met Billy Grant. She said to me on the phone: "I want you to remember everything about that day and meeting Billy Grant and the reason we met him and what happened next, up until the time when Billy and the other guys put the sundial in my garden. Remember that is the reason he knew my address. Remember the sundial.'

She paused and shook her head. 'Why would the police

want to know that?'

John scribbled for several minutes. 'All right. Start from the beginning of that day until the moment he left having delivered the sundial.'

Cassandra, occasionally interrupted by John, went through the full day from the car journey there, to looking around the market, eating cupcakes, drinking cider, making jokes, and then the victim seeing the sundial, deciding to buy it, and Billy Grant offering to follow them in his van. At one point she stood up and beckoning John over to the window at the back, she pushed aside a net curtain and said: 'There it is. That's what all the fuss is about.'

After both were seated again, John thought for a moment before he continued his questioning.

'From the moment you all saw the stall and the sundial to him getting in the van to following you, can you remember any of the conversation?'

Cassandra screwed up her face and John could see that she was close to tears again.

'Well, we were all sort of together. We saw a stall and, at that time there was a girl there rather than Grant -'

'Hang on,' John removed his phone from his pocket and after a moment or two turned the photofit image of Fiona towards Cassandra.

'That looks like the girl,' Cassandra said, without any prompting.'

'Thanks. Did she say anything?'

'She was about to when Billy Grant came forward from the van and sort of elbowed her away. She looked a bit upset about it, now I think about it. But we didn't speak to her.'

'Do you remember anything else about her?'

'Not really. She wore jeans and a shirt, and I remember seeing on the table what looked like a small helmet, so she may have a motorbike or something. I saw a lightweight one near the van. There was also a large black motorbike in the van which I saw when they were lifting the sundial into the back of it.'

'You definitely saw two motorbikes, one outside it and a larger black one inside the van. Can you describe them?'

'Not really, I saw the one in the van only briefly. The one outside was, like I said, a lighter kind of motorbike, a moped, light blue I think, more girly. That's about it.'

'I just need to make a brief call,' he told Cassandra, getting his phone out and dialling Rory. When Rory picked up, he described what Cassandra said about a second lightweight bike so that the guys could look out for it on the CCTV. What if it was a motorbike which could fit in a vehicle which she drove to a location for Billy Grant to pick up after torching the van?

'Is that important?' Cassandra said, anxious to have been of some help.

'I don't know but it could be. You're very observant.'

'I'm an interior designer and I do up houses for a living.'

John smiled. 'That explains it. Okay, go on from when Billy Grant came forward.'

Cassandra picked up her thread and when she finished, John summed up.

'So, you said you told her that her parents would have wanted her to buy the sundial,' John began, thinking that Grant would have picked up on the past tense, 'a price was arranged, she paid in cash, and then there was a discussion about how to get it to her home. He followed in his van, helped place it in her garden, and then left, leaving her a card with very little information on it, and getting her to sign another one. From then on, he would know what her signature looked like.'

Cassandra sniffed and looked keenly at John. 'He would know that, yes. Is that important?'

So, the victim hadn't told Cassandra about her post going missing. 'At this stage everything's important,' he said. 'Now look, I want you to go through my notebook, line by line, and if you think of anything else, tell me, and then I need you to sign your statement and date it. Is that all right?'

She took his notebook, read it slowly, and then signed and dated as requested.

'Thank you very much, Cassandra. You have my card, if there's anything else you can think of, just phone me. If I don't answer leave a message, I'll get back to you.'

She rose and walked to the door with him, her brow furrowed. As he turned to say goodbye she blurted out: 'You must tell me, you must tell me what happens. Please.' Tears began to fill her eyes again. 'She was right though, I didn't understand. He is an evil man.'

John nodded and said with sympathy: 'Cassandra, don't start blaming yourself. People like Billy Grant are very convincing liars, remember that.'

He looked at his watch. 'I have to get on,' he said.

'Yes, she said, but then stalled him again by saying: "When she said that I must remember the conversation we had and, if anything happened, I must tell you, I thought about that all last night that's why I came round. I didn't like her saying: "if anything happened," that's why I came over. I was going to insist she come home with me.'

John nodded. 'Okay, thanks. Cassandra, I can't stress enough how important it is that you don't speak about what's happened or what's been said to anyone.'

'I won't say anything. I won't say anything to anyone,' she said in a choked voice. 'I won't do anything that might make things worse.'

'Good,' John said in a bracing tone of voice, walking towards and opening the front door.

As Cassandra was about to leave, she turned.

'Will you let me know?'

'As soon as I can, I'll get back to you,' he promised.

After following Cassandra out of the door, John turned to lock it securely. Seeing a neighbour pop out of a door a few houses down, John turned purposefully towards his car, thankfully parked in the opposite direction.

CHAPTER 41

The sound of heavy rain on the roof of the building she was in, startled her. But it stopped as suddenly as it had arrived a short while later, restoring silence to her surroundings, cocooning her in a tomb-like existence. Finally, she heard an engine, but only one this time, and anxiety gripped her. Her face, hot inside the balaclava was a mass of prickles, and she felt that she couldn't breathe. What had happened to the girl? Had the evil invader done anything to her? Why would he leave a witness? But then she heard him speak to someone and the door of the office was thrown open. It didn't matter how often she had seen Billy Grant another sighting was always accompanied by dread. But she saw that the girl was standing right outside the door, alive and staying there as Grant strode to the table, picked up some keys, and returned.

'Now don't forget. Pull over where I told you. Make sure no one's around and change the plates, just as I taught you. Understood? Screwdrivers and the tool kit are at the back. Go now and the moment you arrive, get to the train station, and wait. You'll have to cycle, so get going the moment you've parked. No buses, no tubes. Right? I'll text you with instructions.' His voice suddenly hardened. 'Are you fucking listening?'

'Yes.'

'Well, what are you looking over at her for?'

'It's just ... she might need the loo, or something?'

'We're leaving no trace of her anywhere here, okay?' He walked straight up to the girl who was now completely shielded from view by his body. 'Don't forget we're in this together so don't get any ideas because you feel sorry for her. Remember what she's done to us, to you,' His words already soft lowered further. 'In this together. Remember? Now get going.'

As he moved, for a second the girl looked at her and their eyes met. Such a fleeting communication, but did she manage to convey something that would make the teenager think. Surely the evil invader's words "We're leaving no trace of her anywhere," followed by a barely disguised threat, a threat that the girl was implicated in whatever he planned to do, an accomplice, must register. Or was his control over the girl so complete that she was incapable of thought or would be too frightened to do anything. The evil invader slammed the door after her and, as they were both now on opposite sides of it, there was no further opportunity for silent communication. Moments later, the sound of an engine broke the silence followed by the noise of a retreating vehicle.

Using gloves, Grant rubbed a cloth over her computer, and returned it to its bag. He then unlocked her chain from the filing cabinet and unwound it from her body. Linking the chain round one arm and shoulder, he picked her up and slung her over his other shoulder.

Reaching the door, the sound of a helicopter stopped him dead in his tracks and he sat her down on a chair against a wall. He was breathing heavily but remained still. After what seemed like an age, the sound died away. He opened the door a crack and then, throwing her over his shoulder again, and shifting her weight, he moved quickly across the courtyard and into the large building. Lifting her head up a fraction she saw that the van had disappeared and, except for a moped, only one vehicle remained. It looked like a long-wheel base Land-rover, but she couldn't see what make. The girl's car had obviously left.

A moment later she was thrown across a plastic sheet at the back of the Land-rover. He bent over her and took off the balaclava. Fresh air washed across her face, as he pulled the tape off her mouth, giving her a moment to breathe air into her lungs before retaping her mouth. To her relief he didn't put the balaclava back but re-tied the looser duvet cover over her head and threw a blanket over her before wedging her into place. She heard something slot into place above her. Presumably she was completely out of sight. The something was a shelf stretching the whole width and length of the vehicle because she heard things landing on top of it. She still couldn't move or speak, and her limbs were cramped and painful, but she felt marginally less claustrophobic. She heard his footsteps walk away, stop, and then faster steps as he returned to the office.

She waited, wondering about the van, until he returned. Various other things clinked onto the shelf above her including, she imagined, her computer bag and his rucksack, before the boot was finally slammed shut and their journey began again. He reversed the Land-rover, stopping only briefly to shut the doors of the hanger-like building before they bumped along the track. It was just as they joined a smoother road that she heard a helicopter again.

Closing her eyes, she fought to beat down the involuntary spark of hope which had ignited at the sound of the chopper. There was no prospect of escaping, and she would only manage to keep some measure of control and dignity if she accepted that he would end her life. She felt some comfort in the knowledge that, having kidnapped her, in view of the evidence she had left behind, he would not escape justice for his crimes against her. She would let him know what she had done, but not until the end. She would hold off until then, it was all she had to savour. He'd want her conscious for his final act, his last twisted evil act. He'd want her able to talk, anticipating her pleas for mercy, his mouth filling with saliva as he watched her helplessness, felt her fear, but she would disappoint him. That would be the time to tell him. That would be the moment the leer would falter.

When she revealed to him that all her evidence was not on the computer he was in possession of, and even that was in a document hidden for the police to find; when she told him about her phone, the evidence that had been sent by her to others, the evidence still to come from her colleague, he would make mistakes in his efforts to cover his tracks. She was sure of it.

But still, even though she had planned to take her own life, she resented this evil invader having power over her to her last breath. She had tried to comfort herself by visualising his panic as his luck began to run out, as the net closed in. Murder and Kidnapping. He would no longer get away with the pathetic misunderstood act. She wouldn't be there, wouldn't witness his downfall but, as her mind's eye conjured up images of DC Johnny Hamilton, and Colin Fraser, Chairman of the Bench, it helped to know that those who had been so easily manipulated by Billy Grant would be forced to acknowledge they'd been duped and that had they done their job properly, more professionally, things might have turned out differently. Even Marcus Jenner may experience a slight pang of guilt, although she couldn't count on that.

His invasion still exercised control over her emotional compass but since the appearance of the girl and her instinct that some of his invincibility was faltering, she felt calmer. With the acceptance of her own fate and the hope that the girl would be rescued from Grant's malign influence, and that she may have played a part in that rescue, a space opened for the good things in her life. There were still many conflicting layers to her current state of mind, her state of being. Deep anger, resentment, and fear were strongly in the mix but there was a space now for memories of love and friendship and if she could focus on that, she believed that she would be able to exercise the control she needed to face her final moments and to witness the evil invader's confidence in his powers of control plummet.

CHAPTER 42

Beginning his journey back to the nick, John was thinking about his conversation with Cassandra. What was it about the Barnes' market the victim wanted him to know? He had looked over the victim's property, the SOCOs hadn't found anything of interest, so what was it?

Still puzzling over the risk Grant took when he kidnapped the victim, John considered whether, hidden in her message to Cassandra, there was a clue. She hadn't reported the missing post or the card with "Vehicle Accessories" on it and, in the latter case, it probably wouldn't have meant anything to her. If there was a connection between what she said to her friend and Billy Grant's obsession and actions, he was missing it. Grant had been seen looking at her fence by Bob, and the photo of him peering over the victim's fence, if he knew it had been taken, was more damning still. Perhaps that made Billy Grant realise he had to stop her before she could report it. Or was the power of his own sick obsession, once the victim prevented him getting at her, the driving force overriding the risks? But Cassandra's words didn't help him, unless she had missed something out, had forgotten something the victim had implored her to tell him.

He decided to try to recall everything Cassandra had said as opposed to the emphasis she had put on it. He liked her and he felt sorry for her, but her theatrics were a distraction, and he must concentrate on the words themselves. The victim's words: "... and the reason we met him," came to mind. Cassandra had focussed on the reason for their trip, but in a flash of inspiration, John remembered Cassandra pulling aside the net curtain and pointing to the sundial with the words: "There it is. That's what all the fuss is about." It hit him like a ton of bricks, the only reason they met Billy Grant was because the victim had decided to buy the sundial. Precariously changing lanes to swing around a small roundabout and return to the property, prompting more than one driver to hoot at him, John put his foot on the accelerator. The one thing he hadn't looked at was the sundial.

Letting himself into the victim's property, John walked rapidly through the kitchen, unlocked the kitchen door, stepped into the garden, and walked straight up to the sundial. He took several pictures of it, and then began to tip it. It was heavy but, as he laid it on the ground, he saw that the sundial was hollow at the centre of its base. He could feel a drumming in his ears when he saw that there was something pushed up inside the base. He photographed it before pulling out a wedge of paper taped to the sides and pages of typed A4 dropped to the ground including a written note about a meeting at a cafe, a statement headed 'phone call' and exhibiting a tape, a further statement exhibiting the photo of Grant looking through the window of a café, the card with "Vehicle Accessories" on it, and the three photographs they all knew about. Now John understood why Grant had been forced to make a move. Evidence was stacking up. Standing, John carefully laid the bundle on the grass as he righted the sundial and, after picking up his find, he returned rapidly to the kitchen. Putting everything on the dining room table, he returned briefly to re-lock the kitchen door, and then sat down at the table and began to read the typed pages facing him.

Never in his life had he experienced such a wide range of emotions as shook him when he read the victim's document. Murder, he was thinking. Don't you realise, you were as taken in by Billy Grant as those you have accused of taking his bait. You allowed him to turn you into a monster. No sooner had this condemning thought occurred to John, than he set out to dismantle it. Remembering, and not for the first time, that beautiful, haunted, face he glimpsed at the door, how could he even use, even think, of the word monster in relation to her? What she was planning was monstrous, but she had been forced to live in a prison of Billy Grant's making, her life as she had known it, as the person "who laughed so easily, and everyone loved . . ." was being systematically destroyed. He could only imagine what it must be like to have nowhere to turn, a living hell. Thinking about her affectionate words to her friend, her ability even to think about future victims, as set out in that brutally honest document, John felt as though his own movements were restricted, his breathing laboured, his ability to think dulled. He stood and took a quick couple of turns around the room. Time was ticking, he had to get back to South-West Central. He knew that, for her sake, he had to calm down, knuckle down, and consider both her document and evidence dispassionately. If it wasn't already too late, the window of opportunity to save her was narrowing by the hour.

Looking at his watch, he rang Rory and explained what he had found, ending with the words: 'Look Guv, I don't think this document should be circulated, at least not now, because I don't think it will help. The evidence she gathered herself is what matters, not judging her."

'I totally agree,' Rory said matter-of-factly, picking up in John's voice his young DCs conflicting emotions. 'The chances of her going through with this were probably nil anyway.'

'You think?'

'I do, and I also think that had Grant not moved when he did, you would have persuaded her to come on board. But enough of that, what we need to concentrate on now is finding Grant and I want you back here. We need to get going, the SOCOs are now at the three sites and we're covering one of them. Separate the evidence from the document, make separate notes about what she says about the evidence, and we'll circulate that.'

John's head swam a little with relief. 'Thanks, Guv. I'll scribble the notes and be on my way.'

CHAPTER 43

The Land-rover was once again on a track, bumping over untarmacked roads, complaining as it did so. Then suddenly it stopped. She heard the evil invader get out and slam the driver's door. Something was upsetting him. To say that she was keyed up would be an understatement. She was filled with conflicting emotions. Delight at his discomfort, regardless of what was causing it. Had the girl text him and told him she was not taking part in anything else or was that too much to hope? Perhaps she simply hadn't text him. But her hope was mixed with fear, a fear that if the evil invader felt vulnerable his plans would change and he would murder her sooner. If so, how? Would he bury her alive somewhere she was unlikely to be found by anyone any time soon, if ever? Was this a track leading to woods? But it was still daylight, early afternoon, she told herself, trying to combat her rising panic at the thought that her life might end in a painful, slow, suffocation. Surely that would be too much of a risk? But if he was now a hunted animal, his options were narrowing. Everything he did, everywhere he went, would pose a risk.

Then the boot opened and, throwing several things on the ground to lift the shelf off her, he removed the top of her blanket and leaned it. A mobile phone was shoved in her face. She read the text message and blinked her eyes, trying to avoid the evil invader reading anything from their expression. She mustn't give herself away, she hoped that her reaction would reassure him. Of course, he might be right, she probably should take the words at face value, but every moment that the girl, she now knew was called Fiona, was out of his orbit, was a moment she was safe from Billy Grant. Closing her eyes she heard him chuckle, a bit of his spittle landing on her face, then the blanket was over her again and he restored the shelf and belongings so that she was hidden. She then heard a crunching sound, he seemed to be stamping on something. It brought back a memory, a memory of the sound she had made when she destroyed her phone. Shortly afterwards, the vehicle was once more on its way.

Just the two of them now. She thought, she hoped, that this meant his plans hadn't changed. The throbbing at her temples eased. Once again, she made a conscious effort to beat down a glimmer of hope having seen the text. Fiona had said that she'd fallen off her bike and was going to hospital, but there was nothing in the text to suggest that she was going to report matters to the police and what the text said may simply be the truth. She must accept the inevitable, must retain her dignity, or her plans for her last moments with Billy Grant would fail. Her last thoughts must be of her family, her friends, her memories, but before that she wanted to witness the effect of her words on Grant, wanted to see the leer falter, wanted to smell his fear as he realised that his control of events was slipping and his freedom to destroy the lives of others was over.

CHAPTER 44

Rory was ready to hit the road the moment John returned, but at his DCs insistence he sat down at his desk and read through the document: "TO WHOM IT MAY CONCERN." Reading at speed, his concentration entirely focussed on the pages and the exhibits, the only reaction Rory's demeanour occasionally registered was intense irritation.

'What a little idiot, she should have contacted us once her colleague had the photo of Grant looking through the café's window, but there was no excuse not to have come to us the moment she had the photo of Grant looking over her fence.'

He rose from his chair and gathered up the sheets of papers and documents.

'I don't think we're in a position to criticise her and -'

'Of course, we're not in a fucking position to criticise her.' Rory interrupted, his words increasing the tension in the room.

'And she may have been planning to come to us,' John continued. 'I thought we could just give the physical evidence to the others at this stage. I've got a draft-'

'Forget it,' Rory interrupted. 'I'm putting this in the safe and telling the others what we have when we're on the way. We'll obviously need to get someone to take a statement from her lawyer and a further statement from her colleague, Colin, but as our priority is to see whether we can find out where Grant is taking the victim, that can wait. You can drive.'

When they were in a police vehicle heading towards a site south of Guildford, Rory looked sideways at John.

'If she's still alive, we're in with a chance,' he said with a slightly crooked smile. 'When it comes to it, this girl won't go down without a fight whatever she thinks.'

'Except that she was going to end her life after ... she couldn't see a way out.'

Rory sighed. 'She may have been in despair but, once she had the goods on him there was a way out and, on a more positive note, she was bloody furious. There's a lot of "this is not about revenge," in that document but revenge is very much in the mix. She wasn't going to let any of us off the hook. Her enjoyment of life had been systematically taken from her by, and I'm going to use her terminology because it's apt, an evil invader, and Grant is an evil bastard. No one was helping her, including the people who were being paid to do so and, yes, going forward things looked very bleak although she wasn't helping herself either. But she was pitching her wits against Grant, she was able, calmly, to set about what we were supposed to be doing, finding evidence, and she was, I think genuinely, thinking about other victims, who we now know exist. But this document shouts anger to me.'

'If you saw her -'

'Oh, for God's sake,' Rory said, cutting off John's sentence and shrugging with impatience despite his seatbelt limiting his freedom of movement. 'You don't have to sell her to me. You're the one who's struggling to find justification for her intentions. I'm not. Right now, she's got my vote, and I hope I'm right, because it's what she does now that matters. Grant has got her computer, so he knows all about this, but I hope to Christ she is keeping quiet about leaving evidence behind for us to find. If he thinks he's still in with a chance of murdering her and getting away with it, we're still in with a chance of finding her. He'll be working out how to cover his tracks before killing her and that may just give us the time we need. All we can do now is concentrate on what we must do because in a few hours we're going to have to accept the inevitable and go public to find him.'

A silence ensued between the two of them which Rory

didn't try to break. John had to grow up sometime and he'd let him digest what he'd said and fume for a while.

The DI's comment that he was the one trying to find justification for the victim's intentions was weighing on John. He had never been so affected by a woman in his life. The break-up of his relationship with his university girlfriend Holly had been painful at the time, but he was surprised by how quickly he had recovered from it. Holly had turned what had seemed a perfect union on its head with the words: "We're just drifting through life, John," before looking at him in a measuring kind of way, the kind of way that told him she had already moved on and there was no going back, and added: "One day, you'll fall for someone like a ton of bricks, someone you'd never imagine you'd have anything in common with, and you'll know I'm right." Well, she had been right. If anyone had suggested to him that he'd fall under the spell of a woman with murder in her sights, he'd have thought that person should probably be sectioned. A woman he'd half seen behind a door and spoken to through a letterbox. Of course, he wasn't saying that . . . oh, what the hell, the DI could say what he liked, he was frantic, his gut tying itself in knots with the worry that he might never again see the victim alive, but the document had shaken him, and John felt that his reaction to it was not unreasonable. Knowing he didn't have time to process his feelings right now, he tried to shrug it off. But he was angry at Rory, all the same.

Although Rory had phoned in an edited version of John's discovery under the sundial, it wasn't until they were nearing Guildford on the A3 that a piece of the information relayed over the airwaves from the DS monitoring the ANPR, overturned the frosty atmosphere in the vehicle.'

'From our instructions, we have narrowed things down to a dozen possibilities that night,' the officer said. 'We've managed to eliminate a lot of vehicles by contacting the owners. We're still working on 8 possibilities due to their size, four of them drove on roads heading into London and we have officers trying to pick up those vehicles on cameras on the outskirts of the Capital. Of the four others, two were proceeding South towards the M25 and two were travelling West. Regarding these 8 vehicles, two don't seem to be registered to anyone, one is reported stolen, two are registered to women and I'm still trying to get hold of the owners of the other three. One of them travelling West is registered to a Mr George Cameron at an address in Gloucestershire -'

'Wait' John said, interrupting him. 'What's the vehicle number and make?'

The DS gave it to him.

'Okay, I just want to check something, and we'll get back to you.'

After muting the DS, Rory turned his head enquiringly towards John who took his hand off the steering wheel for a moment to pass his mobile to him.

'Paul Cameron's number is in my contacts,' he told Rory. 'He's the student at the property Grant re-directed the victim's post to. It's the beginning of the autumn term. Let's just check that his father isn't called George and that he didn't drop his son back at his flat in a Land-rover when Grant was around.'

Rory found and rang Paul's number and a sleepy voice answered. Putting the phone on speaker phone, Rory identified himself, after confirming that it was Paul on the line, and said: 'Paul, DC John Carter is sitting beside me.' John interrupted simply to explain that he was driving, and Rory continued: 'Can I just ask, do you have a father called George who lives in Gloucestershire, and does he own a Land-rover?'

'Yeah,' Paul replied.

After a sharp intake of breath and a further conversation in which Rory gave Paul details of the registration and make of the Land-rover for confirmation purposes, which he received, Paul confirmed that Grant was at the London flat on the date his father dropped him off.

'Paul, can I have your father's mobile telephone number?'

After a few more words, Rory ended the call by telling Paul that he will, in due course, be required to give a statement and impressed upon him the necessity of not mentioning their conversation to anyone.

Rory went back to his DS, and not long after he'd relayed the information the DS said that he'd spoken to George Cameron who confirmed the details of his vehicle and told the DS that he could see his car in his drive and, no, he hadn't been driving it on the previous day.

'So cloned,' John said. 'Let's hope it won't be long before ANPR gives us the information we want.'

The atmosphere in the vehicle was suddenly charged with optimism.

CHAPTER 45

She was bound tightly, could hardly move, her mouth was taped, the blanket covering her made her face hot, she couldn't see him, couldn't read his expression, but she knew, without knowing how, that despite his apparent triumph over her when he received the text from Fiona, doubts were creeping in. He'd ensured that, in the office building, she could not talk to Fiona and rebut anything he told the teenager but, all the same, as the vehicle continued its journey, she sensed Billy Grant's growing anxiety. She could smell his sweat even through her covering or perhaps she imagined that, but his driving became a little erratic, slowing down sometimes, then speeding up, without her hearing other vehicles driving past on the smaller narrower roads to explain his change of gears. Was he beginning to wonder whether, seeing his captive bound and gagged, might have played on Fiona's conscience? If so, could he be sure that her explanation for not boarding the train was the true explanation? Was he worrying about whether his total control over her might be slipping? When he told Fiona she was his accomplice, he was threatening her. It was a warning that she'd be implicated in any of his actions, and this made him confident that she'd toe the line. But this was probably the first time he had lost control of her, and he was rattled.

She felt the car stop, heard him get out of it, and waited to hear the clink of numberplates drop to the ground, but it didn't happen. It hadn't happened since they'd driven in the van just after he'd kidnapped her, when the sound of police sirens filled the air. Now, she heard his footsteps walk away from his vehicle,

188

then his voice. He was making a call on another phone, having destroyed the first one. Finally, she heard the click of the vehicle locking and the sound of footsteps receding. She was alone and helpless. She didn't know where she was, how far away from Devon which she hoped and prayed was their destination, but she was so tightly secured that, even if she heard a passing vehicle or people walking past, she was powerless to alert them to her situation. She strained against her ties, but after a short struggle gave up. She had no idea where he had gone, no knowledge of what he planned to do, but the one thing she was certain of was that he would return.

For a moment her helplessness overwhelmed her. Tears were once again streaking down her face, her body aching from the strain of trying to free itself. Her nose was running under the blanket, the heat of her face was increasing, and her exertions had made breathing more difficult. Then as suddenly as the onslaught of her attack of nerves, she surrendered to her situation and, as her body slumped and her breathing became less laboured, she realised that this may be the last and only time she would be alone. Now, in the silence, in a space not currently invaded, the words of her document: "TO WHOM IT MAY CONCERN," surfaced and had a steadying effect.

She'd found out that she was incapable of murdering another human being too late to save herself. But directing her thoughts firmly back to her document, she remembered her certainty that there were other victims before her, and would be after her, and that hadn't changed. After all, what had happened to Fiona and her family for the teenager to be under the evil invader's control? Fiona could and must be saved.

Despite being physically constrained, letting go of what she could not control to concentrate on what she could achieve, allowed her mind to roam freely giving her the strength to plan, just as her document had done when the evidence against Billy Grant had begun to stack up. In her last moments, it was essential that she find the power to unsettle the evil invader, to shake his confidence, instil doubts, and add another brick to the building block which would ultimately bring him to Justice before any other victims became his prey.

But this time alone was also an opportunity to look back and remember, without the constant anxiety of where the evil invader would appear next and what he would do clouding those memories. She knew what he was going to do. Closing her eyes, she looked back to a time before Billy Grant, a time of love and friendship and happiness which had been so much a part of her life. Remembering and feeling those days, her imagination took her to a cliff on a headland, and she heard surf on a pebble beach, saw boats in the distance turning with the tide, and felt the spray on her face.

CHAPTER 46

The optimism didn't last. The mood within the police vehicles heading towards the three locations in the Guildford area, which seemed to be the most likely places Billy Grant would have taken the victim in his van, was dipping by the minute. There had been no further ANPR results on the vehicle with Mr Cameron's number plates.

Inside their own car, John turned his head briefly in Rory's direction. 'It's extraordinary, ANPR covers huge areas of road, he must have crossed somewhere which has it by now.'

Rory sighed deeply. 'He may have switched plates again. They're now looking for the same make of vehicle as well as the numberplates, but of course there are many more cars about. But he might simply be holed up somewhere. We may yet get lucky.'

The helicopter which had most recently circled the three locations had reported back that their instruments hadn't picked up any sign of life within them. However, when John and Rory were a few miles north of Guildford, a report came in of an earlier helicopter flight which had picked up evidence of human life within a squat brick building at a location which consisted of a large barn and other outbuildings. It was the site where Rory and John were headed.

Finally, further news came in on the George Cameron numberplate, but it didn't take them much further. It had disappeared somewhere to the West of the A3 after Guildford.

When they reached their destination, the first thing a SOCO showed Rory and John was two sets of partial tyre tracks.

'There was a brief downpour last night,' he said. 'It's likely that one set of the partial tyre tracks will match the make of Land-rover you're looking for.'

Then, not long after they had been shown the tyre tracks, an officer came up to Rory, drew him aside, and told him some further news. A VW Estate had crossed a camera near Malden linking with the A3 towards Kingston which was registered to a William Clarke at the same address as Fiona Marsh's. After the two men had discussed the implications, Rory walked over to the outside of the brick-built office from which John had just emerged, and with a jerk of his head indicated that they return to the car.

Once inside, Rory said: 'Some interesting news,' as he told him the latest. 'Apparently it looks as though only one person wearing a hood was in the vehicle.

Noting the colour drain from John's face, Rory wished he'd put things differently, but facts were facts. 'Our guys are now descending on Fiona Marsh's home address to see if anyone's there and whether that vehicle can be found in the vicinity.'

Continuing, he added: 'Looking on the bright side for a moment, there is no forensic evidence of a body or bodies in the field where the van was set on fire or at our three locations. Because of the evidence that water from a hose was sprayed over the brick office you've just come out of, and the large farm building, The SOCOs clearly think this is where Grant initially brought her. Plus, we have tire tracks.' He paused. Although John nodded it was clear he wasn't really listening and, from his demeanour, Rory judged that he wasn't seeing any advantages to Grant's vehicle travelling north. If it was only Grant in the vehicle, well what had happened to the victim?

They were now travelling back on the A3 towards London and the turn off towards South-West Central via Sutton, John still driving. Rory thought it was better not to remind his young DC that they could only proceed along their agreed lines for a few hours more. After that, they had to release photos of Grant to the press and appeal to the public for information. It was just as Rory was turning over in his mind the significance of the vehicle being driven in Malden, that John suddenly, without warning, signalled and took the lane for the M25.

Rory looked across at him and said without heat: 'Would you mind giving me a steer on why we are now travelling towards Heathrow?'

The frown had left John's face. 'Guv, I think the bastard's playing us. He's been one step ahead from the moment he kidnapped her. Nigel's right, this is a planned operation. We have a van, reported stolen, being torched, another vehicle, or others, taking its place, and now one, registered to him travelling in the direction of London. There were more than two types of tyre track at the site we were on. There's a second vehicle, the one we know is owned by George Cameron, and that's the one he's driving, the one which has disappeared, probably along a series of C roads without cameras or, as you say, with different plates.'

'So, you think it's a decoy?'

'I do.'

'Are we to assume then, that he knows we're onto him.'

'Not quite, but he'll know that if we've found out that our victim is missing from home, he'll be our prime suspect if we think she's been kidnapped, and he's setting himself up with an alibi. I think Fiona Marsh may have been driving the vehicle to Kingston. If so, she's clearly only gone onto a road with ANPR at a time when she can probably make it back to her address without being stopped.'

Rory shrugged within the confines of his seat belt. 'Until we know-' The phone on the display unit beeped and, Rory picked up, and listened to the DS speaking at the other end. 'Okay,' Rory said, 'thanks, keep us posted.' He ended the call and turned back to John. 'The VW is parked near Fiona Marsh's address but she's not there. Let's hope the SOCOs working on the vehicle for any traces they can find for DNA purposes come up with something.' Passing a hand over his jaw, he added: 'I wonder why this girl is going along with all this, if she is.'

'We don't know the time he left. He may have gone before the car was torched, leaving Fiona Marsh to set the match.'

'You know I doubt it.' Rory said, frowning at the road without seeing it as he turned things over in his mind. 'We know she's dependent upon him but, judging from what we've been told, there's no love lost there, and Grant will know that. He won't have taken a chance that she might not have followed his instructions. If she's seen the victim, she may be unsure as to what she should do.'

'Well, then why doesn't she contact us or at least someone who will?'

'Apart from the money, he may have persuaded her that, if she calls the police, she's implicated in anything he does. I don't know.' Drumming his fingers on the dashboard, Rory looked ahead and said: 'Where the fuck are we going?'

'The West Country. Devon, to be precise.'

'Devon,' Rory repeated in astonishment.

'He has her computer,' John reminded him.

The penny dropped. 'He does. Remind me again of the name of that place in Devon.'

'Welcombe,' John replied, with a bitter cut-off laugh at the irony of it.

Rory punched into his phone. 'Which part of Devon.'

'North Devon, near Bude and Bideford and the main police station in that part of the world is Barnstaple.'

CHAPTER 47

It took a long time for the evil invader to return but return he did. She knew and accepted the fact that she would be subject to further, perhaps unexpected, mood shifts as their journey moved into its final phase. Acceptance, accepting her fate, was necessary for her to hold the line, to retain her dignity, to keep to her plan. There was a graph she'd once seen which showed that those who accepted their fate in the latter stages of a terminal illness, were able to control their end, to say goodbye in their own way, to comfort others even. That had been the case with her mother.

The boot opened, Billy Grant raised the shelf, threw back her cover, ripped off the tape, and put a bottle of water to her mouth. She drank. He smiled down at her. Was it her imagination or was the smile forced, as though he was going through the motions?

Taking another strip of tape, he taped her mouth again. She didn't resist. Looking up at him she felt a momentary jab of fear before the leer overlaid the naked venom in his glance. He was rattled all right.

'Not long now,' he said, then the blanket was over her again and the light disappeared. The day was fading fast, soon it would be evening.

When the vehicle began moving again, his voice drifted back to her.

'She's in hospital, just as her text said, and coming round from an operation on her foot,' he told her. 'That's all that's happened. Knocked off her bike, the idiot. She'll be back with

195

me . . . well, until she stops being useful. Then she'll go the way of her mother, a poor child unable to deal with the grief of loss.' He chuckled. 'It is what it is.'

He would be anticipating the effect of his words on her. Anticipating them chilling her to the bone, closing that space called hope. But she was ahead of him, and she would turn the tables and make him afraid. Fiona would be saved. DC John Carter wasn't DC Johnny Hamilton. He would get to the truth in time and Fiona's recovery from an operation should give him that time.

Moments later they had joined a road which allowed the Land-rover briefly to travel at speed, as though he wasn't overly concerned at being stopped by police. This was odd, she thought, because Billy Grant hadn't changed any number plates in this vehicle. Where had he been? He'd come back and told her about Fiona's operation, so had he taken his new phone, a burner as they say, elsewhere? Had he dumped it, despite receiving confirmation about Fiona's accident; as a precaution, so his phone couldn't be traced, his way of leaving a false trail, just in case? She thought it was likely. But then why suddenly on roads which would have number plate recognition? Was he so confident that the police wouldn't know his numberplate because it had no link back to him?

With the fading light, he must want the journey to end and to get back to relative safety after murdering her. She didn't know how far they still had to go, but her belief that their journey was now to be an uninterrupted drive to the location proved wrong.

After a relatively short time, they were again bumping along down a slope. Were his plans changing? She began to panic. Would he stop, get out and then put the car into drive, lift off the handbrake, and let it run into a reservoir or pond or somewhere it would sink out of sight? Perhaps that's why he's not bothered by cameras. But, the Land-rover did stop, and he did get out and open the boot and, after some unexplained moments when she heard his footsteps go back and forth, he once again, removed the shelf and sat her up. This time, she was facing the open boot of another smaller vehicle. The blanket was thrown off her, and she looked around her, before he blocked her view by pulling the duvet cover over her whole body and tying it over her head. she was picked up in a single movement and tossed into the boot of the car. Then the blanket was thrown back over her, and the boot lid slammed shut. A moment later, it opened again and something heavy fell over her legs which were folded into a foetus position.

'Nearly forgot the rope,' the evil invader said before slamming the boot shut again.

For a moment she had to fight the claustrophobia of being in such a contained space but with determination she managed to calm her agitation. It was a tight space compared to what had been, but the boot was spacious enough for her to breathe for some time. His actions showed he must still want to end her life the way she had planned, except for the method of her end by hanging, which he had now edited in her document to fit his intentions. Concentrating, she registered more sounds, things being thrown or placed on the ground, the numberplates, and then a whirring noise, like a hoover. She was cocooned under the blanket, but her hearing was good, and it sounded as though the evil invader was hoovering the Land-Rover's interior. A splashing noise followed the whirr. He was erasing any possible trace of her, any evidence. Concentrating on honing her instincts to take on board everything she could, had a calming effect, and prevented her from panicking within her tomb-like resting place. Eventually, she heard things being replaced in the new vehicle, but he didn't open the driver's door of the car; instead, she heard the Land-rover leave.

She stayed still, trying to keep her breathing calm to use up as little oxygen as possible. She was alone again but this time, it wasn't long before he returned by foot and, once again, their journey continued, up a bumpy hill, onto a tarmacked area, and then with a left swing, presumably onto an A road, as the speed of the car increased. Surely there wouldn't be any more such stops.

CHAPTER 48

John cursed as the traffic began to increase on the M4 and it would increase further when they joined the M5. Rush hour.

His personal phone bleeped, and Rory picked it up from the central console and saw that it was a text. 'Okay if I see who it is?" he asked John, who nodded. He pressed the button. 'Christ,' he said. 'It's from a Fiona and it says: "he's tied the woman up. I don't know what he's going to do." He tried to call her on the number displayed. 'Damn she's cut off her phone. I'll keep trying. But first he rang through Fiona's number for the team to trace.

John took a deep breath. 'So, she's still alive or was when the text came through,' he said before amending his comment to: 'They're both still alive but it sounds as though Fiona is anticipating that, where our victim is concerned, it won't be for long.'

'It's difficult to know what's happening. I mean, after our last update we thought Fiona Marsh might be riding her lightweight motorbike in London. If that's the case, and he's close enough to the two women to kill them we could be heading in the wrong direction.'

John didn't slow his speed. 'I know,' he conceded after a moment. 'I just think he's setting up an alibi. Also, I don't think she'd dare text if he was nearby. Everything I think will be wrong if he has any idea that we broke his alibi at the pub. But so far, we haven't arrested him and, like I said, I don't think any of the people in the pub will tell him anything. He may worry that our victim has reported her photograph of him outside the doctor's surgery, he might also be concerned about Bob the postman and that his plan over the café didn't come off but after the last two court cases the chances are that he'll have been lulled into a false sense of security. He'll figure that we won't charge a third time without a cast iron case. The thing that will worry him most is the camera shot of him looking over the victim's wall. He made his move almost immediately afterwards. But a dead victim doesn't speak and can't counter any explanation he comes up with.'

After mulling things over a bit more, John continued: 'He made sure he took the camera so it will have increased his anxiety, but he might have thought that the photograph, if there was one, would be contained within it. We don't know. But we should keep an open mind for the time being in view of the amount of planning that went into this kidnapping. He may still believe that he will get away with murder provided the place she is killed, a place she identified as a favourite location, a location which her friends can confirm she loved, can be made to look like suicide, particularly as it will be bolstered by her confessions on her laptop. But all this is conjecture, a guessing game, because he's got her laptop.'

'All conjecture, but plausible. Plus, the fact that he seemed to be travelling towards her chosen destination when the ANPR caught his vehicle with the Cameron's numberplate.'

'I'm guessing that the laptop will be left at the scene, and he'll force her fingerprints onto it after wiping off his own.'

Rory stroked his chin thoughtfully, as he considered John's hunch. 'He will be wearing gloves his fingerprints won't be on anything. We may also be wrong about his intentions if she has told him, or tells him too soon, that she left a document behind for the police to find.'

'I know, but I'm banking on her keeping quiet about that for as long as she can. I mean look at the way she built up that case against him, she's not an idiot and she won't want to precipitate any actions on his part.'

'Fair point but John, by tonight, if nothing breaks in the

meantime, we're going to have to go public with this to find him.' He saw the strain in his young subordinate's bleak profile and felt profoundly sad for him. But in the real world, the cavalry turning up on time other than in a case where a ransom was being demanded, was the exception rather than the rule and it was no good sugar-coating things.

'I know,' John replied quietly.

'Barnstable are co-operating and doing whatever they can to cover Welcombe without drawing attention to themselves.'

'If we find Fiona, we need a plan. If she's not contacting him or following his orders, she needs an excuse which will satisfy Grant.'

'You're right.' Rory was about to ask for an update when the DS got there first.

'We've got Fiona,' he said. 'She was just sitting on a bench at Waterloo station. She's in a bit of a state. She had already text Grant to say that she couldn't board a train because she'd fallen off her bike and is about to go to hospital by ambulance.'

'Damn, I wish she'd text us before texting Grant. Well done tracking her down. How long ago did she text him?'

'Not long, twenty minutes or so.'

'I'll get straight back to you,' Rory said.

A few minutes later, Rory contacted his contact again.

'Listen carefully. We need a team at St Thomas's Hospital, and this is what I want you to do.'

Several minutes later, the call ended.

'We just have to hope Grant hasn't rung St Thomas's Hospital yet, but that he tries to verify her account when the team is in place.'

'Yes, what train was she getting?'

'One to Southampton and he was giving her instructions from there. Right direction anyway.'

It took five minutes for the DS to confirm what they feared, they couldn't track Grant's phone from the number Fiona had given them.

'Keep her phone on, he may try to get hold of her.

Someone must be with her all the time.'

'Don't worry, we're onto that.'

'We need as much information as you can get from her, particularly any information about numberplates he uses.'

After a few more minutes of discussing actions required, the call ended.

John said: 'Well, he'll still be ahead of us, damn it! It's going to rattle him that he's lost control of Fiona, but we'll have to hope she can tell us something.

'Yeah.'

'The worry now is if he thinks Fiona is with the police,' John continued anxiously. 'It's all over then and we won't know any change of plan.'

'True. But I think he'll try to verify what she's told him. Let's hope so. Judging by Fiona's text to you, he didn't mention to Fiona what he was going to do with our victim.   All we can do now is to keep going and hope for the best,' Rory said. He wanted John to stay focussed and there really wasn't much mileage in speculating until they had more.'

CHAPTER 49

She would find it difficult to explain to anyone how she felt, imprisoned in her confined space, and she wouldn't have to. It was a strange opposing mix of anxiety and peace. She simply knew that the end phase of her captivity had begun. The car turned off a main road and, although there were no bumps, there was repeated slowing down as corners were taken. The speed had dropped, sometimes the vehicle stopped altogether to let a car past, so that if they weren't yet in Devon, they were close by, Somerset, or possibly Dorset, depending on his route. The West Country had only ever held wonderful memories for her and recalling some of those memories had a calming effect, reducing her anxiety.

Aware that whatever she planned, it might be thrown off course by events, she tried to construct a plan based on what Billy Grant would have to do before he could hang her. He'd been very careful in the way he had bound her, taking care to ensure that there would be no obvious signs of violence or of struggle. He had made her helpless by roping and chaining her over cloth so that nothing directly cut into her wrists or ankles. But he would have to remove all her bindings to achieve his purpose and there would be a moment when her hands were free.

Before that, the evil invader would take off the tape around her mouth. He'd wash her face and let it rest so that the redness would fade. He'd be waiting for her to plead with him for her life and when she didn't do so, he'd try to increase her fear by other means. Just as he had when he'd thrown the rope into the boot of the car, a move designed to increase her anxiety. Perhaps he'd add some detail to the method by which she would die, rope cutting into her windpipe, blocking her airwaves and then . . . That would be her opportunity to interrupt him and to tell him that nothing he now did would prevent his arrest and his trial for her kidnapping and murder. There were things he didn't know, she would tell him, the evidence she had left behind would ensure that his days of outwitting the police and others were over. From there . . . what she might or might not be able to say would depend upon how he reacted to what she will already have said. But it would be too late for a change of plan by then, he would have to get on with things, get what pleasure he could from his final act. But the pleasure would be offset by uncertainty.

Once the rope was around her neck, that would be the time when he'd have to unbind her hands. She visualised that he would limit any opportunity for her to get a hand under the rope around her neck. And into her mind came the thought that he'd done this before, and she remembered his conversation with Fiona when he'd mentioned her inheritance. How had Fiona's mother died? He'd done this before. He would force her to the ground close to where she'd fall and stand behind her, one large hand gripping her wrists the moment her hands were free and, before she could get a hand under the rope at her neck, his other hand would push her over and she'd be falling. This meant that her only chance of trying to get one more piece of evidence was to dig her nails into him to get his DNA and that meant by digging her nails into whatever part of him was nearest to her hands, not by trying to get a hand under the rope.

Then she would be free, and her last thoughts would not be of the evil invader at all.

CHAPTER 50

News filtered in as Rory and John continued their journey. Like a pack of cards folding, the moment the threads of what they now knew about Billy Grant's life were pulled, the stack of evidence against him started piling up. The will of Fiona Marsh's mother showed Gerald Marsh as the executor of her estate, leaving everything she had to her daughter. Gerald Marsh had not received any correspondence about her will, had not even known his sister had died. They'd drifted apart because of her drinking and drug problems. He had, however, received a speeding ticket for a car he'd never owned being driven on a road he'd never used. He had his driving licence in his wallet and, no, he had never applied for a replacement because his had not been stolen or lost. Fiona Marsh, now in possession of the information about her mother's will, was giving two female detectives a full account of everything she could remember from the first moment of Billy Grant entering her mother's life and, consequently, her own. At this stage the detectives were skirting around the manner of her mother's death.

Miranda, the tenant from the block of flats in Coulsdon, had given her statement to police about Billy Grant stalking her until her boyfriend Bob had stepped in and bloody well threatened him. He'd been away for a while doing a Masters' degree at Lancaster University and Grant, she was sure, was unaware she had a boyfriend. Miranda confirmed that she would, definitely, be prepared to give evidence if required. She still woke up sometimes feeling anxious. When he rented a flat in her block, she remembered having seen his face from somewhere before and later recalled, from a conversation she'd had with him, that he'd sold her a kit of required items for going abroad from a "Vehicle Accessories" stall at a Greenwich market.

But the two men in the vehicle travelling West, were focussed on only one thing, saving the victim's life. Rory had been looking at Google maps and garnering as much information as he could about Welcombe. To that end DS Clarke Emery had rung Cassandra at their request to find out what she knew about her friend's favourite Devon location. It turned out Cassandra had been on holiday with the family and knew all about Welcome.

'It's the wrong time of the year for beach worshippers and anyway it's not that sort of coast, no sand to speak of, so people swim out from a stony beach in summer, but it is a beauty spot. It's bleak though, with jagged shards of shale emerging from the sea. When Cassandra stayed with the victim's family, they couldn't persuade her into the sea. It's the right sort of geology and there are trees for cover but not on the edge of the cliffs themselves. Homes do overlook parts of the coastline in places, but not many.'

Thinking over Clarke's description after the call ended, Rory said: 'Billy Grant is not likely to throw the victim off a cliff until he's sure that no one's around.'

'How close can he get to the cliffs?' John wondered.

'Well, if he's still in a Land-rover when he arrives pretty close, I guess. But he's taking a hell of a risk, all the same, so whatever the victim's most loved location is, Billy Grant is going to go for the easiest option from his point of view. Although the place has several cliffs, it will still have to be somewhere with no chance of survival. We'll have to rely on local knowledge.'

'It will be at night.'

'That's going to dent his alibi a bit. It's not following the script of her document. Her last view of her favourite place.'

'Well, she won't be discovered until daylight, but I suppose he could wait until dawn, hiding up somewhere.' John said. He then went silent but was clearly thinking through

Grant's options. Remaining patient and not interrupting his young subordinate's train of thought was becoming a habit, Rory thought. 'Guv, I think he might sus out the lay of the land himself ahead of time,' John continued. 'But it's no good us locating and arresting him without our victim. If she's in a boot of a vehicle, and he's changed the vehicle again, we may not get to her before she's suffocated.'

'We'll plan a surveillance strategy with the Barnstaple officers,' Rory said.

So far, there were no further sightings of a vehicle with George Cameron's numberplate.

'We really need to find him before he's in Devon lanes without ANPR or other CCTV footage,' John said, thinking out loud.

'True, but there's more ANPR in remote areas than people realise due to a countrywide increase in fly tipping. Nigel Sheridan told me that. What we're missing is local knowledge.'

'The problem we have is that Grant may have local knowledge.'

Rory turned his head to look at John.

'Don't forget that line of questioning in the second trial, the so-called discussion with the victim about North Devon,' John finished.

Rory opened his mouth to respond, thought better of it, and simply said: 'Let's just get to Barnstaple."

CHAPTER 51

Her conviction that they were now in or close to Devon was boosted by the brief sight she'd had of the landscape during the switch of vehicles before the duvet cover had blocked her view. The Land-rover had been sheltering inside an open wooden shed on the edge of a field and she'd seen windmills in the distance, a common feature now of the North Devon coastal region. Another hour or so and the windmills wouldn't have been visible; it was dusk, but the night would soon be closing in.

The car suddenly stopped on a road which was winding but without the bumps or potholes of a B road. This time, the evil invader got out of the vehicle, and she heard him speaking to someone. She was close enough to pick up a West Country accent. She was in the boot of a vehicle and totally helpless to alert the person he was talking to of her plight. She tried to shift herself, tried to reach up with her feet to bang on the lid, but by the time she'd dislodged the rope enough to do so, the voices had drifted into the distance, and the next time she heard footsteps, it was only Billy Grant's. Too late.

When the car moved off, it took her some moments to recover. She had managed to control her feelings, discipline herself to a stage of complete acceptance of her fate, everything depended on this, but the sound of another human voice so close, had been unexpected. Hope had risen unbidden and unsettled her but slowly, she regained control by focussing her mind on why Grant had stopped. Had he been asking for directions? If so, she reasoned, they must be close to their destination, and her final one.

More winding roads, slower speeds, hills being climbed, dips into valleys and, once again, she felt herself calmed by Devon's familiar embrace. Then, suddenly, the spell was broken.

'You must be wondering where I went earlier on,' Grant said. 'No harm in telling you, it's not something you'll be passing on. I rang the hospital and then disposed of the phone. I've got others no one knows about, not even Fiona. She always does as I tell her, but you never know, just as well to check. I got the confirmation I wanted. You'll be glad to know she's out of surgery.' He chuckled. 'I'd already hired a car, the one you're in. I never leave anything to chance you might have noticed. Not too long to go now. There'll be a bit of a wait at the other end, everything's got to be right, and then the freedom you were longing for. Freedom for both of us, but I'll keep living to enjoy mine.' he said, finishing on a sigh: 'It is what it is.'

Now all she could hear were the tyres on the road, the sound of the engine, and from time to time, a few passing cars, but not many.

You'll have a few surprises coming your way when you are forced to remove the tape on my mouth, evil invader. You'll find that you are not the only one with foresight.

There was another silence, but she waited, tense with anticipation, guessing he had more to say, enjoying his power over her. She was right.

'You must have wondered why my barrister asked you all those questions about Devon and Hartland. I couldn't believe my luck when it turned out you knew the place. Did you think I'd hacked into your computer? No, I tried, but you're a suspicious one, aren't you? No, it wasn't a conversation we'd had, as you know. But it was one I'd had with one of your witnesses. I wanted them to know that I have a good memory. Like I said, I never leave anything to chance.

CHAPTER 52

'Why?' John asked.

Rory shrugged but didn't immediately answer. Inevitably, as the focus of the chase was honing-in on the West Country and North Devon in particular, information from those who had been concentrating on vehicles heading in that direction had filtered through to other officers on the case who had access to the same encrypted frequency. Word had just reached Rory and John that DCs Johnny Hamilton and Michael Flynn were on their way to Devon.

'Billy Grant knows Johnny he went through an entire court case with him. If Grant sees him without him knowing -' John didn't finish his sentence.

'Stop panicking,' Rory said. 'We're meeting up at police headquarters in Barnstaple, you'll get to voice your concerns there. My understanding is that Johnny played a major role in rescuing a missing child when he was a police constable in Launceston. Okay, it's Cornwall I seem to remember he lived in Bude, but it's pretty close to where we're headed.'

'Guv, that's what I'm worried about,' John said impatiently. 'That's why I think it's important that there's no chance that, in his efforts to make amends, he makes himself more visible.'

'Listen, we'll hear what he has to say and then I'm calling the shots. He'll do what I tell him to do.' Rory took in John's stubborn expression and added in a softer voice: 'He knows that he screwed up in the harassment case. It's a hell of a burden to carry around, feeling that you're responsible for someone being kidnapped and, well, not knowing what will happen. He won't do anything that will make matters worse.'

The silence in the car lengthened then suddenly Rory's temper snapped, his voice cutting through the space between them like a knife. 'I know some of what he's going through. You're the only one involved in this harassment case who, if the worst happens, can look back without feeling guilt at our handling of this case -'

'No guv,' John interrupted, raising his voice to a shout, determined to be heard. 'I'm not actually blaming him, if that's what you think, well except for the threat of Wasting Police Time. Things could always be handled better on every bloody case in an ideal world, but we don't live in that world. I know that. We prioritise dependent upon the seriousness of each case. Even though it's a stalker case, on paper it was a relatively low-level one compared to many we come across, no deluge of phone calls, texts, violence. But we know now that we were wrong, and we know that because, despite our workload, you gave me the green light to investigate this case. Billy Grant is a monster and any risk, however, small, is a risk too far. The stakes are too high. If there's any chance that the bastard sees Johnny Hamilton, well . . .' John's voice paused before he went on, 'there might be no chance left.'

'I'll make sure he doesn't muddy the waters,' Rory said in a milder tone, suddenly hugely relieved, John's words softening the burden he was carrying regarding own responsibility.

'It will be good to have Michael there,' John added after a moment or two, making a concession of his own.'

'How much longer?' Rory asked, looking out of the window at the rolling hills and wishing he was in this glorious part of the world with Thommi rather than as part of this grim mission.

'Forty minutes.'

A call came through the car's speakers, and Johnny Hamilton's face appeared on the central Display Unit. Rory put him on speaker so that John could hear the conversation. After the preliminaries, Rory said: 'Johnny, I was about to ring you, there's a meeting at Barnstaple Police Station in an hour. We're about forty minutes away, where are you?'

'Honiton, Guv. I wasn't asking to be included in any searches because Grant knows me. I wasn't aiming to get out of the car much at all, other than maybe in a wet suit on a board in the sea later. I just thought that my experience on a kidnapping of a child in Launceston might come in handy. I'm thinking along the lines that Grant may be looking to ditch his phone and get another if he hasn't done so already. Also, that he may be planning to hire a different vehicle with a full tank of petrol, again if he hasn't already done that. My guess is that if he does either of those things, it's going to be before he crosses over from Somerset to Devon, although places like Bideford are possibilities. I'm also thinking about car parks. When it comes to Devon, I'd like to check out Air B&B's and holiday places to rent with garages within striking distance of where we think he's aiming for, small villages, some in Cornwall, Morwenstowe, places like that.'

'Right,' Rory said, receiving a nod from John and a thumbs up. 'I see where you're coming from.'

'He plans ahead.'

'He does, but town carparks have cameras, he'll know that.'

'In the case I did, our kidnapper parked at a site with cameras, it was the General Hospital.'

After an intake of breath, Rory said: 'Clever.'

'We thought we'd check out all car hire firms, mobile phone retailers, car parks for food stores, hospitals etc. in the towns leading towards North Devon and then, when we're in Devon, make enquiries with people renting properties and Michael can go and have a look at them. Grant's never seen Michael. I know a lot of rentals on that coast already, I used to use them myself. The owners of the ones I know will be discreet.'

'Good.'

'Are you setting up roadblocks, Guv?'

'Part of the discussion when we get to Barnstaple.'

'Right.'

'Good work, Johnny. Keep in touch with us.'

'Will do. One more thing, have you seen the statement from Fiona Marsh?'

'No, but I've been told what's in it.'

'Were you told that she listed what Grant carries in the van?'

'The number plates, yes. Vehicle Accessories were his thing.'

'Yeah, but I was mainly thinking about rope.'

'Rope?'

'Fiona Marsh's mother apparently hanged herself and he always keeps rope in his vans and other vehicles.'

'Christ.'

'We need to look for a spot with a view, but where trees may do more than give cover.'

When the call ended, Rory looked at John, who briefly turned his head before turning his eyes back to the road.

'He's making a lot of sense,' John said. 'We shouldn't assume that he's going to toss her over a cliff where either he may be seen or where she may be injured but not killed.'

'No.'

After another moment of silence, John said: 'You know, she's not that specific about the exact location she wanted to take her last view of life. He may figure a village close by may be just as good.'

'That's the problem with roadblocks. We don't know when he's going to arrive in the County or at any likely sites, or where exactly he's aiming for. If we stop vehicles too soon, it's bound to be picked up on airwaves and he'll double back or decide to kill her in some other way and take his chances. The sooner we can rely on local knowledge the better.'

'Not far away now, Guv.'

CHAPTER 53

She felt paralysed once more, her confidence that she could turn the tables on Billy Grant, knowing that justice would be meted out to him and future victims saved, imploded. "One of your witnesses," the evil invader said. She had only one witness and that was Cassandra, her greatest friend, so how could Cassandra have said anything or done anything to harm her. Remembering Marcus Jenner's success in getting Cassandra to concede every point he made in the second court case, she felt that her head was about to explode. What hold could Billy Grant possibly have over Cassandra? She must think, she mustn't let Billy Grant triumph now. She concentrated on her breathing. Dividing people, leaving victims helpless without support, his modus operandi, getting people to turn against each other, and he was at it again. He was an evil man, skilled at undermining victims, twisting the knife, the master manipulator and suddenly, a lightbulb flashed in her brain, she remembered that Cassandra wasn't there when Marcus Jenner questioned her about North Devon. She was in a witness waiting room, ready to be called to give evidence.

In control of herself once more and now able to think rationally, she remembered looking at Billy Grant when Marcus Jenner questioned her about Devon and the surprise on his face when she accepted that she knew North Devon well. Even though it seemed at times as though the police officers were not on her side, technically they were prosecution witnesses. Marcus Jenner had accepted their evidence, so their statements were simply read. As the OIC, Johnny Hamilton remained in court during the whole of the trial. Another recollection, Johnny Hamilton looking at the photograph of her and her father sitting on a harbour wall. It led to a brief conversation between them about Cornwall and his love of water sports. Neither Devon nor Hartland were mentioned. But was Hamilton, falling for Grant's act, stupid enough to open-up to him? Were Billy Grant's instructions to his brief meant for a different audience to the one being questioned? A third recollection, Hamilton threatening her if she went near any of the witnesses. What hold did Grant have over Johnny Hamilton. She didn't know but, DC John Carter had taken charge of the case now, and she trusted him.

To her surprise, and relief, the vehicle pulled over onto a bumpy surface. She heard the driver's door open and shortly afterwards the lid of the boot open.

'I'm giving you some air, we don't want you conking out before your view, not that you'll see much of it.'

He took the blanket off her, undid the duvet, and looked down, checking that she was still alive, she thought. Then smirking, he half lifted her so that she could see they were in a parking layby facing a field full of shadowy trees, but little else. Evening had drawn in and there were no house lights or lamps to reveal more. The temperature had dipped though, so the night to come may be peppered with stars and, unless obscured by clouds, a clear moon.

'We have two more stops. Not long to go now.'

She turned her head, pretended to look around, and nodded. His expression changed the moment she swivelled her head in his direction but not quickly enough for her to miss his disappointment at her placid acceptance of her situation.

'Still hoping for rescue, I expect?'

She continued looking at the view.

'Okay, that's enough, treat over,' he said, a decided snap in his tone.

The top of her head banged against the boot lid as she was

roughly lowered into position in the well of the boot. He was in a temper, his control was slipping, she was spoiling his fun. She would be spoiling it further soon.

Once more in her prison, she realised that she didn't mind not seeing the view when the evil invader completed his final hateful act against her. Her memory would fill in the details she wanted to remember, and she'd smell the air and hear the sea. There was even a part of her which suddenly recoiled from too much view. Her love of North Devon was derived from its wildness, the dangerous ancient shale rocks rising above the sea, their edges ready to slice through anything coming their way with their Samurai sword sharpness. This was Daphne de-Maurier county and visions of smugglers braving a treacherous coast came to mind, as well as 'Rebecca's' watery grave in the roiling waters. She'd be joining the line of those who perished in this sea, but perhaps an inability to see her final resting place was now a comfort rather than a loss

CHAPTER 54

Shortly before their arrival in Barnstaple, Rory received a call from the DC who was still taking notes from Fiona.

'Guv, by using Bluetooth, Billy Grant can change the registration on the numberplate of his Land-rover using his phone.'

'What?!'

'LCD, liquid crystal display technology. I don't pretend to understand it, but it can function on a certain kind of numberplate and, within a certain radius, be controlled by a mobile phone.' the DC continued. 'He also carries around a lot of advertising stickers which he can put on the car, so the images of a particular vehicle with another registration looks different on camera. According to Fiona, he has only used this technology so far on the Land-rover, and the registrations he uses, match the registrations of genuine vehicles of the same make as his. He told Fiona that the DVLA checks are making it much more difficult to buy and manufacture false numberplates.'

'Christ,' Rory said. 'No wonder we lost him.'

'Another thing,' the DC continued. 'Fiona also said that Grant does know the South-West quite well because he did some fly-tipping for a client for cash at one stage down in that area. Mainly Dorset and Somerset. He hasn't done it recently because he nearly got caught.'

After the call, Rory turned to John and shook his head. 'Always one step ahead of us. I'm getting too old for this game.'

When Nigel Sheridan rang through for an update, Rory briefed him on the DCs call. Expecting Nigel to comment on

Grant's knowledge and use of technology, he was surprised when, instead, he said: 'Fly-tipping. Rory, if that's the case, do I have your permission to widen the number of people on the investigation to include a couple of Covert Rural Observation Post officers. When it comes to intelligence, fly-tipping, a big problem in farming communities now, has become part of their brief. I know a Dorset CROPs officer and if Grant decides to ditch the Land-rover and hire a vehicle, he might know places Grant might choose to hide it. I know it's a longshot.'

'Everything's a longshot. Go ahead, let's leave no stone unturned.'

The call lasted a few more minutes and then, when it was over, John said: 'Grant might hire a vehicle,' then seeing the sudden exhaustion etched on Rory's face he added: 'Nearly there, Guv.'

On arrival at Barnstaple Police Station some twenty minutes later, Rory and John were ushered into a police conference room and introduced to senior Barnstable, and Bideford, police officers, both uniform and plain clothes. It was still too early for Grant to carry out his plan without risk, if they were right about the plan, but everyone in the room was aware of the clock ticking. Rory and John were shown large Ordnance Survey maps of the coast and surrounding hills and wooded areas. Roads leading in and out of Welcombe were pointed out, essentially two roads, and all the buildings and potential parking areas were indicated from photographs taken from a helicopter.

'These are flats to let and Air B&B's,' DCI Cyril Harding said, pointing at the maps. 'You can see one or two have garages, but we've made discreet enquiries and none of the available ones have been let today. An officer has gone over and will be speaking to the owners of the flats. We want to be told the moment they get any request, if there are any, for new bookings, and we've impressed upon the owners the necessity of informing us without letting on to anyone, particularly the person wanting to rent.'

John frowned at the map on the wall. 'It looks pretty remote. How close can a car get to these cliffs, and this wooded area?'

'Depends on the car. Pretty close if you have a four-by-four but unless you attempt it at night, and even then, you've got to be careful with headlights, you might be spotted. It's a close community and the locals all know each other.'

Rory sighed. 'I can't believe that Grant won't know the difficulties. He can use Google Maps just like anyone else.'

'I suppose he's not anticipating anyone knowing what he's up to,' John replied. 'At least that's what we hope.'

DCI Harding's bushy black eyebrows, which contrasted with his grey hair, pulled together in a frown as he looked across the table. 'From what you tell me, he seems to be covering his tracks pretty well and, now that his assistant has bailed, he can't be sure that she won't give away anything to the police. How certain are you that he's coming down here at all?' he asked, with a rueful expression.

'We can't be absolutely sure,' Rory admitted, 'but the hospital confirmed that his assistant had been operated on, and there are a few pointers indicating he was travelling West after torching his van, including the cell site information when he used his phone.' He then went on to explain why, in Grant's mind, once he had possession of the victim's computer, by staging managing the victim's suicide, he might believe it would be impossible for us to prove he had any involvement in her death.'

'Provided he doesn't know about the other evidence we have on him,' John added.

At the end of the briefing, Harding asked one or two questions, then nodded.

'Are there easier areas close by for someone like Grant to carry out his plan, if he is down here?' John asked.

Harding took them on a pictorial tour of the surrounding areas. All agreed that at least three villages needed surveillance.

'One other thing,' Harding volunteered, 'although you see

trees on the way to the cliffs, there are very few, almost none, at the cliff edge itself. It he continues to want to hang his unfortunate victim, it's likely that he'll do so in a wooded area rather than over a cliff. I'm afraid that makes a rescue more difficult because we can sweep the coastline with a helicopter, but although we might be able to pick up the fact that there are bodies amongst trees and in the undergrowth, we can't land there, although we can use a loudspeaker.'

John nodded at the map on the wall, taking in all too clearly what he was being told.

'We've got a lot of police volunteers. Of course, it's fairly dark now but if this Grant is doing any surveillance of his own, we're confident that nothing that our officers are doing in their old walking clothes, some of them with children, will attract his attention.

The later it got, the more depressed Rory and John became. Suddenly John's hunch seemed a longshot. He fell into a mood of total despair. That is until a call from Nigel came through, which Rory put on speakerphone so that all the officers could hear him.

'My Dorset guy thinks he's got the car Grant came down in,' he said. The atmosphere in the conference room electrified. 'No sign of Grant or our victim, but it's a Land-rover which has been completely cleaned and some of the interior of the vehicle is still damp. The numberplate is thinner and different from most others, and it looks as though it could be compatible with LCD technology. We've sent over to the SOCOS a shot of its tyres, and they'll do a thorough analysis, but they think they are of the same type as one of the tyre tracks at the scene you were at. We're now leaving it alone for the time being.'

'My God, what were the chances you'd find it?' John exclaimed.

'We got lucky,' Nigel said. 'I'd given a description of Grant to my contact and of his van and, it turns out, he was already on their radar having escaped their attention after a fly-tipping incident. Anyway, they looked in the places where this incident had taken place and in one of them, "Voila!"'

"Brilliant work, Nigel,' Rory said. 'So, he's down in the South-West and it looks as though he's following the plan on our victim's computer. What we need now is to find out where he's got hold of another vehicle.'

DCI Cyril Harding's hands gripped each other: 'We need to check every car hire place within a twenty-mile radius, but most will be closed so we'll need to dig around for contacts. We'll go flat out on anything ANPR cameras can tell us. Of course, once you get nearer villages, there are not quite as many cameras, but more than people think and, of course, ANPR is on the roads from which you turn off for the coast.'

Not long afterwards, Michael Flynn was on the line. 'We called quite a few car hire places on the way down here,' Michael said, 'but they'll need to be checked again.'

'Listen Michael,' Rory said, looking at the DCI for approval. 'Can you stay where you are for the moment? It's probably easier if we check from here because of the contacts the police have now that places are closed. Stay put and I'll get back to you.'

'Will do,' Michael confirmed.

As the phone calls were divided between officers, John piped up: 'Look, it's not good enough just checking the Billy Grant, or William Clarke, names, we need the names of any person who has hired a car this afternoon. We know that Grant has had vehicles in other people's names. Remember, Gerald Marsh, the uncle of Fiona, has had a speeding ticket for a vehicle he doesn't own on a road he hasn't driven along. But we must concentrate mainly on what we do, now that we know Grant is not in his own vehicle.'

'I suppose he could have planned ahead and that he's driving another of his vehicles,' Rory said.

'I doubt it,' John said, shaking his head. 'He didn't know about the victim's document until after he'd kidnapped her.'

Rory hit his forehead. 'I'm an idiot,' he said, with a rueful grin. 'Okay, well we need to concentrate on vehicles on the road which have the capacity to contain a prisoner, probably in a boot, without the victim dying.'

'Agreed,' DCI Cyril Harding told his squad. Finding the vehicle Grant is now driving is our main priority. We need to use unmarked police vehicles on the roads leading to and from the coastal areas we think Grant is aiming for and clocking the numberplates of Estates and medium sized vehicles with a single male driving them. Any intel needs to be relayed back immediately and the ownership checked. We'll then know if it's registered to a car hire outfit.'

CHAPTER 55

Suddenly the vehicle was travelling at a decent speed, but it wasn't for long. It stopped and once again Grant opened the boot and prodded her, but this time just to check on her. He didn't speak to her or remove her covering. But, In the moment between opening the boot and shutting it again, she thought she could hear the sea and sounds of activity, cars driving, doors shutting, and people laughing and speaking. We're in a town or a village she thought. Again, her helplessness to cry out and alert others momentarily threatened to overwhelm her, but, after a struggle, she managed to steady herself. If you begin to hope, you will lose control at the end, you will start pleading for your life and you won't be able to leave this world the way you planned, control will have been taken away from you again. When you have told the evil invader what to expect, you want to witness its effect on him, he won't be able to disguise his feelings, his anger and, more importantly, his helplessness. Your torment will almost be over, his will be just beginning. He will know what it is like to be tracked, to be stalked, like a hunted animal with nowhere to turn.

It was odd that he didn't remove the covering and leer down at her or try to taunt her but, from the sound of the car door opening, he simply climbed back into the driver's seat. She waited for the engine to start, but it didn't. All was quiet. He was waiting until later, she thought, too many people around still. But wasn't he taking a chance waiting until there were fewer cars on the road? You're getting back to hoping for the cavalry, she told herself, no one knows where he is or what car he's driving. If they did, they'd have stopped him by now. Concentrate on your plan to shatter his confidence at the very moment he's hoping to savour you pleading for your life.

CHAPTER 56

Michael Flynn opened the car door after his walk about and sat back down in the passenger seat.

'Nothing come through yet?'

'Not yet.' Johnny Hamilton was looking tired. After a moment he said: 'You know, this Grant did such a job on me, I think he's very dangerous. I'm not getting a good feeling.'

'Look, none of us think we'd have done anything differently over Grant's alibi.'

'It's not only that and you know it. John would, and did, do things differently. The bastard had me believing that not only was he innocent but that he was the one being victimised. I left the real victim helpless.'

'Johnny, we have to concentrate on the here and now.' There was a bite to Michael's words. There was nothing he could do to comfort Johnny he had let the victim down, but now was not the time for recriminations.

But Johnny shook his head and raised his voice in his urgency to communicate his thinking. 'You need to hear what I'm saying. You won't understand having not seen him in court. Now that I know what he's capable of, I'm thinking we need to think outside the box a bit.'

Some of Johnny's anxiety transferred to Flynn. 'Okay, what are you suggesting?'

'I don't want to wait for the call on the cars, by the time we trace the car it will be too late. I want to view the landscape from the sea. I have a wetsuit and you can hire one here. You can swim, right?'

Michael nodded. 'I can and I surf.'

'I thought that if we had time to swim from different directions along the coast a bit, we'd get a better view of the more feasible places to throw a body over or hang a body from. We might get a better idea of whether he's likely to change his plan or not.'

Michael shifted in his seat. 'If Rory agrees, I'll drop you off wherever you want so that you can do a recce from the sea, but there are officers who will have a far better idea of the lay of the land than us. People who live here and swim, surf, waterboard, and so on.'

'I know, but their concentration is on the sea and the tides and the sport, not so much on where a dangerous felon can hide and at the same time murder someone and then get away again. Grant is going to surprise us, I'm sure of it. We may catch him, we will catch him, but not necessarily before he's killed her.'

Michael nodded. 'The trouble is that daylight is running out.'

'I know, and that's another reason I want to be in the water. The wind is dying down a bit and it will be a clear night according to my phone. There's not much light pollution in the villages and less as you approach the hills down to the sea. I'll stay here, you go and find yourself a wet suit. One positive is that I won't be recognised in a wet suit with night coming in.'

There was something in Johnny's manner which was bothering Flynn.

'No, I'm not leaving you until we get to Welcombe.'

'For Christ's sake.'

'Listen, if she has any chance of survival, we need to act as a team. I'm getting back to Rory and suggesting we go to Welcome and get into wet suits, like you say. I think he'll listen as you've worked down here. If he's okay with that, you drive me to where I can hire the stuff and sit in the car outside while I go in to hire it and you're giving me the car keys.'

Johnny gave a short laugh, but Michael was right. He knew the DI well. After a short silence at the other end of the line, followed by a short conversation between Rory and the DCI in the operations room, Rory replied.

'Okay, the police down here can cover Bideford. Keep me updated. But I don't want you both in wet suits. If one of you does pick up something, we need someone to be able to cover dry land quickly. Sorry, wait a minute.'

Johnny and Michael heard voices in the background, then Rory's voice was back.

'Michael, I'm going to pass you to DCI Harding. There's a fishing boat pulled up on the shore which you can be on with the son of one of the local fishermen. He's going to give you directions. I'll put him on.'

After a short conversation, Flynn said: 'Will do.' After a nod from his colleague, Johnny reversed and moved their vehicle forward while Flynn began punching a postcode into Google Maps.

CHAPTER 57

The road wound round in curves, slightly downwards, the car braking so that they were travelling at a very slow speed. It seemed to her a long time before it came to a stop. She heard him exit the vehicle and tensed as his footsteps walked towards the boot. Was it now? Was this the time? The lid of the boot rose, and he removed the blanket from over her and then her head covering but not the tape from her mouth.

Evening had given way to night, but she could see marginally better, once her eyes adjusted, than when they had last stopped. There was a three-quarter moon and stars were beginning to appear. A wind still gusted intermittently but the clouds were wispy and outlines of buildings visible. She could hear the sea now clearly. The tide must be up because the waves were lapping against rocks. Turning her head, she saw that their vehicle was parked in a car park which was empty of other vehicles. A few lights were scattered from the direction of, presumably, a village or town she noticed and almost simultaneously she saw the evil invader glance in their direction. Behind her were hills covered in trees, and nearer to them foliage and scrub bordered part of the area of the car park which ended abruptly, presumably where it fell sharply towards the sea. But there were no trees there. This wasn't Welcombe but the sound of the sea and the landscape was North Devon, she was sure of it. Then she saw the rails on the edge of the cliff adjacent to the building she'd spotted. That's where he'll hang me, she thought.

She could sense Billy Grant tense as he looked towards

the lights. Then suddenly he swung her up and out of the boot and walked towards the rear passenger door behind the driving wheel. Resting her on the ground for a second, he opened its door and then lifted her into the vehicle across the whole of the back seats, with various things, felt even through her covers. For a second, he looked at her and his expression was one of fury and hatred, gone were the leers, the little blinking eyes, the pretence had slipped completely and, in its place, the naked face of unmasked evil. He threw the blanket over her but didn't cover her head so this must be it, she thought. This must be her last resting place.

'Not yet,' she heard him murmur, 'not yet.' She braced herself for what was to come, trying to compose herself.

CHAPTER 58

Everything was a different shade of black, including most of Johnny Hamilton himself who, clad in a wet suit, had begun to wade through the water holding his board, his face the only bit of light showing when he turned his head to scour the coastline. He waved at Flynn, just before Michael rounded a bend out of sight, bound for the fishing boat and the fishing nets. Michael returned the wave and then disappeared.

As the night was advancing further stars came out, lighting some of the darkness. Johnny looked at the pile of clothes, a dark mass on the shore, and then at his waterproof watch with the luminous dials. He gave himself another ten minutes of manoeuvring the board in the choppy waters. Then, checking the time again, he threw his mobile phone into the water and headed back to shore. Removing his wetsuit, he dried himself and put on his clothes. Picking up a black backpack, he felt inside. A moment later his hand clamped around another phone and bringing it out, he switched it on.

He looked towards the corner Michael had disappeared around. No sign of anyone. Breathing a sigh of relief Johnny reached once more into his backpack, this time bringing out some keys.

To the right of the cliffs was a path which led upwards, then disappeared, before continuing, more steeply, to where their vehicle was parked. Johnny jogged towards it and moments later he too vanished into the night.

CHAPTER 59

It seemed to her that she had been lying quietly across the back seat, listening to the breathing and odd grunt from the front of the vehicle, for an eternity. He was waiting, waiting until more lights faded, or perhaps one light. In the space between the evil invader placing her on the ground and him tossing her along the back seat, she thought she had seen a light from the dark shape of a building with some scaffolding around it. It was for only a moment, but she thought she had glimpsed it moving, such as from the beam of a torch before she was picked up and pushed along the back seat of the car, where her only view was the car roof. Had she seen a vehicle too? She didn't know. They were certainly the only car in the car park. Was there someone in or around the building who had to leave before Billy Grant could carry out his plan? Her heart seemed to leap as Grant's voice broke the silence, seemingly confirming her guess: 'Fucking cunt.' he said. 'Fucking get going.'

As though wondering whether his spurt of temper may have given her some sort of advantage, he spoke again. 'He'll be gone soon. Just locking up, I expect. Better make your peace with the world now, you won't get another opportunity.'

She was unable to reply but wouldn't have done so anyway. Now wasn't the moment. Then, as though a link had been established between her actions in the past when she had determinedly maintained control as she gathered evidence, and her situation now, her thoughts returned to her document and, almost in prayer, she continued it:

TO WHOM IT MAY CONCERN, my friends and colleagues,

Bob, my lawyer, I want you to know … particularly you, CASSANDRA, that I'm fine. I don't know much about telepathy, but do you remember, CASSANDRA, how my mother could seem to tune in to me sometimes and we'd have the same thought? Sometimes she seemed to sense when I was sad or having a tough time. She was a creative, imaginative, person, as are you. Just in case, I know it's a longshot, but I want you to know that I'm going to fight the evil invader to my last breath and that, even though I'll lose, I'm in Devon. It's my favourite county and it's wrapping around me somehow and when Billy Grant is forced to free me before his evil deed, I'll hear the waves, and smell the air, and see the stars and the moon.

One big thing to tell you though, is that I know where I am. Do you remember CASSANDRA, coming with us to Devon after our first year at Uni? Dad drove us through various villages on the way to Welcombe, and one of them was Hartland. We both loved Daphne de Maurier books, Jamaica Inn was my favourite, Rebecca yours, and Hartland was big Daphne de Maurier country with its wild coast and pointed shards of ancient slate rising high and threateningly from the sea, treacherous for smugglers. Where we parked is where the evil invader has parked now. The weather was atrocious, but we got out and went to some railings and the rain was slapping our faces and the waves were crashing and it seemed we were in the middle of a De Maurier book. But we were so wet, we didn't stop and have a meal at the Inn as planned but drove on to Welcombe to dry out in our rented cottage. Here's the funny thing I want to tell you though. At court in the second case, the evil invader's Counsel suddenly began asking me if I'd ever been to Hartland. You weren't in court because you were in the waiting room ready to be called as a witness. I said that I had been to Hartland but that we'd just driven through it. I couldn't, still can't, make out why he asked me. He probably thinks that if he ends up in court again, that he could use my admission of knowing Hartland to prove I hanged myself here. I want you to remember CASSANDRA to tell DC John Carter, that Welcombe was where we had such fun that holiday, that was our destination, not Hartland. Please remember that. I love you and want nothing better than that you have a full and wonderful life and to know that I am fine, and that my end will be quick in a place that I love. Please don't be sad about anything I said in the document they will find. I wasn't myself and you know that, but I am strong now and glad it's soon going to be over, particularly knowing that it is just the beginning for the evil invader and that he won't be able to hurt anyone anymore.

CHAPTER 60

A puzzled DCI Harding, handed Rory a landline desk phone and said: 'One of your officers wants to speak to you but doesn't want to use the encrypted airwave.'

Rory picked it up and identified himself.   DC Sarah Montgomery was on the other end.

'Sorry guv, but I have something to tell you that's not for general release.'

'Okay.'

'Sir, I've got the footage from a neighbour's doorbell of the argument between the tall dark male and Billy Grant. The male arguing with Grant is Johnny Hamilton.'

There was a silence on the line.

'Guv?'

'I'm still here, Sarah, go on. '

'Johnny does tell Grant to move quickly, and Grant says to him: "But you knew, you said it was too late to change things and unless I kept to the script I'd end up in prison." Johnny then makes a move towards him telling him that he didn't have much time and had better get going, and Grant backs off, says something but it's not clear, it sounds like heartland, or heart something, and then legs it, back into his building.'

'Christ. Thanks Sarah. I'll be in touch.'

'Sorry Guv,' Sarah says, and the call ends.

Five seconds later, Rory forestalls John from asking a question with the wave of a hand and focusses on DCI Harding. 'It's possible we've got a rogue cop.'

'I'm going to ring Johnny,' he continues. 'I'll do it on the secure line and tell him I've got something for him to do and I want him back here.'

John's face was the colour of parchment.

But Johnny's phone is dead, and Rory puts his own phone down and rings another number, using the landline.

'Flynn, can you go down the beach, find Johnny, and then contact me straight away. I can't get hold of him. Can you ring the moment you've found Johnny? Use your own frequency and ring this number, I want to keep the secure one open.'

Tension had gripped nearly every officer in the room. It seemed an eternity when the call came through the landline, but it was no more than ten minutes later.

'Guv, I've found Johnny's wet suit left on rocks. I walked around the cliff to where we left the car and it's missing.'

'Christ. What was the registration?'

Michael Flynn gave it to him and then added in a tight voice: 'Guv, I have to report that Johnny may have tried to get rid of me earlier, but he then fell in with this plan, I never thought-'

'It's okay, Michael. We've got to go, unless you've got anything further that might help. We must put an alert out for Hamilton. I'll keep you posted.'

Rory swivelled his chair, and then gave the entire room the registration of the vehicle Hamilton was driving.

'We've got to find it -.'

'What did Sarah say?' John demanded.

Impatient but sensing John was not about to be fobbed of Rory told him.

'Guv, 'Remember Hartland?' John says interrupting. 'Grant's Counsel asked our victim in the second court case if she knew a place in North Devon called Hartland. She said she and her family had driven through it, but she didn't know it well. Thommi showed me the clerk's notes.'

'Where's Hartland?' Rory asked DCI Harding, and the room in general.

'Not far from here.'

'Right, that's where we're going now,' Rory said, nodding to John.

'One moment,' DCI Harding said. 'I'm contacting the Air Service. We need the choppers out.'

Rory stopped walking towards the door to consider this.

'I'm not throwing this out for debate, Rory,' Harding said, indicating to a DC that he wanted him to ring the National Police Air Service. 'We now need every tool in the box.'

Rory saw that John had reached the door. The time for secrecy was over.

'Thanks Cyril,' Rory said, just before he and John left conference room.

CHAPTER 61

The sound of another vehicle was coming closer, for a moment it seemed to stop, and then it passed them as it slowly wound its way towards the village, the sound of its engine becoming fainter. There was nothing she could do now except prepare herself for her final confrontation.

Grant stepped out of the vehicle, and she heard something drop to the ground. The rucksack with her computer, no doubt. She heard the boot open and knew that he was getting the rope. Finally, her door opened, and the blanket was thrown aside. He dragged her body towards him by her feet, and then stood her up against the car, one hand holding her upright while using his other hand to slam her door shut. She would never have another car journey, she thought. Pinning her against the car with his body, he opened the top of the duvet, tying it loosely round her neck. She saw that the rope was wound round his right shoulder. Then he picked her up, throwing her over his shoulder in a fireman's lift but struggling a little as he bent to pick up his rucksack. She twisted, and threw her head back, connecting with his for a second, clearly taking him by surprise.

He swore. 'I thought you wanted this all to be over,' he jeered. 'Well, now-' and then another expletive as she managed to lower herself further down his back causing him to tighten his hold on her lower limbs, the rope adding to his difficulties. She wasn't going to make it easy. He continued ahead, but his footing was uneven, at one stage he stumbled before regaining his balance, his breathing laboured. No, she wasn't going to

JENNIFER FREELAND

make it easy.

CHAPTER 62

John was driving, breaking all speed limits, while Rory sent various instructions to officers. Suddenly, a piece of news came through the encrypted channel. Devonshire police thought they knew which car Billy Grant had hired and it was picked up earlier on a camera travelling in the direction of Hartland. The tension in the vehicle was almost unbearable. This was now a race against time. How long did it take to hang a person? Hardly any time at all. How long before they were dead? No time at all.

'The clerk's notes regarding the second trial of the victim,' John said, suddenly.

'What?'

'Johnny Hamilton was the OIC and was present throughout the two trials. He knows all about Devon and Cornwall as we know. That line of questioning was aimed at him, and it was just a piece of luck from Grant's point of view that the victim knew the area?'

Rory thought this over. 'I suppose by choosing Hartland, and I hope to God that's what he's done, he's ensuring he has some kind of hold over Johnny.'

There was another silence.

'What was it Grant had on him for Hamilton to threaten him?' Rory asked.

'I've been thinking about that,' John said, taking a corner so fast Rory had to grab hold of his seat. 'Could it be the CCTV? It's possible he found out late in the day that it wasn't our Grant's party and that Hamilton thought that he'd be criticised for not getting the CCTV in time if the court case had to be adjourned.'

'That's what I wondered myself,' Rory agreed. 'He thought he'd get rid of a nuisance caller and made threats to Grant using the alibi as his leverage, maybe telling him that, if he didn't stop harassing the victim, he'd be charged with Perverting the Course of Justice, without appreciating the obsessive nature of a stalker.'

'Or the guile of his opponent. In his turn, Billy Grant used the same leverage to turn the tables on Johnny. Remember Sarah's words on the tape: "You said it was too late to change things."

The two men heard the helicopter at the same time, and Rory looked up through his window.

CHAPTER 63

She saw the outline of the building with the scaffolding, shadows dancing across it as the light dipped in and out when the clouds momentarily crossed the moon, leaving at other times a clear and starry night. Then she saw the bars, the bars where she would be hanged, and heard the sea smashing against the jagged rocks, black and menacing, and further from them, towards the horizon, the water shining in parts, shimmering across the black water in patches.

He put her on the ground, still bound, still gagged, but able to watch his movements. He took the rope, made a noose, and took it over to the bars. A few clouds obscured the moon for a moment, but it re-emerged, and her eyes which were adjusting to the night could pick out most of the outlines within their immediate landscape. She returned her attention to Grant who was now securing the rope around one of the bars. He still had to deal with her, he had to remove her coverings and the tape from her mouth and that's when she'd have her chance to remove the leer from his face. The one downside to his plan, something he didn't seem to have anticipated is that by hanging her from bars he would have to control his temper. If he simply threw her over the cliff, any injuries might be explained by the fall and landing on the shards of rocks below. But not hanging. Once a person's modus operandi, always the MO, she thought.

She saw him tug at the rope and give a satisfied shake of his head. He turned and walked purposefully back towards her. Suddenly, without warning, she knew that she was going to fight for her life. She'd tell him what she intended to tell him, but she wouldn't make it easy. She didn't want to die, and she'd fight for her life, and she felt a surge of adrenalin and her ears drumming, or was it the drumming of her heartbeat? It didn't matter which. His hands were removing the duvet, then they ripped off the tape from the silk covering round her ankles and moved on to the tape binding her hands and, finally, the tape around her mouth.

. . . .

Johnny Hamilton could hardly think for the rush of emotions coursing through him. The bastard, the fucking bastard. From the moment Johnny heard the drip feed of information coming through the encrypted police channels, he knew what Grant's plan would be. But he had to lose Flynn first. Now, travelling as fast as was possible down the narrow roads through Hartland towards Grant's chosen place for murder, he knew it was up for him if he didn't get there first. Otherwise, he was going down too, and prison was no place for a police officer. All Grant had to do was to keep away from the victim, that's all, disappear. Stay away for a while, choose another name and another victim in another county with a different police force. But now, now...

He remembered when he first thought he'd given away too much of himself, too many opinions of entitled women, shared too many thoughts with – what was it she called him? - the evil invader, that's it. - "You don't really get it," she'd said, begging him to do more to protect her, "he's an evil invader," and it was all he could do not to laugh. He'd been way too chummy with Billy Grant, trying to cajole him into leaving her alone, trying to ...what did it matter now? What mattered now is that he had to save himself.

He remembered the court case when Grant's lawyer suddenly questioned the victim about Devon. He actually asked her about Hartland but, although she conceded she knew and loved North Devon and had driven through Hartland, she was clear that she'd never discussed Devon or the West Country with Billy Grant. The Magistrates had looked sceptical, but she was telling the truth. He was the one who had discussed his favourite parts of Devon with the bastard, not her. He'd told him about an inn near Hartland, and Billy Grant was taunting him through his instructions to his lawyer. It was sheer coincidence that it was a part of the world she loved. He remembered that Grant had said to him, during one of their conversations, that he didn't know the West Country himself. Liar, fucking liar, he'd been fly tipping there. An image of Nigel Sheridan came to his mind as he had to slow his speed to accommodate an oncoming vehicle. Nigel lecturing him publicly in front of his colleagues about the evil of stalking.

He was almost shaking with rage as he neared his destination. Grant had all but threatened him over the pub CCTV. The biggest mistake of his life. Grant had asked him the night before the court case what he should do because his lawyer had told him that he had an airtight alibi because of his birthday party, but it wasn't his birthday party. Fool that he was, he could only see, feel, whatever, the derision of his colleagues at his mistake, perhaps even disciplinary proceedings over his handling of the case, stalking being the big fucking buzzword. So, he told Grant to do what he wanted, it was too late to stop the case. Perhaps he'd better plead, he'd suggested, and get it over and done with. But Grant hadn't, he'd gone along with the lie, he hadn't told his lawyer, and when he told Grant that another officer was making enquiries and that he should leave the area immediately, he threatened him, threatened him with exposure of his knowledge of the CCTV. He'd made him an accessory to Perverting the Course of Justice. He hadn't told Grant to do lie, but he had sat through the trial and kept quiet so it amounted to the same thing, and he was not going to let his career, his marriage, his life be brought down if he could help it.

He saw the car in the carpark.

· · · · · · · · · ·

News came in over the secure line, the number plate of the police vehicle Hamilton was in had been clocked by ANPR approaching Hartland. John increased his speed but was then forced to slow down in the town itself, just as Hamilton had been.

· · · · · · · · · ·

'You're a liar,' Grant told her.

'I'm not. They'll find what I left they'll find all of it. I sent a copy of the photo of you looking over the fence to my lawyer, my phone they'll find in the garden of my neighbour, they'll find the statement from my colleague and his picture of you outside the café, they'll find all of it, and they'll know you murdered me.'

She saw doubt changing to fear in his expression. He grabbed the fingers of her left hand, forcing them down onto her computer, just as the nails of her right hand dug into the folds of his neck. His fist slammed into her jaw, and she fell back stunned. As he lifted her, she began to struggle, and then the sound of a car approaching arrested him and he dropped her near the bars as he turned. A tall dark male both knew as DC Johnny Hamilton was racing towards them and from his rucksack Billy Grant produced a knife. He grabbed her, pulling her towards the noose, holding Hamilton at bay.

'You're in this with me,' he said.

'They know all about you,' Hamilton replied.

'But not yet about you, but they will unless you help.'

'Okay,' Hamilton said, looking directly at Grant. 'What is it you want me to do?'

'Get the noose round her neck while I hold her.'

Hamilton picked up the noose. It's all over, she thought, I can't fight them both.

The sound of an approaching helicopter cut through the air.

'Hurry,' Grant said, as she kicked and struggled, while he

bent over her to grab her hands for just a moment. She closed her eyes, waiting for Hamilton to put the noose around her neck, but he didn't. She opened her eyes to see him put the noose over Grant's head instead, and as Grant realised what had happened, he let go of the grip on her hands, and picking up his knife he slashed it towards Hamilton, catching the edge of his arm. Dodging sideways, Hamilton grabbed Grant's shirt and, before he could slash again, tipped him over the edge into oblivion.

A tight scream and then silence except for the sound of the helicopter and an approaching car.

. . . .

The officers in the helicopter saw a figure hanging from a rope, swinging, and for a moment their throats tightened, then: 'It's not a female,' one of them said. 'There's a female sitting on the ground her arms around the rails the rope's attached to and a male standing up beside her. Two other men are running towards them.'

. . . .

John Carter, with Rory behind him, ran towards the figures. Taking in the scene but focussing on the victim, John stopped running a few feet away from her and, catching up, with him Rory said: 'Step away, Johnny, and move over here.'

'I was just trying to persuade her to let go of the rails and come away from the edge,' Johnny said, holding his arm.

'That's fine, but John's got this.'

As John moved further towards the victim, Johnny turned his head and saw that, although she hadn't let go of the rails, she was looking at John as though her life depended on him. Johnny shrugged and moved towards Rory.

'You're going to be all right,' John told her holding his arms out from just a couple of feet away from her, 'you're going to be fine Lillian, it's all over.' She didn't take her eyes from John's face as she slowly let go of the rail with one hand. He took it in a warm clasp, then suddenly letting go altogether, she reached out, and into his arms which folded around her. Very slowly, John guided her away from the edge, her steps faltering, her legs numb from having been in cramped conditions for so many hours. As they drew level with Rory, Hamilton at his side, the victim said:

'He stabbed him. Billy Grant stabbed him.'

'Where's Grant?' Rory asked Johnny Hamilton once John and the victim had passed them.

Johnny tilted his head towards the rail with a rope tied to it and Rory walked over and looked down. He saw Grant swinging from a noose, his own noose presumably.

'Johnny,' he began, having walked back to him.

'I know,' Johnny said, sighing.

'I'm arresting you-' then he stopped speaking as he noted the blood dripping from Hamilton's arm.

'This can wait,' Rory said, taking out his phone, there were two people, both injured in different ways, who needed attention.

'A second ambulance is required,' Rory said to the operator, after dialling 999.

CHAPTER 64

DI Rory Hoskins sat back in his deck chair in the garden and surveyed the crowd milling around, voices raised in laughter, Nigel Sheridan's kids playing games under the supervision of Nell's daughter, Harriet, the champagne flowing, and then closed his eyes. It had been one hell of a year.

The death of Fiona Marsh's mother by hanging had been reopened but many more cases were being looked at. Manipulation ends with the death of a master manipulator and, bits of missed evidence about the man calling himself Billy Grant, as well as many other names, were surfacing, almost daily. It began as a trickle, but then as new facts gave rise to new leads, the trickle increased in volume. Other cases, which had been reported, but ended with the death of the victim, purportedly by suicide, had been reopened and a team of special, effectively cold case, officers were investigating them. It would take time, a lot of it, but what was certain now was that those fooled by the benign persona of a pathetic little man, had been forced to acknowledge that he was a major criminal, potentially a serial killer.

But when it came to the extent of the culpability of one of their own officers in the evil invader's crimes, the onset of Covid and its effect on police and prosecution manpower, contributed to the slow pace of the investigation into Johnny Hamilton. This not only affected the process itself but also the emotional wellbeing of Lillian which, in turn, had its effect on John Carter. In view of his involvement in the case, John was limited in the amount of contact he could have with Lillian and had to rely on updates from Cassandra.

But finally, there was closure. The criminal trial of Johnny Hamilton had ended with a hung jury and the prosecutor made it clear that in his view they were lucky to get that. 'Bottom line, evidence aside, it's tough for a jury to convict a man who's saved a victim's life,' he told them.

The decision was taken not to put Lillian through the trauma of a second trial. Hamilton was then sentenced on the Misconduct in Public Office count, to which he had already pleaded guilty, and he left the police force with immediate effect.

John telephoned Lillian with the news immediately after he left the courtroom, and that night he moved in with her.

Opening his eyes for a moment, Rory saw John and Lillian chatting to Nigel and Marla and, in another group, Cassandra showing Nell a portfolio of designs. Thommi had invited Cassandra as well as John and Lillian to a dinner party to celebrate the return of her friends from Australia and Nell and Cassandra had clicked immediately, two creative beings. Cassandra was now re-designing Nell's drawing room. Noticing that Thommi was still passing round small eats, Rory closed his eyes again.

Sometime later, a hand on his shoulder jerked Rory back to the present. It was Bruce handing him a can of beer. These days Rory was more of a wine drinker, but he took the can and had a swig from it. The family's return from Australia was another happy thing to celebrate. Looking at Nell, Rory saw that she was now tipsy, waving her champagne glass around expansively and spilling most of its contents.

Bruce laughed. 'I hope it wasn't vintage,' he said.

It was but what the hell, Rory thought, there was plenty more. He just had to get Thommi to the plane tomorrow and they could then sleep off their hangovers on their way to Italy. His flat was sold, and they were going to hunt for their new Italian home near his relatives. He'd been dreaming of this holiday for many months and now it was going to happen. The Covid restrictions had been lifted and it was going ahead. Nigel was kicking a ball around with the kids, John was walking with Thommi back towards the kitchen to return the empty small eats platters and, with a sigh, Rory began to rise but Bruce pushed him firmly back.

'I'll get it started, you stay and rest a while longer.'

'Thanks, but I'd better come cos I've got the meat and fish marinading in the kitchen and -'

'You're not seriously going to tell an Aussie how to put grub on the barbie, are you? Really mate?' Bruce said, raising an eyebrow.

Rory laughed, sighed, and gave up the fight to stay awake.

ACKNOWLEDGEMENTS

My great thanks to Finn Slevin for designing my book cover and managing my book's progress through all the steps to publication on Amazon Kindle, within a very tight timescale. Huge thanks also to Elizabeth Fisher for proof-reading my book in record time and giving me sound advice on the plot.

My colleagues working within the Criminal Justice System have, as always, helped keep me up to date with current criminal case law and police procedures.

As ever, my gratitude to Nyckie Hargreaves, and Amanda, and Rebecca Slevin, for their support and help in the project.

Printed in Great Britain
by Amazon

85015850R00150